Praise for

New York Times and *USA Today* Bestselling Author

Diane Capri

"Full of thrills and tension, but smart and human, too. Kim Otto is a great, great character. I love her."
Lee Child, *#1 World Wide Bestselling Author of Jack Reacher Thrillers*

"[A] welcome surprise... [W]orks from the first page to 'The End'."
Larry King

"Swift pacing and ongoing suspense are always present... [L]ikable protagonist who uses her political connections for a good cause...Readers should eagerly anticipate the next [book]."
Top Pick, Romantic Times

"...offers tense legal drama with courtroom overtones, twisty plot, and loads of Florida atmosphere. Recommended."
Library Journal

"[A] fast-paced legal thriller...energetic prose...an appealing heroine...clever and capable supporting cast...[that will] keep readers waiting for the next [book]."
Publishers Weekly

"Expertise shines on every page."
Margaret Maron, Edgar, Anthony, Agatha and Macavity Award-Winning MWA Grand Master

JACK KNIFE

by DIANE CAPRI

Published by: AugustBooks
http://www.AugustBooks.com

ISBN: 978-1-942633-61-7

Original cover design by: Cory Clubb

Jack Knife is a work of fiction. Names, characters, places, and incidents either are the product of the author's imagination or are used fictitiously, and any resemblance to actual persons, living or dead, business establishments, events, or locales is entirely coincidental.

Published in the United States of America.

Visit the author website:
http://www.DianeCapri.com

ALSO BY DIANE CAPRI

The Hunt for Jack Reacher Series

(in publication order with Lee Child source books in parentheses)

Don't Know Jack (The Killing Floor)

Jack in a Box (*novella*)

Jack and Kill (*novella*)

Get Back Jack (Bad Luck & Trouble)

Jack in the Green (*novella*)

Jack and Joe (The Enemy)

Deep Cover Jack (Persuader)

Jack the Reaper (The Hard Way)

Black Jack (Running Blind/The Visitor)

Ten Two Jack (The Midnight Line)

Jack of Spades (Past Tense)

Prepper Jack (Die Trying)

Full Metal Jack (The Affair)

Jack Frost (61 Hours)

Jack of Hearts • (Worth Dying For)

Straight Jack • (A Wanted Man)

Jack Knife • (Never Go Back)

The Jess Kimball Thrillers Series

Fatal Distraction

Fatal Demand

Fatal Error

Fatal Fall

Fatal Game

Fatal Bond

Fatal Enemy (*novella*)

Fatal Edge (*novella*)

Fatal Past (*novella*)

Fatal Dawn

The Hunt for Justice Series Due Justice
Twisted Justice
Secret Justice
Wasted Justice
Raw Justice
Mistaken Justice (*novella*)
Cold Justice (*novella*)
False Justice (*novella*)
Fair Justice (*novella*)
True Justice (*novella*)
Night Justice

The Park Hotel Mysteries Series
Reservation with Death
Early Check Out
Room with a Clue
Late Arrival

Short Reads Collections
Hit the Road Jack
Justice Is Served
Fatal Action

CAST OF CHARACTERS

Kim Otto
William Burke
Jake Reacher
Margaret Reacher
Carlos Gaspar
Charles Cooper
Lamont Finlay
Petey Burns
Hugh Sullivan
Susan Turner
Greg Jones
Leonard Dover
Michael Flint
Brad Coda
Rupert Adams IV
John Templar
Dr. Felipe Sanz

and
Jack Reacher

Perpetually, for Lee Child, with unrelenting gratitude.

JACK
KNIFE

NEVER GO BACK
By Lee Child

Reacher said, "I'm a detective and I know what you're going to say."

Turner said, "Do you?"

"It was always fifty-fifty. Like flipping a coin."

"I can't just walk away."

"And I can't stay. Not here. Not anywhere."

"The 110th was your creation, if that makes you feel any better."

"And now it's yours."

CHAPTER 1

Tuesday, May 24
Chicago, IL

FBI SPECIAL AGENT KIM Otto was all too aware that life could pivot from comfortable to catastrophic in an instant. Particularly in Chicago.

Always vigilant, she carried threat level awareness in her body at the cellular level.

Twenty minutes into her run, a driver mashed the grabbers and laid on his horn. Kim jumped several inches off the sidewalk and turned toward the danger.

The sedan stopped mere inches before he would have mowed down a jaywalker wearing earbuds who was crossing the street, oblivious to the danger.

Kim's heart picked up a couple of beats.

The pedestrian increased his pace and jogged across the street out of the sedan's path. The driver accelerated on his way, perhaps a bit more carefully.

And that was the end of it. No one got hit. No one died.

The driver didn't jump out and shout at the careless pedestrian.

The pedestrian didn't flip the guy off or yell obscenities about driving recklessly in a residential neighborhood.

Kim's heartbeat returned to normal and the tension in her shoulders eased as she moved along. Crisis averted.

In general, Chicagoans were polite Midwesterners. Which was one reason Kim enjoyed the city. The vibe felt normal and comfortable to her. Very similar to her home in Michigan.

Like law enforcement everywhere, she was hyper-aware of Chicago's increasingly violent crime statistics. More than six hundred homicides had been committed here last year alone.

Her situational awareness kept the needle pegged in the red zone on her internal threat meter at all times.

But it felt great to be outside, using her body, stretching her muscles. Forced inactivity was against her nature as well as a waste of time and she hated it.

She ran in the posh neighborhoods where, statistically speaking, the population was less likely to kill each other mid-week in broad daylight.

She had spent too many hours waiting, doing paperwork, and sitting on the sidelines the past few days.

Which had motivated her to run twice a day. Meaning she'd completed her usual five-mile fitness routine in the morning and now a more relaxed five miles in the afternoon.

Running was automatic and soon she was in the zone where her body did the work without conscious volition while her mind was free to wander back to problems with her job and her new partner.

Her assignment was to find Jack Reacher, and he was slipping through her fingers. Every minute she spent here in Chicago instead of tracking Reacher's movements gave him time to widen the gap between them.

It was her new partner's fault and she couldn't forgive him for it. Not yet, anyway.

Nor could she simply leave Burke here alone. He was her number two. She was responsible for him. She didn't have it in her to blow him off, even though he'd abandoned her more than once.

But as her mother often said, two wrongs didn't make a right, no matter how you did the math.

She'd demanded a new partner after her previous one retired. Twelve days ago, The Boss had assigned FBI Special Agent William Burke.

On paper, Burke was perfect. He had served as a Navy SEAL before joining the FBI, which meant he should have been both supremely capable and reliable.

He should also have understood the chain of command. She was the lead agent on this assignment. She'd been on the hunt for Reacher since the beginning.

Burke was the new guy. He'd been reminded of that status by The Boss more than once, yet he blew off his orders as if they'd been written in sand. He took risks he shouldn't take, with his life and with hers.

She'd never warmed up to Burke and her gut said the lack of appropriate feelings of loyalty, camaraderie, and friendship was mutual.

In short, he made her uneasy and she couldn't put her finger on the exact reason. Which made her even more uneasy.

For the second time since he'd come on board, Burke was in the hospital. He'd be released tomorrow, which might be the good news or the bad news.

She'd been expecting a full report about Burke from a confidential source at the NSA. The report hadn't come through and she'd waited in Chicago waiting as long as she could without arousing undue suspicion. Time to move on and hope the NSA report would catch up with her soon.

She'd finished the mountain of official paperwork late last night and sent it all off to The Boss.

Today, she'd written more extensive, confidential reports, which she'd uploaded to her secure server—secretly paying her insurance premium.

This whole assignment would go wickedly, horribly wrong at some point. She was certain. She'd find herself testifying about the hunt for Jack Reacher. Heads would roll. A few souls would end up in Leavenworth.

When pompous bureaucrats looked her way for a scapegoat, which they would, her contemporaneous reports could save her ass. She hoped.

After the last report loaded, she'd closed down the server and disconnected her laptop's parallel operating system. The only way to eliminate all traces of her cyber activities from the laptop was to destroy it, but at this point destruction was not an option.

Satisfied with her progress, she'd suited up and headed out for her run.

She intended to clear her head and work the kinks out of her body. The day was glorious. Nothing better than springtime in Chicagoland. She smelled the fragrant mixture of spring tulips and forsythia and daffodils that lined the streets in cheerfully bright colors after the long, gray winter.

Covering five miles of ground seemed to pass in five minutes.

When she slowed to walk the last few blocks back to her hotel, she noticed an independently owned ice cream shop on the corner of a busy street.

The throng of people coming and going and the unmistakable aroma of freshly brewed coffee drew her closer. She wondered what all the enthusiasm was about.

The whimsical metal sign swinging from the top of the door depicted a single scoop of caramel-colored ice cream perched atop a Wedgwood china cup.

The caption read, "Coffee. With Attitude."

What coffee addict could resist?

She grinned, stepped inside the coffee ice cream emporium, and deeply inhaled its wonderful bouquet.

Shelves and displays filled with trinkets and collectables lined the walls. All the items sported coffee and ice cream images and slogans.

Patrons were licking ice cream scoops, drinking coffee, laughing at the silly slogans, and generally amusing themselves. In short, people were acting normally for springtime in Chicago. The atmosphere was refreshing.

The mean streets of the city's unsafe areas seemed a thousand miles away.

Kim stood at the end of the line, reading the menu board as she waited her turn. The patient customers were well mannered and the queue moved quickly.

When she reached the confectioner behind the counter, the wholesome young man flashed a smile that promised expert and friendly service.

He brandished his scooper and flashed a flirty grin when he asked, "Which of our flavors might you enjoy most today?"

"How is the Totally Awesome Dark Mocha Toffee Crunch?" she replied, reading from the list.

His smile broadened to light up his whole face when he exclaimed, "It's totally awesome!"

She laughed. This place was infectious in the best of all possible ways. "One scoop, please."

"Two scoops are twice as good," he suggested, holding the scooper poised for action.

She shook her head. "I've already run ten miles today. I don't have the oomph to pound out another ten to run off those calories."

He cocked his head and gave it one last try. "Work hard and play harder, my mom always says. She's a size two. After six kids."

"Nice try." She laughed again. "Just one scoop, please."

He wagged the scooper and gave her another big grin. "It's tempting, isn't it? You know you want it."

"You're an incorrigible flirt. You know that?" Kim smiled back because she couldn't help herself. "But no. Just the one totally awesome scoop, please."

"You got it." He shook his head as if she were making a life-altering mistake, but he dug into one of the big cartons in the freezer, muscles moving under the skin of his arms as he worked the scoop like a pro.

In less than thirty seconds, he'd created a softball-sized scoop of the smooth caramel- colored ice cream and plopped it into a takeaway container decorated like the china tea cup on the sign out front.

"Nuts? Whipped cream? Sprinkles? Shaved chocolate? Espresso beans?" he asked, waving his palm over the toppings like a magician. "You're really well-toned for a woman your size. I'm sure an extra scoop and a few toppings would look great on you."

She regretfully declined, shaking her head.

"Can't blame a guy for trying," he said as he shrugged and handed the ice cream to her with a silver plastic spoon and a flourish.

"Thank you," Kim replied as she took the treat and tasted it. "Wow! Totally awesome is right."

"You be careful out there," he said with another grin and a twinkle in his eyes before he turned his attention to the next customer in line.

Kim pulled a twenty-dollar bill out of her pocket and paid for the ice cream at the register, leaving a generous tip for the scooper. He certainly deserved it.

"Watch yourself. It'll be dark soon," the cashier said as she thanked Kim for her business.

"I'm from Detroit. Where the weak are killed and eaten," she joked in response, but the cashier didn't smile.

All the chairs inside the shop were already taken, so Kim wandered outside with her ice cream. She meandered along the sidewalk, enjoying her treat and the warm afternoon sunshine.

"You know, that scooper might have been right about the toppings, too. He didn't steer you wrong on the ice cream," she said to herself. "Why not?"

She turned back toward the ice cream shop for a few chocolate-covered espresso beans.

She'd taken half a dozen steps when she heard shouting, and a woman ran out of the shop screaming. "Help! He's got a gun!"

Kim heard the unmistakable sound of two gunshots fired inside the shop. She tossed the ice cream into a nearby trash bin, pulled her weapon, and told the woman to call 9-1-1.

Kim ran toward the ice cream shop.

CHAPTER 2

Tuesday, May 24
Chicago, IL

WITH HER GUN DRAWN, Kim approached the shop and scanned the interior through the windows from the sidewalk.

Murders, rapes, shootings, and car thefts were all up sharply in the area, prompting warnings everywhere she'd been. The numbers were horrifying, to be sure. Even in areas like Lincoln Park.

She saw two men inside threatening the others. One held a gun. The other brandished a knife.

The patrons were down on the floor.

The gunman was behind the counter, standing with his foot on the back of the ice cream scooper who had been flirting with her just a few minutes ago. He'd shot the young man, who was unconscious and bleeding.

The man with the knife stood by the cashier. He was holding a knife to her throat and shouting.

"Give me the cash or I'll kill you." The man pressed the knife against her flesh and drew blood.

Kim shoved the door open and stepped inside. "FBI! Hands up!"

The cashier used Kim's entrance as a chance to scream and elbow the man sharply.

He swore and lifted his arm to slash her with the knife.

She scrambled toward Kim and slapped her hand over her neck to stop the bleeding.

The gunman behind the counter raised his pistol and aimed it at the cashier.

Before he could shoot off another round, Kim fired. The gunman staggered and fell on top of the young man already on the floor.

The man at the register moved toward Kim.

"Drop the knife! Drop the knife!" she yelled.

He lunged forward, moving fast, closing the distance between them.

"Stop!" she tried one last time.

He kept coming.

She put two bullets in his torso.

Momentum propelled his body forward another few feet and pitched forward.

Kim jumped aside, out of his path.

His body landed face-first on the cheerful parquet floor. Blood oozed slowly as gravity pulled the life force from him.

The other patrons ran into the far corners of the shop, screaming now that they could release their shocked voices.

Kim yelled, "Call 9-1-1!" before she checked the carotid pulse on both men to confirm they were no longer threats to the patrons and then hurried toward the victims.

The cashier was leaning against the wall, holding her hand to her neck wound, moaning in pain. Kim hurried to check on the others. The young man was still breathing. The two armed robbers were not.

Several of the patrons pulled out cell phones. At least one must have called the police. The others were probably shooting video or getting back on their feet.

A small crowd gathered outside the ice cream store.

A man hurried forward bringing bandages for the injured woman. "Just got these at the drug store on the corner."

He applied a white gauze patch to her neck, telling her to keep the pressure steady until help arrived. She moaned and nodded as if she understood the instructions.

Within minutes, two patrol officers arrived at the scene and called for more backup. One administered a dressing to the woman's neck to stop the bleeding and addressed the wounds on her torso. The second officer attended to the server. Both attackers were beyond the need for medical attention.

The scene unfolded predictably, according to procedure.

An ambulance arrived for the injured cashier and the young man who had been so full of life just an hour before. Kim hoped both of them would recover.

More squad units arrived for crowd control. One officer said the medical examiner's office was on the way to deal with the dead men.

There was no role for Kim to play at the moment. As far as the FBI was concerned, she shouldn't have been there at all. The Boss wouldn't be happy about it, either.

She shrugged. What was she supposed to do? Stand by and let two armed robbers kill innocent citizens? Nothing she could do about any of that now.

She stood off to the side out of the way until one of the officers approached her.

Kim showed her badge and gave him a quick report of the events as they had played out.

"Good thing you shot them," the officer said. "Both of them were most likely hyped up. Heroin probably. Maybe meth, too. Given the chance, they would have killed the two clerks and you, and who knows how many others."

Kim shook her head. "This is crazy. It's mid-afternoon in one of the best cities in America."

"Absolutely," the officer replied. "It's worse at night and on weekends. Daytime problems like this are less frequent. It's the drugs and the gangs, mostly."

"The crime situation has got to be eating everyone alive," Kim said. "Aren't people fed up with living in fear like this all the time?"

"Of course. Yeah. Cops, too. We're all fed up with it," the officer replied before returning to his post. "You got any answers? We'd all love to hear 'em."

Kim waited. Detectives would want to take a statement. Departments handled some things differently, but they'd want a ballistics match to her bullets in the two bodies.

Of course, there would be paperwork. There was always paperwork.

The bottom line was, she wasn't going anywhere for a while.

CHAPTER 3

Tuesday, May 24
Columbia, SC

"GOT ANOTHER BOTTLE OF water?" Jones, leader of the three-man crew, stretched and yawned with boredom. The sun rested low in the eastern sky, bathing the city in a warm orange glow for the last hours of daylight.

"Man, I hate surveillance," Smith groused from the backseat for the thousandth time as he handed the warm water bottle across the console of the van.

"Yeah," Jones replied, twisting off the cap. He took a long swig, disappointed that it tasted nothing like cold beer.

"Give me one, too," Manny said from the driver's seat.

Surveillance was the worst part of any job and they'd been sitting around waiting for two days. "Almost time to move," Jones said.

"Finally," Smith replied. "What's all the bother about? We've done this a dozen times. Neutralize the mother. Wait for the kid to arrive. Snatch them up at the same time. Get back down here to the van. Manny drives us back to the compound. We wait for further instructions. Bingo, bango, bongo. We're done."

"Yeah. Just babysitting, really," Jones said as if he believed it. He'd already grown tired of Smith's complaining. Smith wasn't the right man for this job. But Jones had needed a replacement and Smith was the only man available.

"I could have done this one alone and with my eyes closed," Smith complained.

Manny shook his head as he swigged the water.

Jones said nothing. Smith was capable enough. But he was no brain trust. He didn't have the sense to know why this was a three-man job. Jones went over it again as if the facts might stick into Smith's head this time.

He held up three fingers on his left hand. "Three disturbing facts."

Smith shrugged.

"First, Jake Reacher won't want to cooperate," Jones said, lowering his ring finger.

"Who cares? No target ever wants to cooperate," Smith snarled, curling his lip as he patted the pistol he'd placed on the console. "We got ways to deal with that kind of behavior."

Manny said, "Lots of ears inside that hotel. Eyes, too. You'd never make it out of there."

"So you say," Smith snarled back.

"Two, the kid is the size of a truck. You've seen him," Jones said, keeping the second and third fingers extended. "Which might not be okay. If he refuses to cooperate, we won't be able to force him. Not physically anyway."

Jones had only seen Jake Reacher from a distance so far, but the kid had been easy to spot. No possibility of misidentification, not with this one.

Smith shrugged. "The kid can be handled. We've subdued more difficult targets lots of times."

"Have we? He's a trained soldier. The army's pretty good at teaching self-defense," Manny replied, irritated now, even as he agreed with Smith in principle.

"The kid ain't the only one with army training," Smith said.

Jones lowered his middle finger, leaving only the index finger extended.

The third fact was seriously troublesome. Jones had been walking through various scenarios to handle the problem in his head since the White Kings had received this assignment.

Smith shook his head. Angrily, he said, "Look, screw it. There's no way around it. No way to finesse it, either. We just gotta tackle the problem head-on and barrel straight through. There're two of us and only one of him."

"Haven't you been listening to me?" Jones asked, explaining the third fact for which there simply was no solution. "You saw him. The kid is the spitting image of Jack Reacher. Fair hair, icy blue eyes. Weighs about two-fifty. Hands as big as turkeys."

"Yeah, yeah. And he's bulked up like he's spent long, hard hours at the gym. So what?" Smith snarled.

Manny chuckled under his breath. "Man, you ask for trouble."

Jones gave up. There was no way to make Smith understand what was happening here because Smith had zero experience with Jack Reacher.

Not like Jones. He'd seen Reacher fight off six guys, more than once, and put a pair in the hospital. He'd seen Reacher send guys to the morgue, too.

What Smith didn't understand was that the kid's physique was pure genetics. The army would use that raw Reacher DNA to turn him into a lethal fighting machine, exactly like his uncle.

Wouldn't take long or be hard to do, either.

And they'd already done most of the work.

Jake had finished his basic training. He was a trained killer now.

"Okay. Just realize the kid needs strong motivation to behave well during the course of this operation." Jones shook his head, giving up the argument. "Very strong motivation."

"Which was why we set things up this way. To motivate the kid," Manny said.

"Look, I'm sorry Rudy died. I'm sorry he's not here with you guys. But I'm not an idiot. We've been over and over all this." Smith frowned and shot a fierce glare toward Manny in the rearview. "The situation ain't perfect. Never will be. Let's stop talking and go. I'm sick of sitting here."

Jones drained the water bottle and mumbled from the passenger's seat, "Every reason it should work and no reason why it shouldn't."

"No such thing as a sure thing," Smith replied, cracking his knuckles the way he did when he was nervous. "We just gotta do it anyway. Hope for the best, handle the worst."

Pop, crackle, pop, pop. Over and over. Ten digits, twenty pops. It sounded like a kid rolling a bowling ball across a big sheet of bubble wrap.FSeriously irritating.

Smith found fault with everything. To Smith, every solution presented ten problems waiting to jump out and bite them in the ass. He'd mentioned everything that could possibly go wrong at least three times in the past hour alone.

Smith wasn't often wrong. But his constant objections weren't helpful, either. They caused Jones to worry when he might not have otherwise.

Why couldn't Smith be more like Manny? Just do the job and keep his mouth shut?

"You got any better ideas?" Jones asked through clenched teeth.

Smith shrugged in reply. He was a follower, not a leader. He could see the issues, but he never had a better idea. This operation was no exception.

Jones did one more quick run through the plan. "Look, we've got no quarrel with Jake Reacher. If the kid plays his cards right, he can go about his business when all this is over."

Which was a lie. Jones didn't expect any of that to happen. He didn't have orders to kill the kid and the mother, but he assumed those orders would come soon enough.

"The mother's a tool to make the kid behave. Take it easy on her. No bruises, no matter what. Nothing remotely threatening about her. Leave her alone." Jones gave Smith a snide grin. "She's too old and too skinny for your taste, anyway."

"Hell, a sturdy twelve-year-old girl could probably take her down with one strong push," Manny replied with a grin.

"We've been over all this. Let's get it done," Smith said.

Jones nodded. "Hold your water. Won't be much longer now."

They'd been watching Margaret Reacher since she arrived in Columbia three days ago. Brunette. Mid-fifties, or thereabouts. Brown eyes. Average height, meaning about five-four. Way too slender. She looked like she hadn't eaten a solid meal in weeks.

She had already made several foolish moves, revealing her total lack of training or expertise in basic situational awareness.

Along with her frail physique, her behavior screamed *easy mark*. Given the difficulties her son presented, Jones was just fine with Margaret being easy.

"No chance she'll be any kind of problem," Smith stated flatly from his perch on the back seat.

"Right," Jones nodded. "Mother and son plan to have dinner tonight at the Magnolia Hotel. The mother is already inside. The kid is due to arrive shortly."

The kid had graduated from basic training today. He'd be granted a short leave.

Kidnapping them both after graduation meant the army wouldn't be looking for Jake or his mother. Not tonight, anyway.

No one should notice either one was missing until Jake failed to report for his duty assignment next week.

"With any luck at all, we'll get in and get out and be on our way long before anyone realizes they're missing," Jones said.

Smith noticed a large group headed through the hotel's entrance. He pointed. "Look. Cover."

Jones said, "Okay. It's showtime."

"Finally. My ass is numb." Smith grumbled as he grabbed his gun, shoved it into his waistband, and left the van through the side door.

Smith tugged his baseball cap lower and ducked his head to shield his face from view. He stepped off, walking toward the hotel until he blended into the middle of the group.

"We'll be back. Stay alert," Jones instructed Manny before he followed close behind Smith a moment later.

CHAPTER 4

Tuesday, May 24
Near Fort Meade, MD

HUGH SULLIVAN'S OFFICIAL JOB title, deployed only when absolutely necessary, was Special Assistant to the Director of National Intelligence, National Security Administration. No one would find him on any organizational chart. He never appeared as the public face of the NSA.

His official duties were few. His real work was done in the shadows, off the books, without supervision or oversight.

He used the code name "Patton," one of the most successful generals the US Army had ever produced. Some said Patton had been a tactical genius. No one called him a failure. Ever.

He viewed his total operation as akin to a global conglomerate, complex and far-reaching and rapidly reconfigured as necessary.

He'd conceived the plan long ago, after watching boys play with indestructible plastic Lego building blocks. The durable blocks snapped together to create vehicles, towers, buildings, animals, boats, almost anything.

For more variety, gears and mini-figures and various other parts could be added and subtracted, destroyed and replaced, and integrated as necessary.

The individual blocks could snap apart without damaging the existing structure. Which could be rebuilt into a completely new object by adding and subtracting different blocks.

The idea was pure genius.

Legos had been successfully sold for generations. They were perhaps the longest-running, most successful toy on earth.

Key features were quality, durability, flexibility.

"Lego" translated from Danish for "play well."

Sullivan had appropriated and adapted the concept for his conglomerate. Well Played served as a slogan, moniker, and operational objective.

As Well Played's sole founder and chairman, Sullivan kept the Lego metaphor in mind and his finger on the pulse of his empire at all times.

Secrecy and security were the top priorities. He was connected to each of his CEOs by a secure encrypted line which refreshed frequently.

Thwarting eyes and ears and hackers and evil-doers had become second nature to Sullivan and everyone on the Well Played payroll.

Five minutes past the appointed time, Sullivan placed his weekly call to the White Kings CEO and Director of Pharmaceutical Development for the operational status report.

Dr. Felipe Sanz answered the call immediately. "How may I be of service to you this evening, Señor Patton?"

"Just give me the report," Sullivan smiled.

Spaniards were all about respect and courtesy, weren't they? It was refreshing. Finding Felipe had been an unexpected bonus, a lucky fluke.

Spain, one of the world's five largest cultivators of morphine-rich poppies, qualified as a high-level supplier of raw material stocks. Spain had applied to the DEA for approval to supply narcotic raw materials to the United States for pharmaceutical use.

Approval was granted.

Sullivan saw the revenue possibilities immediately.

When processed into heroin and opium by the White Kings, Spain's excess raw materials could be sold as pharmaceutical grade product on the black market. Rich Americans would gladly pay inflated prices for the it.

The plan had morphed beautifully into a significant money maker, both for the White Kings and Sullivan's other operations. Everything fed his coffers to fund the good works he did worldwide. Good works the U.S. Government couldn't legally do otherwise.

When he'd hired Sanz away from one of the richest producers in Spain, Sullivan sought a top Ph.D. chemist to create the medical-grade pharmaceuticals he intended to manufacture. He hadn't expected to like the man. The relationship they'd developed was a bonus.

"Production slowed down a bit the past few days, I'm afraid," Sanz reported. "We're running behind on the heroin. We have a big shipment going out tonight to Texas, and it may be early morning before we get it loaded."

"And the opium? How's that coming?"

"Better. The helicopter will be ready to depart for DC as scheduled," Dr. Sanz replied.

Sullivan chewed his lip. The report was straightforward enough. But to his trained ear, something important had been omitted.

After he'd put his finger on the missing piece, Sullivan asked, "What caused the slowdown in production?"

Production at the White Kings compound rarely missed schedule. The place hummed along like clockwork under Dr. Sanz's direction. They'd never had a delay before. During their last call, Sanz had reported receipt of the raw materials. No indication then that any sort of delay was anticipated.

Dr. Sanz cleared his throat. "I'm sorry to report that we had a fatality yesterday, sir. We're one man down. We haven't had a chance to replace him."

Sullivan sat upright in the chair. "A fatality? On the premises?"

"Yes. He died in his quarters."

"Cause of death?"

Sanz cleared his throat again. "It appears to have been a heroin overdose, sir."

"What? We've got addicts on the payroll?" Sullivan demanded, his jaw clenched hard. "I thought you solved that problem."

"Our products are pure, as perfect as we can make them. No one else creates products like ours. Which is why we can sell at top dollar," Sanz replied. "Some men are better able to resist temptation than others."

Sullivan could almost see Sanz shrug as he delivered the truism. "What was his name?"

"Rutger. We called him Rudy. Good man, before he got in too deep," Sanz said. "Such a shame."

"Where's the body?" Sullivan said, controlling his anger one small breath at a time.

"We buried him on the grounds, well outside the fence, near the poppy field. Where we buried the others. We had a little service for Rudy, too," Sanz explained. "That's why we lost so much production time."

"No survivors, right?"

The last thing Sullivan needed were mourners banging on the door. Eliminating the grieving presented logistical challenges and consumed valuable time he preferred to spend otherwise.

"He was an orphan, sir. Like they all are. Parents deceased. No siblings. No kids. We're meticulous about the background checks," Sanz replied. "But now we're short-staffed. And we have a full schedule for the next few weeks. We may need to adjust our deliveries."

Sullivan rapped his fingers on the desk, one after the other. "Yeah. I'll send you a suitable replacement soon."

"Thank you, sir," Sanz said obsequiously. "Was there anything else? I need to get back to the floor."

"Yeah. I'm sending you two house guests," Sullivan said, using the euphemism for hostages. "I'd prefer they were well tended while they're with you. But it's not essential. Do whatever you need to do."

Sanz paused for a long moment. "I'm sure that will be no problem, sir. We'll take care of them. How long will they be with us?"

"Not sure. As long as it takes," Sullivan replied before he hung up, still gnawing his lip.

He turned to the databases. A dozen files populated his screen instantly.

Sullivan scanned the lists until he found Rutger. He was an army vet, which was okay.

Most of the White Kings had served at one point or another. They weren't the military's best or brightest. But they'd had solid training, which the White Kings needed.

The White Kings recruited from Fort Jackson, Rutger's last duty station, which made sense, too. The White Kings once had a base near Fort Jackson before they'd outgrown those quarters.

Rutger's army personnel files revealed he had served his time without much distinction. No real problems noted, either. He'd been a standard grunt, no more, no less.

He'd done two tours in Afghanistan with a few of the other White Kings. That was okay, too. More than okay. It usually meant they worked well together as a team.

Sullivan was feeling better about the situation until he noted the name Rutger had listed as his emergency contact.

Lt. Colonel Susan Turner, CO of the 110th MP Special Unit, United States Army.

"What the hell? Are you kidding me?" Sullivan said aloud.

Rutger had probably listed Turner because he had to list someone and he didn't have anyone else. She might not even know she was his emergency contact.

And he'd been discharged five years ago. She'd probably forgotten a guy like Rutger in the first thirty seconds he'd been gone.

Hopefully.

CHAPTER 5

Tuesday, May 24
Columbia, SC

THE GROUP HEADING INTO the hotel was noisy and preoccupied and didn't seem to notice they'd acquired two more men tagging along behind.

Jones and Smith peeled off when the tourists headed for the restaurant on the south side of the first floor.

Smith moved to the elevator. Jones joined him. They rode up with two couples who were too busy talking to pay close attention to anything else. Noisy conversation filled the space to overflowing.

Smith and Jones kept their heads low, staring at the carpet, avoiding a full-face capture by the CCTV inside the elevator car.

After the car stopped on the fifth floor, Jones exited the elevator nonchalantly and turned left. Smith followed. They walked slowly until the elevator's doors closed, the system dinged, and the car continued its upward journey.

Then Jones and Smith did an abrupt turnaround and approached the room three doors down to the right of the elevator.

The doors to each room were arranged in pairs. There were three sets of pairs on each side, numbered from the end of the hallway toward the elevator lobby.

Margaret Reacher was booked into room 504. The kid was in room 502. The door was next to hers, and the rest of his room filled the remaining space at the end of the corridor.

While Jones kept a lookout, Smith drew his pistol from his waistband and held it out of sight of the cameras. He placed his thumb on the peep hole and knocked on her door.

"Housekeeping," Smith called out.

Margaret Reacher opened the door wide, wearing a bewildered smile and casual clothes. No shoes.

Jones shook his head. The woman exhibited no situational awareness at all. How had she managed to stay alive so long?

Before she could fully comprehend what was happening, Smith made his move.

He covered her mouth with his big palm, pushed the door wide with his hip, and rushed her inside, brandishing the pistol to reinforce the threat.

The woman's eyes widened and her nostrils flared with fear, but she barely resisted the backward momentum.

Smith barreled forward, shoving hard as she stumbled backward across the carpet.

When she plopped down on her ass on the bed and whimpered, Smith clamped his hand hard across her mouth and shoved her down onto her back.

Jones took a quick look along the quiet corridor. There were no guests milling about. With any luck, they had not been seen.

They had breached the room and neutralized the woman in less than five seconds. The inevitable CCTV cameras in the corridor shouldn't have captured anything remotely useful.

"So far, so good," Jones murmured under his breath.

He hurried inside, quickly put the "Do Not Disturb" sign on the knob, closed and locked the door. He exhaled a long breath and took a look around.

Smith pulled a sleep mask from his pocket and settled it on her face. She offered no resistance.

"Keep this on at all times," Smith told her gruffly. "The less you see, the better for you."

Margaret donned the sleep mask. She stopped whimpering and remained still, making no effort to escape.

Jones gave Smith an approving nod.

The woman was smart enough to guess that she shouldn't see too much or offer too much resistance. Not that she'd actually survive. But she'd be more compliant and easier to manage if she thought she had a chance.

Her suitcase was open on the luggage rack across from the foot of her bed. Her purse gaped open on the bed near her feet.

Swiftly, Jones walked through the connecting door to check both bedrooms and bathrooms. He shoved the shower curtains aside, just in case. But no one was hiding in either tub, hers or the kid's.

"All clear," Jones said as he returned.

He picked up the remote control and turned up the volume on the television. He found one of those twenty-four-hour cable channels broadcasting the deafening war news from the battlefield, complete with heavy artillery fire and flying helicopters.

The noise would cover her screams if she decided to do something stupid. Hell, that racket would dampen anything. Perfect.

Margaret Reacher lay on her back on the bed as if she was too terrified to move.

Smith shoved his gun into his belt and took his position as lookout at the window. He stood off to one side, between the bed and the wall, opposite the entry doors.

He held back the heavy drapes, staring onto Gervais Street. From that angle, he could see the front steps leading into the lobby.

When the kid arrived, Smith would see him immediately.

Jones shoved his pistol into the waistband of his jeans and glanced at the bedside clock. The kid was due to arrive soon. Not long to wait.

"I gotta take a leak," Jones said, regretting that last bottle of water he'd downed in the van. Better get rid of it now, while the docile Mrs. Reacher was their only hostage.

Jones went into the bathroom and closed the door behind him. He unzipped and urinated what felt like two gallons of excess water.

He zipped up and reached across the toilet to flush.

Which was when he heard a gunshot explode in the bedroom.

Jones pulled his pistol, yanked the door open, and took quick, long strides across the threshold into the room.

"What the hell is going on?" he shouted over the television's volume.

Neither Smith nor the woman replied.

In two more steps he had a clear view of the situation.

Smith was lying flat on his back on the carpet between the bed and the outside wall with his right leg slightly bent at the knee. His left arm slid down but still held the heavy drape between his fingers.

Margaret Reacher, the sleep mask pushed up on her head, stood in front of the prone Smith, holding a Glock 17 in both hands, pointed straight down at him.

Jones rushed toward her.

Before he could reach the woman, she fired a second shot into Smith's chest.

Jones knocked her arms aside and shoved her hard.

On the way down, she dropped the gun and Jones kicked it to the side.

She landed on her ass on the floor, staring straight ahead at her victim, hands empty, mouth rounded, eyes wide and horrified.

One quick look at Smith was all Jones needed to tell him the man was dead.

The room smelled of blood and gunfire.

The stench of death would come very soon.

"What the hell were you thinking?" Jones managed to spit out, followed by a stream of curses he'd learned doing time in some of the roughest places on earth.

Margaret Reacher seemed to shrink to half her normal size. Her teeth were chattering.

He glared at her shocked face and ordered harshly, "Don't move. Not even an inch. You got that?"

The instruction was unnecessary. She looked like a statue of a five-year-old child cemented to the spot.

He spent another moment looking at the body while disjointed thoughts zipped through his head faster than the bullets that had killed Smith.

The kid's room next door was undisturbed.

A quick scan of Margaret's bedroom revealed nothing that could tie Jones to the murder. The only thing he'd touched in here so far was the "Do Not Disturb" sign.

He went back to the bathroom, grabbed a washcloth, and used it to wipe his prints from the toilet handle and anything else he might have touched.

He walked through to the kid's room and collected the "Do Not Disturb" sign, using the washcloth to hold it. He touched nothing else.

Back in Margaret's room, he wiped the doorknob, the lock and replaced the sign on the outside. He used the washcloth to close the door and relock it from the inside.

Still using the washcloth, Jones picked up the hotel notepad next to the phone and forced the bitch to scribble a message onto it.

He tossed the note onto the bed along with the unused burner phone from Smith's pocket. He sent a quick message to the burner with a tag that said "Jake," just in case the kid wasn't any smarter than his mother.

Then he crammed the hotel's pen into his pocket along with the first "Do Not Disturb" sign.

"Come on." He grabbed Margaret's arm and pulled her up off the floor.

She didn't struggle. She was still in a weird state of shock. Surely this was the first time she'd ever killed anyone.

Jones's surprise had subsided. What he felt now was searing hot rage he was barely able to control.

The bitch shot Smith. She killed him. Smith wasn't a genius, but he didn't deserve to die like that.

If Jones had any concerns about what was supposed to happen to the bitch, those concerns were gone now.

He hauled her over to the side of the bed.

Angrily, he said, "You'll come with me. Give me any trouble, and I'll kill you like you killed him. And then I'll kill your son. Do you hear me?"

She nodded.

He gave her a hard shove toward the bed.

"Stick your feet in the shoes."

She did as she was told.

He kept a firm grip on her arm and pulled her across to the door. He pulled the sleep mask off her head and stuffed it into his pocket.

He kept his hold on her arm. "Open the door."

Like a pliant rag doll, she complied.

Jones pulled her into the corridor and waited until the hotel room door closed firmly behind them.

With luck, and the "Do Not Disturb" sign in place, the maids wouldn't enter the room until after Margaret's scheduled check-out time on Wednesday. Maybe.

They'd be gone long before then.

He forced her to grab a third "Do Not Disturb" sign off the door of another room and put it on Jake Reacher's door.

The signs might work to keep everyone out of those two rooms. And if staff violated the requests and entered anyway, there was nothing else he could do about it all now.

He strode to the stairwell, pulling the bitch along. Once inside the stairwell, he stuffed the cloth into his pocket and firmly closed the fire door.

"Down the stairs," he ordered.

She looked up, bewildered.

"Do it!" he said, giving her a little shove to reinforce the direction.

She seemed to comprehend. She started down slowly, one step at a time, holding onto the railing.

They trudged down five flights to the main lobby with the speed of charging turtles.

At the first-floor stairwell exit door, he shook her hard to get her attention. She looked at him through terrified eyes.

He jabbed her ribs with the barrel of his gun. A brutal reminder. "Act normally."

She nodded.

Jones watched through the small glass window in the door for a chance to mingle with other guests. As soon as he identified a reasonable opportunity, he tightened his grip on her arm and tugged her through the crowd.

Outside, he pulled her across the street to the parked panel van. He rapped on the side door and Manny pushed the button to slide it open.

Jones shoved her inside. Then he stepped inside behind her. He closed the door.

Manny gave him a puzzled look from the driver's seat but asked no questions. He started the engine.

"Give me both wrists. Right now," Jones growled, stifling the urge to punch her in the face.

She clasped her hands together in front of her body and he zipped a cable tie around them, pulling it hard, tighter than necessary. She winced. He didn't care.

He fastened her into the shoulder harness in the backseat where he could keep an eye on her. He opened the waiting pillowcase and tugged it down over her head.

On top of the pillowcase, he settled heavy over-ear headphones and sent loud music through them to block conversations and other noises from her hearing. With a remote control, he started the specialized soundtrack to fill the space between her ears for the duration of the drive.

Still breathing heavily, Jones climbed up front and settled into the passenger seat as Manny slipped the engine into drive and rolled out into traffic.

The White Kings compound was an hour's drive southwest, without traffic. More if they hit any kind of snag.

Jones pulled a new encrypted burner phone from the van's console and punched a preset key. After three rings, voicemail picked up.

"Ten-sixteen. Ten-sixteen." He paused and then added, "One man down."

Manny's eyes widened and he turned his head to stare. He opened his mouth to say something.

He saw the expression on Jones's face and thought better of it. Manny clamped his jaw shut and turned his attention to the traffic.

Jones worked to control his rage, breathing hard.

Through it all, Margaret Reacher never said a word.

Fortunately for her.

Jones didn't need a weighty excuse to pop her right here.

CHAPTER 6

Tuesday, May 24
Fort Jackson, SC

JAKE TOOK A FINAL look around to be sure he hadn't left anything behind when he'd packed up and stowed his gear in the Jeep.

One of his buddies walked past on his way out. "See you around, Reacher."

"Copy that," Jake replied.

Overall, his army basic training experience had been better and worse than expected.

Total confidence in his physical and mental abilities had settled deeply into his pores during boot camp. At the cellular level, he felt like a different man.

Not so long ago, he'd been a typical American college grad waiting for his real life to start.

He'd graduated today.

Now he was a trained soldier. A professional.

He would not be coming back here tonight. Fort Jackson, South Carolina, was firmly relegated to his past.

The world beyond Fort Jackson's gates was his future.

A few of the new soldiers had been apprehensive about the changes. Better the devil you know, they felt. Not Jake.

His nerves fairly hummed with excited anticipation. His life was about to expand exponentially in ways he had never imagined.

He couldn't wait to start.

Jake had a few days' leave before he was due to report to officer training school in Fort Benning, Georgia. His mother had hoped for more time together, and he hated to disappoint her, but the schedule was set in stone.

He was in the army now. Limited leave after basic was the army way, and Jake loved everything about the army way. He was completely satisfied with his career choices so far, even if his mom didn't understand.

Mom had wandered around the Visitor Center and the Basic Training Museum on family day like a lost child, bewildered and confused. She seemed to feel as if her son had become a stranger. Jake tried to reassure her, but he'd made little progress.

Dad had died months ago, but he would have felt the same as Mom. Dad was a college professor. He had not raised Jake to be a soldier. He'd have been as bewildered by Jake's choices as Mom was.

His parents were good people, solid citizens, and Jake loved them like crazy.

Which didn't mean he wanted to live the life they'd planned for him. Not even a little bit.

"But you're set to become a lawyer. Admitted to Harvard," his mother had said when he told her about the army, uncomprehendingly shaking her head. As if he'd gone off course somehow after Dad died.

Jake had tried to explain his feelings, but Mom simply widened her eyes and seemed more bewildered than a fawn caught in headlights.

She didn't mention any other Reachers or lay the blame for Jake's change in direction on his genes.

Reachers had been soldiers going back a good long while. Jake believed the army was baked into his DNA. Mom said that was nonsense. But was it?

Even if he couldn't explain it satisfactorily to his mother, Jake felt at home here. A sense of belonging he had never felt anywhere else. He certainly couldn't tell her that after she'd devoted her life to Jake and Dad.

So he laid the blame squarely on the army's rules. He had the same amount of leave time after basic training as the other members of his unit. Everything was easier that way.

He was running late tonight. Mom wouldn't mind. She still simply wanted him to be happy. She probably always would.

Still, he glanced at his watch to confirm his uncanny sense of the time, which he thought of as the clock in his head. The clock in his head had never been wrong. Not once.

No more nostalgia. Time to get a wiggle on, as one of his college buddies used to say. Or, as his drill sergeant would have put it, time to haul ass.

Jake grinned as he scanned his bunk one last time.

He planned to meet his mother at the Old Magnolia Hotel for a dinner celebration tonight. They'd spend the day together tomorrow before she drove back home to Laconia, New Hampshire, on Wednesday.

Jake wanted this to be a pleasant evening. Something she could remember while he was off traveling and saving the world.

He had Reacher blood in his veins, but he was also Margaret's son. He wanted her to start living her life again. Dad would have wanted that, too.

Whenever he asked, she said she was okay, but Jake noticed how her clothes were too large for her frail body, and the sadness that lingered in her eyes tugged his heart.

He worried about her, and he supposed he always would. He was the man in their little family of two now. It was his job to protect her from anything and everything. He wanted her to be more than okay, and really good with whatever life offered. Always.

He didn't know exactly how, but he meant to try his best to make it so. Margaret Reacher deserved that much, at the very least.

Jake swiveled his neck for a quick final scan, turned smartly on one heel, and strode purposefully through the barracks' exit into the heavy, humid air that covered everything in Columbia, South Carolina, like a shroud.

Perspiration dotted his upper lip instantly. He pushed through the heavy air. Smelled it, tasted it.

He wiped the sweat away with a knuckle as he hustled toward the parking lot, climbed into his Jeep, started the engine, and reversed out of the space.

A few days' leave.

It seemed like a lifetime.

He had not had a few days to himself since he walked into the army through the gates at Fort Jackson ten weeks ago. They'd kept him busy. He hadn't really noticed how little free time he'd been allowed while the hours rushed past.

But now…whole days off.

A big grin split his lips and deepened the creases at the corners of his steel-blue eyes.

At the exit gate, Jake slowed and lowered the window. The tall, broad-shouldered sentry was busy with another vehicle coming through on the other side. A green sedan, driven by a dark-haired woman wearing an officer's uniform. Jake couldn't see much of her through the sentry hutch. Her hair was pulled back. Small-boned and slender, she removed her sunglasses to allow the sentry to confirm her ID. She had amazingly huge brown eyes.

The sentry checked her in and offered an appreciative but unnecessary salute. She flashed a megawatt smile bright enough to light Las Vegas, replaced her sunglasses, and drove onto the base.

"Who knew the army had such spectacular officers?" Jake grinned as the sentry's attention finally turned his way. He handed over his ID.

"No kidding," the sentry replied, glancing toward the retreating green sedan with a woeful expression on his face.

"Who was that?" Jake asked.

"Lieutenant Colonel Susan Turner, CO of the 110th MP Special Unit."

"Seriously? Why do we need the CO of the 110th MP on base? Something happen?" Jake asked, wondering how he could have missed that level of excitement.

"My policy? Don't mess with the 110th," the sentry replied. "You should adopt it as a mantra."

"Okay, but I've never seen a cop that good-looking before. You?"

"Yeah, well, quit looking. She's way above your pay grade, soldier." The sentry grinned as he gave everything a quick once over, handed back Jake's ID, and waved him through. "You're backing up traffic."

"Too bad," he replied and rolled the Jeep out into traffic, still smiling.

Jake raised his right hand and waved goodbye to his past as he left Fort Jackson in his rearview.

He hit the redial on his phone. The electronic buzz sounded four times before the call clicked over to voicemail. She must be in the shower. He waited for the tone.

"Sorry I'm running behind, Mom, but I'm on my way. I'll see you in twenty minutes. Thirty, tops, if the traffic's bad."

Jake disconnected and tossed the phone onto the passenger seat. Up ahead, traffic was already backed up. The drive into downtown Columbia would consume at least the next thirty minutes.

Damn. He slapped the steering wheel with his big paw. He'd be late. Again.

He grinned. He had a clock in his head, but he wasn't a slave to it and never had been. His mother already knew as much.

On its outskirts, Columbia was a mix of new and old, a town filled with history and promise. Jake had tried to convince his mother to stay a few days to explore the city, but she'd said she needed to get back home. She had a list of excuses.

People were counting on her. People she cared about. She volunteered at the library on weekends, and she didn't want to inconvenience the other volunteers, who were mostly neighbors she'd known all her life. There were bridge games scheduled, and she couldn't find a substitute at this late date. And so on.

No, she needed to get back.

Jake had kept trying, but none of his arguments made any difference.

Mom was leaving Wednesday, bright and early. She'd made up her mind.

On some level, he was glad she had started to rebuild her life and had solid reasons to head back home. Dad's death had been a terrible blow, but mom seemed to be emerging slowly from the unrelenting grief.

Margaret Reacher would be just fine.

And Jake was already feeling a little less guilty about joining the army and leaving her alone.

CHAPTER 7

Tuesday, May 24
Chicago, IL

KIM FELT NAKED AND vulnerable without her duty weapon. Most criminals were taller, heavier, and meaner than she was.

She had solid training, strong self-defense, close-quarters combat skills, and tactical chops most criminals didn't, which leveled the playing field a bit.

But her marksmanship was her greatest equalizer. The gun was absolutely necessary.

The detective in charge had promised to get the gun back to her as soon as possible, but he'd also told her about the backlog of work facing Chicago PD lab techs these days.

"We've got more than four thousand gun violence cases we're processing," he'd said, not by way of an excuse. Just the facts. "We'll fast-track this one for you, but it could be a few days or even weeks before we can get it done."

"Thanks," she said with a nod.

He grinned. "I'm sure the FBI has plenty of weapons you can use in the meantime."

"Right," she replied, without elaborating.

Chicago had some of the toughest gun control laws in the country. She couldn't simply buy a new gun tonight. Not legally, anyway.

"I'll work it out," she'd told him.

He didn't ask how she planned to solve the problem, which was a good thing. Because the truth was that replacing her gun was a bigger issue than it might have been for another agent.

Under normal circumstances, an agent on active duty would receive a replacement weapon swiftly and through channels. Not for her. Working off the books wasn't for the timid and weak-kneed.

When Kim finally made it back to the hotel, she brewed fresh coffee first. When in doubt, drink coffee. That was always her plan B.

Kim poured the coffee into a paper cup and sipped for fortification. Then she located the encrypted burner phone that connected her directly to her former partner like a tether connects a spacewalker to the ship.

She settled onto the bed with her feet up and her eyes closed. She pushed the direct dial button and listened while the signal clicked through cyberspace like an arrow aimed directly at the bullseye.

"I was just about to call you, Suzie Wong," Carlos Gaspar said with a smile in his voice. "I've been looking at video footage for so long my eyes are glazed over."

"Found anything?" She heard hope in her voice and he probably could, too. She sipped the hot coffee while he talked.

"Maybe. As car thieves go, your convict has more talent than most," Gaspar said with something close to admiration in his tone.

"Don't I know it," Kim replied sourly.

Petey Burns had escaped from a federal prison in Bolton, South Dakota. His mug shot had been circulated to law enforcement all over the country. He'd been sighted a few times, but each time he'd escaped like a Las Vegas magician before law enforcement could recapture him.

Tracking a car thief shouldn't have been all that difficult. The manhunt should have succeeded in the first forty-eight hours. It had not.

Worse, Kim had had more than one chance to recapture him and she'd failed.

Burns had somehow remained at large for twelve days and counting.

Gaspar said, "Because of his preference for German cars, I had been limiting my focus to the top German manufacturers."

"But you've changed your approach," Kim guessed. "Because you saw Burns somewhere driving something not German."

"Give that girl a cigar," Gaspar replied. "A Volvo, to be precise. Traveling south from Gary, Indiana. But even better than that, he was not alone."

Kim nodded and smiled, even though he couldn't see her. Gaspar had never let her down. Not once. And he wasn't even her partner anymore.

Petey Burns was a goofy and endearing serial offender. Even with all that charm going for him, he'd never managed to evade arrest for more than a few days before. There was no reason to believe he'd suddenly become a tactical genius.

Which meant Burns wasn't the one calling the shots here.

A wiser man was running this game.

Someone with training and experience.

One who understood law enforcement and criminal minds.

A guy who was competent and clever and supremely confident.

When there's only one choice, it's the right choice.

Jack Reacher was leading this little posse. Had to be.

Reacher had hitched a ride with Petey Burns back in South Dakota ten days ago. They'd been seen together several times since then. It appeared they were traveling together, at least for a time. They'd split up. But now, it seemed they were together again.

It was a stroke of good luck on Kim's hunt for Reacher. She'd never been lucky before. Never believed in luck. Never had any cause to. Certainly, she never relied on luck for anything.

Chasing Burns while the whole country was looking for him was a hell of a lot easier than finding Reacher, operating alone and in the shadows, without any official support.

Reacher traveled the country. No fixed address. No assets. No credit cards. No driver's license. No reason to stay anywhere more than a few days.

He had an ATM card which he used to withdraw money from his pension account now and then. But those transactions happened randomly and were only reflected after the fact, not before.

Sometimes Reacher took the bus. More often, he hitchhiked.

Which was how he ended up in the passenger seat next to Burns.

No doubt in Kim's mind.

Reacher was the brains of this little crew of two. Burns had been free as a bird for almost two weeks, a lifetime for his track record.

Had to be Reacher's doing.

Which was why she'd called Gaspar, her secret weapon.

Right at the beginning of this assignment, she'd learned that Reacher and Gaspar think alike. They were identical in all the important ways that made it so.

Men. Cops. Veterans. Same foundation. Same training. Same early life experiences. Same prism.

If the brains weren't precisely the same, they were a lot closer to each other than either one was to Kim's way of thinking.

Her second secret weapon, why Kim had been chosen and why she would win was simple. Reacher had no idea how her mind worked.

She'd exploited both weapons more than once. As a result, she was closer to finding Reacher right this minute than she'd ever been.

She grinned again. "That's great, Chico. Do you know where they are right now?"

"Not yet. So far, we've only seen recorded video footage. Some of it's a couple of days old. But the Gary Indiana video is solid. It's definitely Burns driving and Reacher in the passenger seat," Gaspar said. "We are tracking from there."

"When did they pass through Gary?"

"The video we found is dated early Monday morning," Gaspar replied. "Which means we've got more than thirty-six hours of video to search through."

"What are you looking for?"

"We'll find the Volvo abandoned somewhere. Burns will switch out to something else as soon as he can," Gaspar explained. "Which will mean we'll need to locate and trace a different vehicle. That will take some extra time."

Kim climbed off the bed and opened her laptop. She pulled up a few road maps, thinking about the logistics.

"There aren't that many roads heading out of Gary, Indiana. That will reduce the number of cameras you'll need to access. And they've got to sleep sometime. Somewhere," she paused thoughtfully. "So how long before you can locate them? Any idea?"

She could jump in a rental and drive like hell to wherever they were, but Burns and Reacher had a solid head start. And Burns drove like a man with a lead foot. She probably wouldn't catch them that way.

Kim grimaced. As usual, flying was a better option. She didn't have to like it, but she'd suck it up to get the job done.

While her mind had wandered, Gaspar was talking again.

CHAPTER 8

Tuesday, May 24
Columbia, SC

UP AHEAD, JAKE SAW the Magnolia Hotel on Gervais Street, within walking distance of the State House and the Congaree River. He parked the Jeep, grabbed his duffel, and ran up the old stone steps to the main entrance.

At the desk, he collected his room key for 502, the room adjoining his mother's, and took the elevator to the fifth floor.

He stepped out into a silent and unoccupied corridor, which seemed both strange and welcome all at the same time.

Jake cocked his head and basked in the sheer joy of silence. At home in Laconia, he'd spent many happy hours engaged in quiet pursuits. Along with everything else, his opportunities to experience solitude had also changed.

He'd spent the last ten weeks in the constant companionship of other recruits. Conversations had become a solid wall of background noise every waking moment of his life in the army.

A constant low decibel level mix of voices, footfalls, music, television, and a plethora of other noises sounded beneath all activity like a score for a movie.

A "Do Not Disturb" sign hung on the door to his mother's room. He gave the door a quick double tap as he passed, just to let her know he'd arrived.

Jake used his key to enter Room 502 next door. He noticed she'd put the sign on his door, too.

Once inside, he took a fast look around, revealing the spacious setup. Traditionally furnished in greens and golds. Queen-sized four-poster bed. Smallish private bathroom. Flat-screen TV mounted on the wall. Heavy drapes pulled across the windows. A bedside lamp casting a warm glow over the furniture.

Not upscale, but a lot nicer than anywhere he'd slept recently. More privacy, too. The room felt both luxurious and somehow lonely at the same time.

The feeling itself was odd. Jake had never been lonely. Not once in his entire life.

The door between the two rooms was slightly ajar.

He noticed the television blasting from Mom's room, roaring the evening news about the war. Oddly, he hadn't heard the TV while he was out in the corridor.

"These rooms must have incredible soundproofing," he murmured.

He dropped his duffel onto his bed and rapped his knuckles on the dividing door.

"Mom, sorry I'm late. The traffic was crazy," he called out pleasantly over the noise from the TV, pushing into her room as he moved silently across the plush green carpet. "Are you decent? I'm coming in."

With a genuinely happy smile, he walked through, expecting her to be ready and waiting. She wasn't always punctual, but he was late enough that she should have been ready.

"Man, it's cold in here," he said. The air conditioning must have been turned as low as it would go, and the room felt colder than a meat locker.

He stopped moving almost instantly.

What he saw didn't meet his expectations. Not even a little bit.

First, Margaret Reacher was not in the room.

Her dinner outfit was laid out on the bed.

The bathroom door was open. He glanced inside.

She wasn't there.

Next, he noticed the odor he should have smelled sooner. He put his forearm across his face to shield his nose, but it didn't help.

Which was when his gaze dropped to the floor.

He saw the man's feet immediately.

"What the hell?" he said, the words barely audible because of the blaring TV.

Jake's eyes widened and his breathing quickened as he approached for a better view.

The man lay flat on his back on the carpet in the narrow space between the bed and the wall. His right leg was bent at the knee. His left hand held the heavy drape loosely between his fingers.

Oddly, the first thing Jake felt was relief.

Because the body with the hole in its chest, blood pooling around it, dead eyes staring at the ceiling, was not his mother.

The feeling lasted but a moment before his heartbeat accelerated uncomfortably hard in his chest.

Jake approached carefully to avoid disturbing the evidence.

He didn't touch the body or reach for his phone to call for help. No point.

Two things were immediately undeniable.

The man was definitely dead.

And Jake had never seen him before.

"Why were you in my mother's room, anyway?"

He scanned the room quickly and noticed several things he hadn't noticed initially.

A pistol on the floor, maybe six feet from the body.

Jake had spent a lot of time around guns lately. But he didn't need to call upon his basic training to identify the weapon instantly.

He'd seen that particular gun many times before. Besides, his mother had told him she'd brought it with her from home. For sentimental reasons, she'd said, she wanted him to have it.

The gun had belonged to Dad, who hadn't liked guns much. Living in a rural community, he'd viewed them as a necessary evil. He might need to shoot the occasional snake.

Dad's entire garage was lined with tools and every single one had bright yellow reflective tape diagonally across the grips, just like that pistol.

In Laconia, neighbors and friends often borrowed tools and didn't return them. The diagonal tape on the handles was Dad's way of identifying his stuff whenever the need arose. As it often did.

Dad didn't mind if people borrowed his things. He simply wanted his stuff returned when the borrower was finished.

Unlike his garden rakes and hammers, the tape on the handgun's grip looked almost as new as the day David Reacher had wrapped it. As far as Jake knew, no one had ever borrowed the weapon.

Jake had seen Dad use the gun only once when a fox couldn't be dissuaded from raiding the nests of Dad's beloved songbirds.

Jake had been about ten years old at the time. He and Mom had cried when they saw the dead songbirds. Dad was incensed. He'd pulled out the pistol and staked out the remaining robin's nest. That very night, he got lucky. Two quick shots ended the fox's hunting days.

Neither Jake nor Dad had the least bit of sympathy for the fox, even as they carried his body on a shovel blade and buried it way in the back of their property.

Jake shook his head to clear the long-forgotten images as he looked again at the body. Definitely not a fox.

But the dead man didn't belong in his mother's room, just like the fox had no business invading the songbirds. Just like the fox, the dude got what he had coming.

"Who the hell are you, and where is my mother?" Jake cocked his head and narrowed his eyes as if the man might actually sit up and answer.

Jake stood, rooted to the spot, with jumbled thoughts running through his head like the fast ticker running along the bottom of the television screen.

It was odd that cops hadn't flooded the hotel already, wasn't it?

The rooms in the old hotel were thick and solidly soundproofed. The heavy fire doors muffled sounds, too. Jake had not heard the television until he'd entered his own room and then only because the connecting door was ajar.

Was the war news loud enough to cover actual gunshots?

But at least two gunshots had been fired, given the two holes in the man's torso. Guns were more than loud. Fired in a closed room like this one, surely someone would have heard the explosions.

So where were the police? Were they on the way? How much time did he have before they arrived?

Not long, probably. Nervous sweat dotted his brow and he dabbed it with his sleeve. He had nothing to fear from the police. He hadn't killed anyone.

But what about Mom?

Had Margaret Reacher killed this guy? Why would she do that?

And if she didn't kill him, who did?

And where was she, anyway?

Had the killer taken his mother?

His gaze fell on the bed again.

Near Mom's dinner outfit, he saw the hotel note paper in plain view and a cell phone resting beside it. Mom's personal cell phone sported a neon pink silicone case he'd bought for her. She said the case glowed in the dark and she could find it easily at night or inside her purse.

This cell phone was cheap black plastic. It was smaller than hers and a different brand altogether.

The note was hastily scribbled with the hotel's cheap ballpoint, but unmistakably his mother's strong handwriting. The words were underlined twice and made her wishes clear.

"No cops."

CHAPTER 9

Tuesday, May 24
Washington, DC

WEARING A GRAY WIG, false goatee, hat, and glasses, Hugh Sullivan strolled along the sidewalk on the National Mall pretending to enjoy the unseasonably balmy evening.

The famous cherry blossoms had long since peaked, and the delicate pink petals were gone with the wind. Verdant spring leaves had sprouted along with the annuals and the grass re-installed every year.

A few tourists were wandering and pointing out the various attractions in the famous skyline. A young couple strolled ahead arm in arm.

A tall, skinny man wearing a jaunty porkpie hat set back too far on his head approached as if there were no reason for caution.

Leonard Dover's nonchalance was meant to convey that they were just two friends meeting up for a walk. Nothing suspicious or unusual about that if anyone was watching.

Of course, someone was.

In Washington, DC, someone was always watching.

Every moment of every day, someone or something had eyes on every corner of the city and every person populating the area for any reason.

Prudence required wiser heads to assume as much. Nothing remained under cover in this town. Even inconsequential secrets were regularly exposed in the most public of ways.

Dover fell into step beside Sullivan, matching his leisurely pace. "We may have a problem."

Sullivan replied, "So you said."

"It looks like an idiot has infiltrated the Club," Dover reached into his pocket for a cigarette and a lighter. "Styled himself as a conscientious whistleblower."

Not many people smoked cigarettes these days. It was reckless to light one up here in the near darkness. Dover should have known better. Operatives with proper training would be able to spot him more easily in person now and on video later.

Sullivan frowned and made a mental note of the infraction. In his experience, a nervous man develops habits to control his worries. Once those habits were formed, they were exceedingly difficult to break. Simply better to replace the man.

He would replace Dover when the opportunity presented itself. Which it would, soon enough.

He'd established his personnel policies early and applied them effectively for decades.

Succinctly stated, no one in Sullivan's orbit was allowed to cause significant potential inconvenience. Dover's tenure was nearing its end.

"What's the Judas crusading about? Nothing about chess is illegal," Sullivan replied.

"He's made an appointment with one of our influential generals to discuss his, er, concerns." Dover paused for a long drag on the cigarette and blew three perfect smoke rings into the night.

Sullivan smiled. "Club members. His *concerns* will be put to rest."

Dover shook his head. "They've tried. He's insistent. Already complained to a second club member who tried to deflect him. No luck."

"Oh?" Sullivan said, pushing his hands into his pockets in a relaxed, unconcerned way for the benefit of watchers.

"He says he'll go to all eight generals. If he gets no satisfaction at the club member level, he says he'll keep going up the food chain until he gets a publicly televised hearing," Dover said, taking a final draw on the cigarette. He pinched off the fire, field stripped the butt, and dropped the mess into his pocket.

Sullivan nodded approvingly. Dover was a nervous man, but he'd been trained well. He hadn't forgotten everything he'd learned.

They walked a while in silence until the lingering young couple behind them moved onto one of the park benches to neck under the stars.

Sullivan advanced another twenty yards out of the couple's earshot before he picked up the conversation. "Who is this guy, anyway?"

"Rupert Adams the fourth," Dover replied, shaking his head. "I mean, giving a kid a name like that, parents have got to expect trouble."

"Don't think I've met him. Name's not familiar." Sullivan frowned. "What is this Judas complaining about, specifically?"

Dover lowered his voice further. "He had a friend. The friend died recently of a heroin overdose. So he's sensitive now, I guess. Recently enlightened is how he put it."

"Why is he complaining to us about heroin? There's no heroin on the premises at the Club."

"We don't know."

"I see," Sullivan nodded, frowning because the problem was more serious than he'd expected.

The mole's personal issue was pushing him, which would make him more difficult to deflect.

And it sounded like he'd made a connection between the heroin that killed his friend and the opium supplied to the Club.

Not good.

"He's a full member, you say? Not a provisional member or a guest?"

"Full member for three years. Takes advantage of everything the Club offers," Dover nodded. "Only recently has he been beset with his attack of conscience. Since his friend died."

"So we have the usual proof that he's been participating fully for three years," Sullivan said flatly. "Just in case he gets some sort of wild hair. We've got enough to bury him."

"Of course," Dover replied. "I checked."

A young woman approached, walking from the opposite direction. Dover stood aside. Sullivan moved ahead, nodding politely as she passed.

"Who else is he talking to?" Sullivan asked when Dover rejoined him, blowing a long stream of annoyance through his lips.

"Club members only, so far as we know. But the more brick walls he hits, the more likely he is to go broader," Dover replied.

"I'm sure I don't know him," Sullivan said, still perplexed. He kept his finger on the pulse of everything. But this guy didn't resonate with him at all.

"You know his people, for sure." Dover shook his head woefully. "He came highly recommended. We vetted him according to protocols. Two of his bosses are members. And he's a legacy through his father."

"His father?"

"The father came over with the group from the old Dove Cottage Club when that got busted up seven years ago. He was killed in Afghanistan a year or so later by an IED," Dover said. "I don't know how we missed the son's self-righteous tendencies. But we did."

Another group of tourists came up from behind, laughing and talking loudly. Sullivan and Dover paused and stood aside to let them pass and then fell into step again.

"Recommendations?" Sullivan said.

"Nothing yet. No real harm done so far. Just thought you should know." Dover shrugged. "We've got eyes on him twenty-four seven. If the situation changes, I'll contact you."

They had reached an intersection in the sidewalk and the end of Dover's report.

Sullivan's instinct was to eliminate the threat first and ask questions later. But he nodded approvingly. Perhaps it was wiser to collect full intel first in this instance.

"Be prepared to act quickly," Sullivan said flatly. "Send me his full background files. We may have more damage control to do. And keep me posted constantly as the situation develops."

Dover nodded.

Sullivan turned left and walked away.

He heard Dover's leather soles slapping the sidewalk as he strolled in the opposite direction.

The conversation had been troubling on many levels. Sullivan trusted Dover. He was a good man. He'd been on the payroll for a while. His job was to identify problems and solve them before they became too big to handle without interference.

But Sullivan was also supremely annoyed. The Four Knights Club was one of his best-performing assets. He couldn't afford to lose it.

Put simply, Dover had waited too long to handle the threat. He'd identified the Judas problem much later in the process than he should have.

Perhaps a different outcome would have been possible if the mole had been identified earlier. At this point, only one solution existed.

The mole must die. Very Soon. Within twenty-four hours.

Where, how, and what to do with the body were the only questions that remained to be answered. He couldn't be buried at the Palace. He had too many connections.

Sullivan sighed. At the moment, nothing could be done about any of that.

He put his head down and quickened his pace. The mole wasn't the only problem on his agenda.

CHAPTER 10

Tuesday, May 24
Columbia, SC

JAKE STARED AT THE note. And the phone. And the body. It was all surreal.

He wanted to call the police. But he didn't because her note was emphatic. *No Cops.*

"What the hell have you gotten yourself into, Mom?"

Once the police arrived, Jake wouldn't be allowed to go after her. Not for a while, anyway. They'd want statements and information. Fingerprints and DNA. Who knew what else?

Hell, they might even think Jake killed this guy. He'd be a suspect, at the very least.

The guy on the floor was already dead. Nothing could be done for him now.

First things first.

His mother was missing. Possibly kidnapped. Possibly by this man's killer.

Margaret Reacher had done nothing but love Jake and take care of him his entire life. She deserved the benefit of every doubt. He owed her that much and more.

The longer he delayed calling the police, the worse it looked for both of them. He knew that.

Jake hadn't killed anyone. He didn't want some South Carolina detective thinking otherwise if he was found standing by the body.

When the police arrived, they'd take the place apart with tweezers. Nothing would go unnoticed. Trace evidence was some of the most powerful in any trial.

Margaret's DNA was all over everything in this room. She'd been staying here for days.

This was the first time Jake had set foot in here.

He took one last look around the room.

Jake replayed the scene in his mind from the time he walked into his room until now. He hadn't disturbed anything.

He was almost certain.

Memory wasn't good enough. When he was interrogated, he'd need more than his word that he'd disturbed nothing inside the room.

He needed insurance.

Jake pulled out his cell phone and shot a long video of Room 504. He recorded the bedroom and bathroom and everything visible in them.

After that, he snapped several still photos of the dead man.

He emailed the videos and the photos to himself so he'd have access to them in case his phone was confiscated. Which it probably would be.

Then he stared for a long time at the gun.

Should he take it? Or not?

Jake hadn't started his law enforcement training yet, but he'd watched enough cop shows to know that everything in this room was evidence in a homicide.

Evidence tampering was a felony everywhere. If he touched that gun now, the ripple effect could capsize his entire life.

He'd done nothing wrong so far.

He could call the police and get them on the scene right now, against his mother's scribbled instructions.

Or he could end his army career right here before it ever really started.

Hell, he might even go to prison for concealing a murder weapon if he took the gun.

Margaret Reacher didn't deserve to be prosecuted for murder.

He'd stake his whole life, and hers, too, on that much.

If Mom had killed this guy, which was still an open question, she would have had a solid reason.

The shooting was absolutely justified. It had to be.

She'd have stayed to face the music, knowing she'd be exonerated.

He felt his head wagging instinctively. She didn't simply shoot this guy for no reason and then run away.

Margaret Reacher would never, ever, have done something like that. He'd stake his life on it. Hers, too.

So where was she? Where did that cheap cell phone come from? Why did she explicitly instruct him not to notify the police?

After what seemed like a couple of moments too long, he figured it out.

The only answer that made any sense was that someone had forced her to leave.

Which meant this dead dude must have had an accomplice.

When Jake found him, the gun could save Mom's life and Jake's, too.

He weighed the options, all of them bad, for a few seconds longer before he shrugged and made his choice.

He had to find his mother and bring her back safely.

Nothing was more important.

Not his own safety, not his career. Nothing.

Mom came first.

He owed her everything.

And he had an ace in the hole. He still had Agent Otto's private number. She'd given it to him when he first met her back in the spring. If he got into so much hot water that he couldn't get himself out, he'd call Otto.

But not yet.

And not from inside this hotel.

His decision was made.

Jake reached down and grabbed the gun. He stuffed it into his waistband and pulled his shirt down to cover it.

Then he swiped the note and the phone from the bed and stuffed them into his pockets as he strode quickly back to his room.

He made a second set of videos of both rooms now that he'd messed with the evidence he'd recorded the first time and sent them to a dummy email address to which only he had access.

Then he deleted all the videos from his phone.

What else?

The yellow shirt he was wearing would act as a beacon. Even the dimmest witness would remember a big guy wearing a yellow shirt.

He opened his duffel and pulled out a denim shirt and slipped it over the bright yellow polo with the sweat stains under the armpits. He turned the collar up to cover his face as much as possible and stuck a denim baseball cap on his head. He pulled the bill down low.

The wardrobe change did nothing to conceal his size and shape, but it was the best he could do for the moment. At least the denim would blend into his surroundings.

He zipped the duffel and grabbed it off the bed and headed out.

He handled the doorknob with the denim shirt sleeve and wiped his fingerprints from the knob as best he could. Then he opened the door and did the same to the exterior knob.

Jake hadn't touched the "Do Not Disturb" sign on his door on the way in, and he didn't touch it on the way out, either.

Still holding the knob with his hand inside his denim sleeve, he closed the fire door solidly behind him.

"I'm coming, Mom. Hang on," he muttered under his breath, stuffing the cheap black cell phone into his pocket.

Jake wasn't a cop yet, but he knew the hotel was equipped with CCTV. It was too late to rewind his behavior and sneak into the hotel. His image would be all over the earlier CCTV video footage, wearing the yellow polo. He shrugged. Couldn't be helped.

He also figured once the body was discovered, some detective would put two and two together and come up with six and start looking for him.

Which meant he could buy himself some time if he could leave the hotel unnoticed. Or, if unnoticed wasn't possible, at least he could be not quite as obvious on CCTV.

Jake had spent zero time in his life avoiding the police. He'd never had to. He'd always been one of the good guys.

He had no idea whether his actions would be effective or laughable to experienced detectives.

In the corridor, he made his way to the elevator lobby. Finally, a lucky break. The hotel had two stairwells, one beside each of the two elevator cars.

He used his shirt sleeve to open the stairway door on the left and slipped inside.

Instead of going down, Jake took the stairs two at a time up to the seventh floor. Then he covered his hand with the denim sleeve again to open the door. He slipped into the elevator lobby and moved quickly into the other stairwell.

This time, he took the stairs two at a time down to the hotel entrance level.

At the bottom of the stairs, he waited until a group of tourists, laughing and talking, entered the elevator lobby and pressed the call button.

When the elevator arrived, a batch of tourists poured out, and the waiting tourists moved in. During the exchange, Jake slipped out of the stairwell and joined a group moving toward the front exit.

Outside, he hustled downstairs to the sidewalk and made his way to the parking lot where he'd left the Jeep.

He pressed the key fob to open the hatch, tossed the duffel in the back, and slipped behind the steering wheel.

Jake rolled the Jeep into traffic and drove a few miles to the nearest fast food joint. He pulled into the lot and parked. He waited a few minutes to be sure he hadn't been followed before he fished the burner phone from his pocket.

When he powered it up, there was a text message waiting. The message had his name on it.

He pressed the button and the full text showed on the screen.

It said: "Tell no one or she dies. Wait for our call."

Jake's worst fears were confirmed. His mother had been taken. If he screwed up, they would kill her. No question about it.

He read the short message three times because the words simply would not stick in his mind.

CHAPTER 11

Tuesday, May 24
Chicago, IL

"I'M WORKING AS FAST as I can here, Sunshine," Gaspar chuckled. "I promise you'll be the first to know when I find Burns and Reacher. And once I do that, I'll keep a closer eye on them, too."

That was a promise he couldn't keep and she couldn't rely upon. He didn't control all the variables and neither did she.

A few weeks ago, Gaspar had retired from the FBI and taken a job with the very high-end Scarlett Investigations in Houston. Scarlett had several exceptionally competent operatives on her payroll.

One of them had helped Kim out a few weeks back.

Michael Flint.

Too bad he wasn't her partner, she'd mused more than once. Flint was a man she could rely on.

As trustworthy as Gaspar, Flint was exceptionally fit, and all his limbs were fully functional. An on-the-job injury years ago had left Gaspar unable to perform the physical aspects of the job.

So Gaspar was no longer a member of law enforcement. He wasn't bound by the same rules Kim was forced to obey.

All of which meant Gaspar had resources Kim couldn't access, along with more room to move when he deployed those resources.

This was her third secret weapon.

She had unknown resources available to her, more than her enemies and many of her friends.

The downside was that The Boss kept close tabs on Gaspar and even closer tabs on Kim.

The Boss was aware that Gaspar had located the Volvo. Once Gaspar found Reacher, The Boss would know about it almost instantly.

She'd learned to stop worrying about what he might do with that intel.

Nothing Kim or Gaspar could do to prevent The Boss's omnipresence or to stop him from intervening, even if she wanted to. She wasn't all that sure about what she wanted in this particular instance, anyway.

Kim reconnected to her secure server. With a few clicks, she found the encrypted files Gaspar had sent earlier.

She located the arrest records for Peter Arthur Burns and scanned through quickly for the relevant intel.

"They were headed south, right?" she asked, skimming over the data.

"Yeah. I mean, roughly in a southerly direction. Not like they had unlimited options. It's impossible to go very far north from Gary, Indiana, without landing in Lake Michigan," Gaspar teased. "Also not likely they'd double back to Chicago. So east and south are the logical choices."

"They will avoid the interstates," Kim mumbled, preoccupied with searching through the intel on the screen to locate what she wanted. "Okay. Found it. Mable Geraldine Burns. Petey's mother."

Noises from Gaspar's clacking keyboard filled the air between them. "What about her?"

"Her last known address is Marietta, Georgia," Kim replied. "Not too far from Atlanta."

She rattled off the digits and Gaspar made a note of them. He'd do a thorough background check on the address and the woman. Soon. Very soon.

"It's a stretch to assume Burns is going home to see his mama, don't you think?" Gaspar said. "And if he is headed that way, why would Reacher go along for the ride?"

Kim pushed back in her chair and closed her eyes to think. "Remember where we started this assignment, Chico?"

"You mean the day you rented that piece of crap Chevy in Atlanta?" Gaspar teased. "How could I forget?"

"Yeah, yeah. Well, after that, we learned about Jacqueline," Kim mused aloud. "Don't tell me you don't recall her."

"Jacqueline Roscoe Trent," Gaspar said, letting her know he hadn't forgotten.

"Born the right length of time after Reacher left Margrave. Nine pounds, two ounces. Thirty inches long. Fair hair, blue eyes," Kim recited from memory.

Gaspar added, "Fifteen years old and a tall drink of adolescent trouble."

"Living in Margrave, not too far south of Atlanta, Georgia," Kim finished.

"So you think Reacher could be on the way to see the girl?" Gaspar asked, sounding unconvinced. "All of a sudden, Reacher wants to be a daddy?"

Kim shook her head slowly. "Stranger things have happened."

"Not since the dinosaurs disappeared," Gaspar grumbled under his breath. "Most guys who love 'em and leave 'em like Reacher don't go back to see if their seeds have sprouted."

"Well, some things have come up recently that might have put the idea into his head," Kim insisted.

"You're talking about Reacher learning he has a nephew a few weeks back?" Gaspar replied, exhaling a long gust of pent-up breath.

"Partly. But if Reacher had a kid of his own, he would feel responsible for her. He'd go back to Margrave and check it out. He'd want to know for sure," Kim insisted. "That's what you would do, isn't it?"

"Yeah, and I get your point. I certainly would check on her. And I'd have done it long before now," Gaspar said quietly.

There were many things about Reacher's behavior that Gaspar didn't approve of. Kim guessed Reacher's sex life was probably one of them.

"Exactly. As soon as you had reason to suspect you had a kid out there, you'd be on the way to find out for sure," Kim said.

"*But he's not me.* Don't forget that, Sunshine. I'm the guy who settled down, got a real job, had a family. Reacher never did any of that and never wanted to," Gaspar replied. "We have zero evidence that he's changed his mind on that score."

"We haven't been looking for that evidence, either." Kim inhaled to fill her lungs with a moment to think. "We know Reacher's got a heart. He feels like he failed with his brother. He was extremely protective of his nephew, once he knew Jake existed."

"Okay, let's say you're right about all that. You're always saying Reacher thinks like me," Gaspar said. "What I would do is head to Columbia, South Carolina."

Kim cocked her head. "Because Jake's there. At Fort Jackson. In basic training."

"Almost," Gaspar replied. "If it were me, I wouldn't go while Jake's in basic training. While the recruits are in basic, the CO watches them like a hawk."

"Okay."

"Even if I went down there, I wouldn't have a chance to spend time with the kid," Gaspar explained, clacking the keys on his keyboard again. "I probably couldn't even see him half a mile away through a high-powered rifle scope."

"And Reacher would know all that, just like you do." Kim swallowed the last of the coffee, wondering what he was looking for with all that keyboard work. "Then why would you go down there at all? Or more importantly, why would Reacher go?"

"Bingo!" Gaspar cackled when the clacking paused. "Looks like Jake is done with his basic training. What's odd, though, is he was scheduled to graduate today. Usually, they have those graduations on Thursday."

"Any idea why this one was scheduled early?" Kim asked.

"Probably something mundane like the venue was booked for something else." Gaspar shrugged. "But the point is, friends and family can attend the ceremony. And now that he's graduated, he's a professional soldier. He'll have a bit of freedom to chat with his uncle that he didn't have before."

"Yes, that's the natural way these things go, right?" Kim asked. "Seems kind of sentimental for Reacher to care about that, though, doesn't it?"

"Nope," Gaspar replied. "You can bet that if I had a nephew, I'd be proud as anything of my brother's boy. No way in hell you'd keep me away from being there to help celebrate the moment."

"Even if you didn't know for sure the kid would want you there?" Kim asked.

"Even then," Gaspar said emphatically. "Sometimes kids don't know what's good for them. I've got five of my own. Trust me on that, too."

Kim let the new ideas soak into her thinking. "Possibly. I mean, maybe just call the kid. Talk to him. Invite him to dinner. That's what a normal uncle would do. Right?"

Gaspar let the question lie there for a bit as he clacked on the keys a few more times.

"Could be a problem, though," Gaspar said.

"What is it?"

"The graduation ceremony already happened. Based on where we found the Volvo on the video feeds, Reacher might have had trouble arriving on time," Gaspar said, consternation plainly evident in his tone. "Drive time is twelve hours and change on the interstates. Probably twice that on the side roads Burns has been running. Even if Reacher had tried to get there, he might have missed it."

"Or he might actually be in the vicinity of Fort Jackson right now," Kim said, still turning the idea around in her head.

"Or not. Say you're right, and Reacher's on his way to Margrave," Gaspar said finally, giving in. "What are you planning to do with that intel?"

"Both Columbia and Margrave are south of Gary, Indiana, aren't they? And Fort Benning, Georgia, where Jake will be doing his officer training, is close by, too," Kim replied slowly, turning it over, looking at the road maps.

"It's still a guess, Sunshine. The only thing we know for sure is that Reacher was in the Volvo," Gaspar said, slowing down the momentum a bit more.

"Right. Keep working on that. Let's find out where Burns and Reacher are now," Kim replied.

"If Reacher actually developed a normal man's soft spot for his progeny, we might just get lucky," Gaspar started clacking the keyboard again. "But even if Reacher was there for the graduation, that doesn't mean he's hanging around. He could be gone by the time you arrive."

"I'll book a flight and figure out how to replace my service weapon," Kim nodded, ignoring that last bit of truth. "Which could take me a while. I'm not going down there unarmed."

"Sounds like you don't want to ask Cooper to replace yours," Gaspar said.

Kim didn't confirm or deny.

"Okay, then," Gaspar said after a brief pause. "Might be easier to buy a weapon in South Carolina or Georgia than Illinois. Want me to figure it out?"

"Thanks for the offer." Kim shook her head, even though he couldn't see her. "I'll take care of it."

The open line seemed abandoned for a few moments while neither spoke.

"I'll keep trying to locate Reacher. It makes sense he could have been headed to South Carolina or Georgia, but we could also be way off," Gaspar said, having refocused his attention.

"Okay," she replied absently. Her mind was already working on the gun problem.

"There's a lot of places Reacher could go between Chicago and Margrave. This could take a while. Be patient."

CHAPTER 12

Tuesday, May 24
White Kings Palace

MANNY DID THE DRIVING and Jones fumed all the way along the narrow roads to the White Kings' headquarters. Two miles back, he had pulled onto the long gravel driveway and followed the van's headlight beams through the trees until they reached the Palace.

At the compound's entrance, he slowed to a stop, lowered the window, and punched his current personalized code into an electronic keypad to open the gate.

"Home sweet home," Manny said with a grin, swiping a palm over his face as if he could wipe away the eye strain and the stress of the failed operation.

Jones leaned back on the headrest and closed his eyes briefly, too. A thick tunnel of trees extending in every direction extinguished whatever ambient light might have existed in the sky. The last hour of the drive had been darker than black.

"How're you doing back there?" Manny asked, glancing toward Margaret in the rearview.

The hostage had remained belted into the backseat with the hood over her head. She hadn't even whimpered during the long ride. Not once.

She didn't respond to Manny's question.

Jones shook his head. Hell, she might have died from fright or dehydration or some other damned thing already. Jones tried to care about her, but he couldn't dredge up an ounce of concern.

If she was dead, it was no less than what she deserved after what she'd done to Smitty. Less work for him and absolutely zero downside.

Her kid wouldn't know whether she was alive or not, after all. Not yet, anyway.

Manny didn't try again. "We're running late."

"We made the first call. He only knows what he was told," Jones replied curtly.

The truth was that the kid hadn't even asked about his mother, which was not a good sign. Jones shook it off. No point in wasting energy on matters outside his control.

He could do nothing about the kid's willingness or lack of desire to rescue her. If he didn't come to the meet-up location, then Jones would have to go get him. Simple as that.

"Looks quiet," Manny said, nodding toward the scene beyond the gate. A casual observer might think residents had retired for the night.

"That's how it's supposed to look," Jones said.

Active personnel were packaging and loading inventory for tomorrow's shipments in the outbuildings at the rear, out of view. The work would continue until they completed the orders just before five o'clock in the morning. Same schedule as always.

"Man, this place is impressive," Manny said as he did every time as if he'd never seen it before.

"Yeah." Jones had seen palaces housing kings and queens of first-world nations that were less grand than this one. Made sense that the compound had been dubbed the Palace by its original owner.

A couple decades ago, a tech titan named Whitey King had bought the acreage from a farmer. With a fraction of his billions, King had built the luxury gated property surrounded by thousands of empty acres and dubbed it the Palace.

King had expected to provide for and control his family and then pass the estate down to his heirs, as the railroad barons and lumber barons and oil barons and bootleggers of yore had done before him.

The Palace was conveniently located near the east coast of the United States. King could easily fly to Washington, DC in an hour by private jet. Slightly longer to fly to Boston or New York City or Atlanta.

King's grand plan for his estate had worked for a while. Until his economic bubble burst, leaving him flat on his financial ass. His property was then sold to satisfy about half the claims against him. He killed himself not long after.

Patton had learned about the Palace somehow. Patton kept his finger on the pulse of everything. The property was more than adequate for his burgeoning pharmaceutical operations.

Thus the White Kings had paid pennies for the Palace and the surrounding acreage. Everything was shiny and new when they had moved in and repurposed the property to suit Patton's plans

These days, The Palace was perfectly suited to the White Kings' most significant needs. It was completely self-contained. It operated off the grid. It was located in the middle of nowhere. And there was ample storage as well as room to work.

Within the Palace, the White Kings lived like royalty.

Only members were allowed to enter through the massive front gate. The White Kings needed privacy, and at the Palace, seclusion was assured.

While Manny waited for the gate to open, Jones rested his eyes. The Palace had become second nature to him. He could have navigated the place blind. Thanks to plenty of floodlights, he never needed to.

The compound's buildings were laid out in a blocky U-shape with Whitey King's personal home sitting at the base of the U, opposite the gate. Even in the dark, with only floodlights illuminating it, the mansion was impressive.

Patton maintained private quarters in the main residence, although Jones had never seen him at the Palace. Also housed there was Dr. Felipe Sanz, arguably the most essential member of the White Kings organization.

Each side of the main building was flanked with three large mansions, reflecting the same design, although slightly smaller.

Outbuildings were located behind the residences. What had once been palatial horse barns, garages, and other essential storage facilities, were now repurposed.

Beyond the outbuildings was the helipad and beyond that, the runway. Private jets landed regularly at the Palace. The runway was always ready and waiting.

Further back, beyond the runway, was a second gate, even better fortified than the front gate.

The grounds were maintained like the Queen of England herself had created them.

Perhaps the most important asset was the high-tech electrified fence that surrounded the entire compound. Whitey King had originally installed the entry barrier and Sullivan had improved it exponentially.

The decorative wrought-iron fence was twelve-feet high and designed to discourage curiosity, should anyone wander out this far from the known world.

A would-be visitor could see the grounds inside and thus wouldn't be enticed to climb over the fence, Whitey King had reasoned. Paparazzi could use their long lenses and shoot photos through the fence, should they be so inclined.

There was a tasteful and unmistakable "No Trespassing" sign prominently affixed to the gate, simply to make the point clear and provide a warning.

King had designed and installed a system to keep persistent intruders off the fence.

Should a potential intruder try to breach the fence for a closer look at the private buildings, a stern electric shock was instantly delivered, strong enough to discourage further attempts.

The first jab was more than enough to do the job.

But Patton anticipated certain types of visitors might be a little too thick between the ears to get the message with the first high charge. The tech was already there, so he ramped up the deterrent capacity.

These days, the system automatically escalated current strength with each attempted breach.

The curious visitors, if they had the temerity to try a second time, would be instantly and much more sharply rebuked.

On the third attempt, a fence climber would be strongly zapped.

The third level charge would reliably disable normal humans and leave lasting reminders, such as burn marks and scars.

No human had ever tried to breach the fence a fourth time, as far as Jones knew. He'd heard rumors, unconfirmed, that the fourth charge could lead to cardiac arrest and death.

Jones believed those rumors.

A few times a year, the White Kings discovered a seared deer, which confirmed the system's efficiency well enough. Human visitors should be smarter than those deer.

But should anyone try, the fourth charge would be deadly. Even healthy human bodies couldn't withstand high wattage electrical charges. After all, the death penalty had been effectively administered by electrocution for decades.

The remote location and the fence were all the fortification the White Kings needed to secure the Palace compound. Heavy artillery, around-the-clock surveillance, and other security methods had never been necessary.

Which meant the member population here was lower than might otherwise have been required. Sentries with weapons were unnecessary.

"Finally," Manny said as the heavy metal gate groaned and clanged and complained as the wheels squeaked, pushing to the right, across the drive, until the driveway was no longer obstructed.

Manny rested his boot on the gas and rolled the van through an opening wide enough to admit a troop transport.

When the van's rear bumper cleared the sensors, the gate reversed, closing the Palace compound securely once more.

"Put the hostage in C building. There's room for both of them in the basement cells." Jones pointed to the mansion in the middle of the left leg of the U.

"Okay," Manny replied as he turned toward the back driveway. He pulled up behind C building and parked the van.

Manny pushed the button to open the van's two side doors, exposing the back compartment. A welcome gust of fresh, cool air rushed through. The hostage might have stirred. It was hard to tell.

Jones climbed out of the passenger seat and stretched the tension from his long limbs.

An average-sized soldier came outside through the back door of C building and hustled down the brick steps. Brad Coda cocked his head. "Where's Smitty?"

"Long story," Jones replied tersely.

"Give me the headlines." Coda and Smitty had served together in Afghanistan. They were tight, then and still. Both had joined the White Kings a while back, around the same time.

Coda had moved up the food chain and Smitty had not. Which told Jones all he needed to know about both men.

Jones swiped a palm over his tired eyes. He had no desire to deal with Coda's infamously fast flashpoint tonight.

"I'll fill you in later," Jones said.

"Can't wait to hear about it," Coda nodded, accepting the excuse but making it plain that he'd expect to hear the whole truth. "Got the cargo in there?"

"Just one, the woman," Jones replied. "We have to go back for the kid."

Coda shook his head but asked no further questions. "I'll take her downstairs. Get her settled. She'll be okay alone?"

"Yeah, she'll be fine," Manny said. "We'll be back in a few hours with the other one."

"Copy that," Coda replied as he stepped into the van and freed the hostage from her seatbelt. "We're running behind on tomorrow's shipment. We could use some extra hands, so be quick."

Coda left the bag over the woman's head and guided her toward the back entrance, perhaps a little rougher than needed. Maybe he sensed that whatever had happened to Smitty was her fault.

Jones watched as she stumbled up the steps. Only Coda's firm grip on her bicep kept her upright. When they reached the back verandah, Coda buzzed the door open, and they went inside.

Manny shook his head, "We figure out where that dude came from yet?"

"Canada," Jones replied. "Isn't that what he said?"

"You ever meet a rude Canadian before?" Manny asked with a smirk.

Jones nodded. "Solid point you've got there."

The truth was that Jones had met Coda for the first time a few days ago. The two men remained wary of each other.

The only thing he knew for sure was that Coda had also been involved in that big multi-state ATM robbery project for Patton recently.

The same big project Jones had completed.

They hadn't worked together, but both had completed the job successfully when others had died trying.

They served the same master, which was all Jones needed to know.

"Do we have time for a piss and a coffee before we go get the kid?" Manny asked.

"Sure. Bring two cups. I'll call when you're back." Jones replied, pacing to stretch his legs and breathe in the fresh air. "The kid's worried about his mom. He'll wait as long as he needs to."

CHAPTER 13

Tuesday, May 24
Columbia, SC

JAKE HAD PARKED IN the dark corner of the fast-food lot and slumped low in the driver's seat of the Jeep. He'd tried to catch a few winks, mindful of the advice from his drill instructor to sleep when he could, but sleep didn't come.

His mother had been missing for hours and he was definitely worried.

But what if the call never came? He'd tried to make a plan B, but every alternative he conjured came up short.

If his mother didn't call, how would he even begin to search for her? He couldn't involve the police. The more he thought about it, the fewer alternatives he could find.

His eyelids were heavy. He pulled his cap down over his face and let his chin drop. He held the burner phone in his lap, with the ringer to full volume, just in case he dozed off.

A few minutes after midnight, the phone's ringtone blasted through to his subconscious. Jake answered on the second ring. "Yes?"

"Judas Tree Park. Come alone, or you'll never see your mother alive again." The electronically altered voice was male, which was the only thing Jake could say about it. He didn't recognize the voice, and no one else would have, either.

He exhaled with relief for a brief moment.

He'd harbored a niggling worry that his mother might have killed that guy in her hotel room and then run away to avoid arrest. He hadn't wanted to believe she was capable of such behavior. But the man was dead, and she'd been in possession of the weapon that killed him.

Jake's good opinion of his mom had been affirmed by the call. But knowing for sure that she'd been kidnapped wasn't all that great, either.

"I'm new to the area. I don't know where that park is," Jake said, keeping his voice as steady as possible, hoping to draw out the conversation until he could learn something useful.

"Check the text," the electronic voice replied.

The only thing Jake heard after that was silence. The caller had disconnected before Jake had half a chance to ask about his mother or anything else.

Jake's objection to the directions had been genuine. He didn't know where Judas Tree Park was located. Hell, until yesterday, he'd hadn't known what a Judas tree was.

His mother had mentioned the Judas trees planted at Fort Jackson just yesterday at his graduation.

"Judas trees are common around Columbia," Margaret Reacher had said. "They're a variety of blooming redbud, also known as the Eastern Redbud tree."

"Yeah, I've seen them around," Jake had replied.

"I'd love to have those in my back garden," Margaret mused aloud. "I wonder if they'd grow well in New Hampshire?"

Jake had shrugged off the question. He didn't know anything about plants and trees. As nearly as he could tell, the secret to gardening was to plant the right thing in the right place and then stay out of the way and hope for the best.

But he'd seen thousands of showy magenta buds splashed around everywhere in Columbia earlier in the spring. There were probably a dozen parks full of Judas trees.

The locals were not all that precise with their directions either, as Jake had learned the hard way. They had local names for places that were not on any map at all.

He'd been lost more than once trying to navigate around South Carolina. If he went looking for Judas Tree Park tonight, he might never find it.

A few seconds later, a text came through on the burner, as promised.

Jake plugged the address into the Jeep's GPS system. The screen displayed a map with a defined route from his current location.

Judas Tree Park was north. The estimated travel time to cover the eighty-four miles was just over two hours along mostly paved two lanes. There was only one road on the map leading to the park.

The route guidance would consume at least two hours of travel time unless he exceeded the speed limit, which could capture the wrong kind of attention.

He punched the button on his GPS to see images of the area. Several photos filled the screen. Each picture had been snapped in springtime and revealed blooming trees and sunshine.

If there were homes or shops or any sort of civilization nearby, none were shown on the map or the images.

Which meant it would be black as pitch out there tonight, too.

He had flashlights in the jeep. He pulled one out of the console's storage box and tossed it onto the passenger seat. He plugged his phone in to charge while he drove and made sure the phone's location services feature was turned on.

If he got lost or something, maybe someone would be able to find him.

Jake checked his gas. Only half a tank. He'd fill up at the first available opportunity before he headed north. The last thing he needed was to run out of fuel alone in the wilderness.

He slid the transmission into gear and rolled out of the fast-food parking lot onto the four-lane. At the first traffic light, he turned north.

A mile up the road, he saw a gas station. He pulled in, lined up at the pump, and filled his tank to the brim.

Keeping one eye alternately on the clock and the illuminated map on the GPS screen, Jake pulled out onto the road again.

The GPS now estimated arrival time at Judas Tree Park in two hours and twenty minutes. He'd dawdled too long. The caller's instructions had clearly implied that the deadline was not flexible.

His vaguely formed plan to arrive early and get the jump on his mother's kidnappers was quashed before he had a chance to implement it. Now, they'd be waiting and watching for him instead of the other way around.

Jake glanced over to be sure his dad's gun was still on the passenger seat next to the heavy flashlight.

He grabbed the steering wheel with both hands and goosed the accelerator.

The Jeep jumped forward and sped along the blacktop away from the city lights of Columbia and toward the darkness beyond.

After a while of solid driving, all ambient light from Columbia was long gone. The Jeep's headlights illuminated the road, shining straight ahead into a tunnel of trees. The red taillights shone weakly, swallowed by the trees behind.

Beyond the Jeep's light ranges, ahead, behind, above, and on both sides, was nothing but blackness. No moon. No stars. No nothing.

Jake slowed his speed. Along this kind of wilderness road at night, wildlife could dart in front of a vehicle and cause a major accident. The last thing he needed was to crash and destroy the Jeep before he reached Judas Tree Park.

He glanced at the GPS. He was still too far from his destination, which was straight ahead in the never-ending blackness. There was nothing to do but push steadily onward.

Further along, a rustic brown sign with white block letters appeared on the right side of the two-lane.

"Judas Tree Park entrance ahead," Jake read aloud. "Rustic. No amenities. No camping."

A park worker had hung a board to cover the operating hours, indicating the park was now closed.

Another mile beyond the sign, the ranger's station was illuminated by the Jeep's headlights. The small, square log structure was settled in the median between the entrance and exit lanes to the park.

During park hours, the ranger checked visitors in, offered directions, and collected fees, most likely. Jake wondered how many visitors came out here and why. Hunting, maybe?

The barrier gate arms were painted to match the rustic brown logs of the ranger station. Both the entrance and exit arms were up, presumably to allow late vehicles to pass without damaging the barriers.

The entrance road was just as dark on the north side of the guard shack. The park was closed and, in theory, occupied only by the wildlife.

"Okay, I'm here," Jake murmured under his breath. "Where are you bastards? And where is my mother?"

He drove slowly past the ranger shack and deeper into the park. On the left sat a pair of industrial-sized garbage dumpsters. The lids were closed and pad locked. A small sign said, "Do not feed the animals."

On the right, another brown sign listed various activities, including parking, hiking trails, bird watching, and so forth, all straight ahead.

Jake slowed the Jeep and advanced toward the flat gravel parking area. There were no vehicles in the lot or anywhere else he could see.

He parked the Jeep and lowered the windows to listen but heard only the quiet sounds of his engine running and his own breathing.

"Did I get here first?" he murmured. It was possible, even though he'd been running later than he should have.

Jake put the Jeep into gear and rolled slowly to the back of the lot.

He reversed to back off the gravel and into the trees.

He placed the burner phone, the flashlight, and the gun where he could find them quickly and easily.

He killed the lights and the engine and settled in to wait.

CHAPTER 14

Wednesday, May 25
Chicago, IL

"ARE YOU SURE THERE'S no way you can help me out with this?" Kim asked the last contact on her list of acceptable options.

"I'm sorry, Kim. You know I would sell you anything you want. I'll even toss in a generous discount. All you have to do is get your background check, and that'll just take about five days. Then I can fix you right up," he replied.

"Okay. Thanks. I'll call you tomorrow if I don't find a better solution," Kim said and rang off with a long sigh.

Buying a legal gun was a big hassle in Illinois. And it wasn't a small problem in nearby Wisconsin, Indiana, or Michigan, either. She'd tried every avenue she could think up. And hit a brick wall every time.

Which wasn't necessarily a bad thing under normal circumstances. Kim was in favor of gun safety. Her dad was a veteran, and she grew up on a farm with brothers who enjoyed hunting. They'd all been taught from a young age to respect firearms of all sorts, just as they'd learned how to use them safely and effectively.

None of that helped her replace her service weapon at the moment.

Local residents might have time for background checks and waiting periods and all the other bureaucracy that had developed around gun control. But she didn't have that kind of time.

She needed to replace her service weapon and preferably tonight.

She wanted practice time at the range to get the feel of the new weapon, too. Which meant she wasn't heading after Reacher again until she'd made it happen.

Plus, she needed sleep. Heavy eyelids slid across her eyeballs like they were scrubbing the delicate tissues with forty-grit sandpaper. Every time she blinked, she struggled to open her eyes again.

She couldn't afford the slowed performance and reduced competence that resulted from sleep deprivation.

She looked at the list she'd scrawled quickly on the hotel notepad. The hour was too late to call more contacts, and their responses were likely to be negative anyway. Options for obtaining an illegal weapon were dangerous and risky, even if she'd been tempted to try them.

Kim had an excellent backup weapon in her gun safe, which wasn't a great answer. Personal weapons were not allowed on the job.

Ask Cooper or Finlay?

She shrugged off both choices as unacceptable, although each had its merits.

Cooper was her boss, and as such, responsible for keeping her equipped to handle the Reacher assignment. He had access to FBI weapons and could easily provide an authorized replacement, which he'd be required to do at some point anyway.

The problem was, she didn't want Cooper involved.

He'd be livid about how she'd used her service weapon, drawing the wrong kind of attention to herself. He'd be asked to vouch for her to Chicago PD at the very least, which he would not appreciate. Not even a little bit.

She kneaded her forehead with her fingers. Thinking about Cooper gave her a headache.

She simply didn't want to deal with him on this issue.

She'd done what she thought was right, and she didn't intend to be second-guessed by some suit sitting behind a desk on the other side of the country. Especially not her boss. Not tonight and not ever, if she could avoid it.

Which left Finlay. He could easily provide a new pistol, too. He would ask fewer questions. Make fewer demands. He'd at least pretend to be concerned and helpful.

But Gaspar didn't trust Finlay. Never had. Never would. Kim often argued Finlay's case, eloquently and with feeling. Yet Gaspar never relented. Never changed his views on the subject, no matter what.

Gaspar had never given her reason to doubt him and he'd been a loyal partner as long as she'd known him.

Which meant Finlay was out of bounds. At least on this issue. For the time being.

The last easily available option was to take Burke's Glock. Which would be easy to do. He'd left it with her while he was in the hospital.

She wouldn't take his gun without asking.

He wouldn't agree to it. And if he did, he'd be the one without a weapon.

Kim wouldn't put his life in jeopardy by leaving him unarmed. She took a deep breath and accepted the inevitable.

When there's only one choice, it's the right choice.

A quick trip to Detroit might be the least worst option.

"The devil's always in the details," she murmured.

She could drive home in about five hours. Be up and going again before noon.

She could sleep in her own bed, pack clean clothes, and pick up the weapon she was familiar with and knew she could rely upon in the kind of tight situations this assignment seemed to present daily.

The only thing stopping her was exhaustion. She might fall asleep at the wheel if she tried to drive to Detroit tonight.

Briefly, she wondered how much it would cost to rent a driver. But she dismissed the idea almost as soon as it popped into her head.

Cooper would never approve the line item on her expense account. Even if he did, some bean counter at the FBI would have a hissy fit and reject it. Then she'd be right back in the untenable position of discussing all of this with Cooper.

She picked up her phone and quickly checked the commercial flight schedules. The first available flight departed at five-thirty, which would be six-thirty in Detroit.

Flight time was less than two hours.

Kim glanced at her watch. The airlines wanted passengers to check in two hours before the flight. The Boss usually handled those logistics, and she usually turned up at the last minute without issues.

Not tonight. Unless she wanted to get Cooper out of bed now, she was on her own.

She had heard nothing more from Gaspar. If he'd located Reacher, he would have let her know. Which meant there was nothing new to report.

Even if she dashed out the door right now, she wasn't likely to find Reacher tonight. He was probably sleeping, anyway. Burns, too.

That's what normal people over the age of thirty did at two o'clock in the morning.

She gazed longingly at the comfortable bed she'd slept in the past few nights. Her eyes closed on their own.

Kim accepted that she'd reached the point where fighting sleep had become counterproductive. She could head out now and catch a few winks before the five-thirty flight. She'd dozed in airport chairs many times, but nothing about the practice was restful.

First things first, her mother would have said.

"Oh, hell," Kim mumbled under her breath. "What's the damned rush?"

She booked a flight to Detroit from O'Hare tomorrow morning at nine o'clock, which seemed like a very long time to be without her gun. She dropped onto the bed and zoned out.

CHAPTER 15

Wednesday, May 25
Judas Tree Park

JAKE WAS RESTLESS. HE'D expected to receive a second call with further instructions. So far, the second call hadn't come. Why not?

He assumed the kidnappers' burner phone was equipped with a tracking device. Once he'd answered the first call, they would have expected him to keep the phone on his person.

They would be able to locate both him and the phone at all times.

A vague plan gradually took shape in his head.

What if he didn't keep the phone with him?

Maybe he could lure them somewhere. Keep his escape and rescue options open.

He'd never dealt with a situation like this before, but Jake sensed his best strategy was to keep the kidnappers off balance instead of secure and complacent.

He gathered equipment from the few options in the Jeep. He stuffed the burner phone in his pocket and the gun into his waistband.

Jake grabbed a pair of small binoculars that had belonged to his dad, an inveterate bird watcher, from the console. He slipped the leather strap around his neck and tucked the binoculars into the pocket of his denim shirt.

He left the Jeep well hidden in the trees and stepped deeper into the woods with his heavy flashlight in hand. Almost instantly, the Jeep seemed to disappear.

After a few moments of complete sensory deprivation, he noticed the sound of leaves rustling in the slight breeze that brushed his skin. The scent of pine combined with noxious fumes akin to the compost pile his mother kept behind the garage back home reinforced his resolve.

Small mammals like rabbits and squirrels and snakes were no doubt aware of his presence. Birds, too. Maybe larger mammals like a deer and bear. But at the moment, Jake couldn't hear or see or smell any of them.

The blackness was nearly total. As his eyes adjusted to the meager ambient light, certain shapes seemed blacker than others. He wandered quietly in a three-dimensional world surrounded by the dark, darker, and darkest elements of life.

His flashlight could have solved the problem because the beam's distance was more than four hundred feet, which made the flashlight simultaneously essential and hazardous.

If he turned it on, an enemy could easily see the beam from a significant distance. If he left it off, he risked injury or death from unappreciated hazards.

"I'm no good to Mom if I fall and break my neck," Jake murmured.

He aimed the flashlight toward the ground and punched the toggle button. He pulsed short, irregular bursts of light, just long enough to glimpse his surroundings.

When he'd located a reasonably clear path through the trees and memorized it so he could find it again in the dark, he moved further away from the Jeep.

Jake hustled silently across the gravel parking lot to the far side where two wooden tables were set up for hikers.

Using brief bursts of the beam, he located a steel trash barrel. The lid was securely latched with two heavy-duty toggle clamps and sealed as if it had been punched into place with a hammer.

Jake shoved the clamps open with the heel of his hand until he managed to release the lid. As soon as he cracked the seal, an overwhelming stench exploded and attacked his nose like a caged animal. The toxic fumes brought tears to his eyes.

He squeezed his eyelids tight, held his breath, and jerked the heavy lid upward, hard enough to fully open the barrel.

The barrel was filled to the brim with garbage, and it looked like a park ranger had stomped on it to pack everything down.

The pickup service was probably due tomorrow because nothing else could be crammed into the barrel once the park opened in a few hours.

The kidnappers would probably show up long before the garbage collector. They didn't intend to wait until daylight to make a move.

Jake considered leaving the lid off the barrel. He imagined it might act as a siren call for hungry animals, which he might be able to use as a diversion somehow. The kidnappers would probably shoot them, though. The last thing he needed was a pile of dead animals here.

He could toss the burner phone into the barrel, replace the lid, and secure the clamps to lock it down again. He grinned as he imagined the kidnappers pawing through the disgusting garbage to find the phone.

But the cell signal could be weakened if the burner was enclosed in steel, and he definitely wanted the kidnappers to find the phone.

So he replaced the lid, turned the ringer up as high as it would go, and set the phone atop the barrel. It seemed like the best he could do, given his limitations.

The setup seemed reasonable. They might think he was sitting at the table and placed the phone on the barrel to be sure he could grab it quickly.

The kidnappers might buy that for a few moments.

Which could be long enough. Possibly.

Once Jake set up the phone, he hurried across the parking lot and into the woods.

The forest floor was covered with years of dead leaves, twigs, and other rotting plants. Underneath the compost were insects of various kinds and who knew what else.

Using the flashlight sparingly, he found a small clearing with a reasonably unobstructed view of the garbage barrel and the entrance to the parking lot.

He chose a sturdy pine to lean against and, while his heart beat like a relaxed adagio metronome, settled in to wait.

He had no idea how long he'd been waiting. It seemed a lifetime ago that he'd bounded into the Magnolia Hotel with a grin on his face and joy in his heart.

He barely recalled the moments before he discovered the horror of a dead stranger in his mother's room.

The normal pace of time halted from sheer terror when he realized Mom had been taken.

Since then, minutes had passed like hours. With the limited data he'd acquired so far, he'd puzzled through things.

Points that seemed more likely than not?

The kidnappers were late. But they were coming.

His mother was of no use to them unless they could leverage her somehow.

But how? And for what?

Margaret Reacher wasn't rich. She didn't have one of those jobs where her employer or some insurance company was likely to pay big bucks to buy her freedom. The widow of a college professor, mother of one adult son, and she volunteered at the library.

Jake's parents had been far from rich, and Jake wasn't rich either. He was a soldier. He could qualify for food stamps on the salary the army paid him.

No, it wasn't money they wanted. He'd discarded that idea almost as soon as it had popped into his head.

Revenge wasn't the answer, either.

If Margaret shot that guy and killed him using Dad's gun, whoever took her could have killed her right then and there.

Revenge would have been swift and sure and final. Margaret's body would have been lying next to the dead guy in her room, too.

But she wasn't there.

Although he'd discarded revenge almost as quickly as the ransom motive, he worried they might kill her, which terrified him.

A sharp pain seized his heart and squeezed every ounce of life from his heartbeats.

His entire body shivered. The kind of shiver that Mom used to tease him about.

"Someone's walking over your grave," she'd say when he was a child.

The curse had frightened him back then, and he didn't much like it now, either.

He shook his head swiftly.

No. That way lies madness. He'd be of no value to her if he let himself descend into despair.

Jake decided to believe the kidnappers wanted Margaret alive. All the available evidence pointed that way.

They'd taken her hostage.

And they'd contacted him.

Which had to mean it was Jake they wanted, right?

But why?

He'd spent the past few hours fighting that question like it was a twenty-foot alligator. He knew exactly how that felt. He'd wrestled a big gator once and almost lost a leg.

The visceral memory washed over him.

The gator had dashed out of the murky water without warning. Jake was the closest of the three guys to the river's edge, and the gator came right at him.

For a terrifying few minutes, Jake had expected to bleed out right there on the riverbank in the warm sunshine.

His buddies fought hard and managed to wrangle the heavy reptile off Jake before it inflicted irreversible damage.

Afterward, the gator ran back into the water on stubby legs that carried him way more swiftly than any of the guys would have believed possible.

The situation Jake and his mother were in now felt exactly like that.

A monster had attacked without warning.

Right now, the monster was winning.

And this time, Jake didn't have any buddies standing by to help them.

A pair of headlights flickering through the trees snapped his attention back to the present.

The headlights were high off the ground, so the vehicle was a truck or a van or maybe a full-sized SUV.

The vehicle approached from the park's entrance along the paved road to the gravel parking lot. The headlights swept past Jake's surveillance point, temporarily blinding him as the vehicle swept around the empty lot in a big arc.

He saw the boxy shape clearly enough to identify it as a van. A big one. A shiny silver panel van with no windows on the sides or in the back.

No way to see into the passenger compartment.

Margaret could be inside. Or not.

Jake couldn't see the driver or anyone else. He blinked furiously, attempting to banish the flash blindness resulting from the bright headlights.

He lifted the binoculars to his eyes and trained them on the van. He memorized the make and model and the license plate, although he figured the vehicle was stolen anyway. But the mental activity made him feel as if he was doing something proactive, at least.

The van entered the parking area slowly, rolled through to the back of the lot, rounded the curve, and headed out again.

The headlights landed brightly on the picnic tables and the garbage barrel with its lid askew.

They must have seen the phone.

The van pulled up in front of the garbage barrel and stopped.

A few moments later, the burner phone vibrated and rang loudly. Jake counted the insistently long ring tones. Four, five, six. Almost as if they couldn't believe their eyes or their ears.

Jake smirked and muttered, "Not quite as green and stupid as you thought, eh?"

The passenger door opened, and a man stepped out onto the gravel. He held another phone in his hand.

Cussing all the way, he approached the barrel and grabbed the burner. He lowered his phone from his ear and punched a button, and the burner stopped ringing.

Then he turned and strode back toward the van with both phones.

He was momentarily illuminated by the headlight beams and Jake got a good, long look at him.

He was tall, maybe six feet, give or take. Fit. White. Broad shoulders, brown hair. Early forties.

Carried himself like a soldier. An officer, most likely.

His body language screamed *I'm in charge*.

Jake had seen plenty of guys who carried themselves just like that in the past few weeks. It was a confident presence that Jake emulated.

"Fake it 'til you make it," his dad would have said.

The van's engine was running, so Jake took a chance and lifted his cell phone.

He zoomed in as far as the camera would allow and shot a burst of photos without flash, never lowering the binoculars or taking his eyes off the target.

The man said something to the driver.

The driver climbed out and walked around in front.

The second guy was shorter. More tentative. He had wild hair that encircled his head as if he'd just toweled off after a shower.

Jake's viewing angle was awkward, but he used his cell phone to shoot a burst of photos of the driver, too.

None of the shots would be great. Maybe the sheer number of photos would produce something he could use to identify these two.

They talked for a few seconds, but Jake couldn't hear the conversation.

Then the driver walked outside to the edge of the light and lowered his zipper to take a leak. After that, the two climbed back into the van and closed the doors.

The driver took another slow roll around the edges of the parking lot, illuminating the trees with his headlights.

Jake released a pent-up breath. He had pulled the Jeep far enough into the woods. They didn't seem to see it.

The van returned to the driveway and turned right to go deeper into the park. Perhaps there was another parking lot back there.

Maybe they thought Jake got his instructions wrong and was waiting somewhere else.

Another thought jolted him.

Was his mother dead in the back of that van? Were they going farther into the woods to dump her body?

He shook his head. That line of thinking would get him nowhere.

More likely, they were late arriving because they'd dropped her off alive somewhere first.

Possibly.

Probably.

Which meant all he had to do was follow them back to wherever they had left her.

Or he could attack now.

If he took them on now, and she wasn't in the van, he might never find her.

If he didn't subdue them now, he might never have another chance to force them to tell where she was being held.

The argument escalated in his head until the van's headlights emerged again and headed toward the exit.

"Come on, Jake. Make a choice," he murmured. "And do it fast before you lose them."

He waited until they were far enough ahead before he scrambled from the forest and hurried back to the Jeep.

CHAPTER 16

Wednesday, May 25
White Kings Palace

IT SEEMED NO SOONER had Jones lain his head on the pillow
that Coda was pounding on his bedroom door. He climbed out of
bed and slipped on his pants.

"Hold your water. I'm coming," he said as he walked toward
the door and pulled it open. "What's up?"

"Jake Reacher is out front," Coda said. "Let's go."

Jones replied, "How do you know it's him?"

"The kid's unmistakable. Looks just like his uncle, only
younger," Coda said. "Plus, I've seen pictures and video. No
mistake. It's him."

"All right." Jones nodded. "I'll get my shoes."

He shoved his feet into his boots, grabbed his pistol off the
nightstand and shoved it into his waistband, and followed. He
pulled a sweatshirt over his head, hustling along behind Coda
down the long corridor on the third floor of Building C toward the
security office.

"Catch me up, Coda. The kid just drove straight up to the gate?" Jones asked, wiping the sleep from his eyes and trying to focus.

"He might have been out there for a while. I don't know. We got an alert on the fence near the front gate. Something got zapped. Could have been a squirrel or a rabbit. Dunno. Not enough juice deployed or absorbed for anything larger. Only happened once," Coda said as they rounded the corner.

Coda placed his palm on the bio reader, and the security room door clicked open.

"When we looked at the video, we saw the kid. Just standing there. A couple minutes later, he started pushing buttons on the keypad at the gate."

"He's alone?" Jones asked. "No sign of anyone else with him?"

"Not that we've found. Still checking," Coda said.

"Did you send someone out to pick him up?" Jones asked.

"Thought you might want to do it," Coda replied. "He was your target. You missed him twice. Third time's the charm, right?"

"Yeah," Jones said, wearily rubbing his palm over his face trying to wake up. He'd had a long series of long days, which was no excuse. "Show me the video. I'll go get him."

Coda pointed to one of the screens. The night vision video camera at the front gate had been activated.

Just like Coda had said, the kid was standing there with his feet apart and arms at his sides. Like he was waiting for a bus.

Jones peered closely at the screen. "What the hell?" he murmured.

"We haven't found his vehicle. He might have parked it out at the road and walked in from there. The sensors in the driveway didn't pick up a vehicle," Coda said. "We're checking the cams along the road now, too."

"Is he armed? That's the mistake Smitty made with the mother. She had a gun. He didn't know it," Jones said.

Coda's jaw clenched. He was still pissed about Smitty. "Could be. Hard to tell on the video. Smart to assume he's armed."

"Okay. I'm headed down there." Jones moved toward the door.

He strode along the corridor to the back exit.

At the door, he placed his palm on the reader and the door kicked open. He pushed through into the cool early morning air.

Floodlights illuminated the grounds. The lighting was bright enough to navigate along the driveway. He stayed out of Jake's sight line, hurrying along the gravel toward Building D.

When he reached the corner of Building D, he pulled his pistol and craned his neck out. The fence did what it was designed to do. It kept Jake outside but gave both men an unobstructed view.

Jones called out. "Jake Reacher. Raise your hands above your head."

Jake did as instructed. Both hands went into the air. He wasn't holding a weapon.

Jones held his pistol pointed as he advanced toward the intruder. When he came within conversational distance, he said, "What are you doing here?"

"You wanted me here, didn't you? Isn't that why you took my mother?"

"If it were up to me and you showed up on time, she'd be dead already," Jones said, keeping the conversation going as he advanced, holding his pistol in position to shoot first.

"Better late than never," Jake replied. "I want to see my mom."

When Jones was ten feet away, he saw the dead rabbit at Jake's feet. The kid might have seen it get zapped.

The only way he would find his mother was to get inside the compound, and he must have realized he couldn't sneak into the compound.

Did he imagine himself as some kind of Trojan horse?

Coda was scouring the exterior CCTV video. If the kid had a posse with him, Coda would find them.

"Are you armed?" Jones asked.

"Yes. I have a pistol in my back pocket," Jake replied.

"I'd rather not shoot you. But I will if you mess with me," Jones said.

"I just want to see my mother," Jake replied.

"Turn around. Pull the gun out slowly. Toss it through the fence," Jones demanded. "Screw this up, and I'll shoot you. You won't die right away. But you'll wish you had."

Jake turned around. He pulled the pistol from his pocket using his thumb and forefinger. He glanced over his shoulder and tossed the pistol through the uprights like a place kicker.

After the pistol hit the ground, Jake turned around to face forward again.

"Empty your pockets," Jones said. "Toss the contents on the ground. Put your hands back up."

Jake complied. He turned his pockets out. Nothing in them. No wallet, no keys, not even a few coins.

"Remember, I'll shoot you in a hot second if you give me any trouble at all. This place is armed beyond your comprehension. Even if you could make it past me, you'd never reach your mother before she dies. You want her to be alive when you find her, don't mess this up," Jones said, giving him the unvarnished truth. "You got it?"

"I understand," Jake said again. If he was nervous, he didn't act like it.

Jones waited a few more seconds. The kid seemed to be alone and sincere enough. It might be smarter just to go ahead and shoot him.

But live hostages were always better than damaged or dead ones, Patton claimed.

"Open the gate," Jones instructed whoever was listening back in the security center.

The wheels screeched as the big gate began its long, noisy trek. Jake stood tall, hands at his sides, waiting.

Jones walked over to the pistol on the ground, stooped, and stared at it.

The Glock with the yellow tape on the handle from the Magnolia Hotel room.

The one that killed Smitty.

CHAPTER 17

Wednesday, May 25
Detroit, MI

KIM FELT LIKE A new woman. She stepped off the plane at Detroit Metro Airport's McNamara Terminal after a solid seven-hours sleep and an uneventful flight from Chicago. She'd been mainlining black coffee for hours, and her churning stomach demanded something to soak up the acid.

She stopped at the women's restroom, washed up a bit, and headed toward the bagel shop. The terminal was a mile long. Her plane had landed at the very end. The bagel shop she preferred was half a mile away.

The terminal was busy this morning. She felt like a mouse in a maze as she made her way through groups and along moving sidewalks.

When she reached the bagel shop, she joined the line behind a young woman wearing jeans and a hoodie, who was intent as she rapidly thumbed the tiny keyboard on her phone screen with both thumbs.

A man dressed in a business suit, carrying a briefcase, walked up a little too close behind Kim. The line inched forward until the girl with the hoodie moved up to place her order.

Kim felt the tap her shoulder.

"Ms. Otto?" he said, friendly enough. "May I speak with you a moment?"

Kim turned around to look him over. She didn't know him. But he looked familiar. He was a type. Fit, reasonably sized, boring haircut. The kind of guy who worked for an employer with a dress code. A three-letter agency, probably.

The girl was still placing her takeaway order. There were plenty of other people around. And Kim knew the terminal security was top-notch.

Even without her gun, she felt reasonably safe here.

"Have we met?" she asked pleasantly enough.

He shook his head, reached into his pocket, and pulled out a badge wallet. He showed his ID briefly but long enough for her to recognize it.

The name was Lester Lester, which was ridiculous on its face. Probably fake.

The ID was DHS. A Homeland Security agent.

He offered her a business card. She palmed it, frowning, memorized his fake name, and dropped the card into her pocket.

Who was this guy?

How did he know he could find her here?

What the hell did he want?

Hoodie girl paid the bill and moved off to one side to wait for her food.

The impatient woman at the counter offered Kim a snarly, "How can I help you today?"

"Plain toasted bagel. Cream cheese, no butter. Black coffee," Kim said, slapping a twenty down on the counter.

The woman punched a few buttons on the touch screen, handed Kim her change and a receipt with her order number on it, and said, "Next."

Kim stepped aside, and the agent followed. He didn't order anything.

She collected her bagel and coffee and moved over to a small table deep into the shop. He came along. She sat with her back to the wall. He moved the second chair to the side of the table rather than sit with his back to the open entryway.

She smiled, removed the lid from the steaming coffee, and bit off a chunk of the bagel. This was his meeting. She waited for him to start. She didn't wait long.

"I have a delivery for you," he said, sliding the briefcase toward her. "It's a replacement for the item you lost recently."

Kim chewed the bagel, swallowed, and said nothing. She imagined the bread plopping down into the lake of coffee in her stomach and made a splash before it sponged up the acid mix.

"I was also told to deliver this." He reached into his jacket and pulled a padded manila envelope from his breast pocket. He placed it on the table between them.

The envelope was similar to many others she'd received from The Boss over the past few months. But it was slightly different.

Which meant Cooper hadn't sent it, but someone who knew about the envelopes had.

She swallowed two more small bites before she replied. "Who sent you here?"

The question was a test of his veracity.

He shrugged by way of reply.

She accepted his response because she'd already deduced the answer.

She'd told no one her plans to come back to Detroit this morning. Not even Gaspar. She'd made no phone call of any kind since she hung up with him last night.

Kim had made the flight reservation online. Which meant the spy had either hacked her internet activity or the airline manifests. Or both.

Cooper watched her constantly, but not always in real-time.

He did have an actual job with significant responsibilities, which kept him from virtually following her around like a puppy.

He might not even know yet that she'd made the reservation.

All of which meant Lester Lester did not report to Cooper.

DHS was the most significant clue.

This guy had been sent here to deliver two packages. That's all he knew and all he needed to know.

He was probably unaware of who originally issued this particular order. All he knew was what he'd been told.

"Was there anything else?" Kim asked as she continued to eat the bagel as if she'd had coffee with him every day for the past hundred years.

"Yes. In the envelope is a plane ticket to Columbia, South Carolina. Your flight leaves in twenty minutes," he said.

"I'm not going anywhere else on a plane this morning," Kim replied, swallowing another bite with a swig of cold coffee.

He nodded and reached into his pocket. He pulled out a burner phone. Similar to the ones Cooper used, but again slightly different.

Lester Lester powered it up and placed the burner on the table in front of her.

Almost immediately, the phone vibrated and the screen lit up.

Kim picked up the phone. "Yes?"

A deep, smooth as silk voice she recognized instantly responded. "You'll want to take that flight."

"I need to go to my apartment. I need fresh clothes." She didn't mention her need to collect the backup gun in her safe. "What's in the briefcase?"

Finlay responded, "A friend from Chicago fast-tracked the tests. Since the suspects died, there will be no prosecution. He asked me to return your property."

She nodded but didn't ask for further explanations.

Her service weapon was back where it belonged as if it had never disappeared.

Nice touch.

Finlay always knew exactly how to motivate her.

She asked, "What's in South Carolina that can't wait?"

"Young Jake Reacher finds himself in a serious situation. Literally life and death for him and his mother. He needs your help," Finlay replied.

Kim cocked her head and offered a cheeky reply. "Have you notified his uncle? Seems like the time."

"Would that I could." Finlay had always denied all knowledge of Jack Reacher after their experiences fifteen years ago when Finlay had been a small-town police chief in Margrave, Georgia.

Kim never believed him.

She'd accumulated no hard evidence either way.

But Finlay was often ready, willing, and able to supply whatever she needed, whenever she needed it.

This seemed like a solid way to test the truth of Finlay's relationship with Reacher.

If his nephew was in life or death trouble, Reacher wouldn't like it.

Things could go south for those who threatened Reacher's family. Fast.

Probably even faster for those who knew his family was being threatened and did nothing about it, too.

Which meant Finlay would do whatever he could to find Reacher and send him to Columbia if he wasn't already on the way.

Maybe he was.

Maybe Finlay knew Reacher would be there when she arrived.

"Cooper won't like it if I do what you ask," she said.

Finlay ignored her perfectly legitimate objection. "Are you going or not?"

"Not sure I can make it." Kim glanced at the clock above the door at the bagel shop. "Only fifteen minutes before they close the jetway door. Anything you can do to help me out with that?"

"It's a federal crime to interfere with air travel," Finlay replied cheekily.

Kim scowled and said nothing.

Finlay offered one last thing. "The intel we have is inside that envelope. We'll have more by the time you touch down in Columbia."

Kim disconnected the call, dropped the burner into her pocket, and picked up the briefcase, which was heavier than she'd expected. Briefly, she flipped the latches open and lifted the lid.

Inside were two items. One was her service weapon, as expected. The other was her backup gun.

She shook her head. Finlay was still an enigma. And despite Gaspar's misgivings, she was still ambivalent about him.

She grabbed her bag and hustled into the terminal toward her gate.

Her mind raced even faster than her feet.

She trusted that Finlay had done whatever was required to allow her to take the briefcase and its contents onto the plane. Cooper always handled that end of things nicely. Whatever Cooper could do, Finlay seemed to do better.

Once settled into her seat on the plane, she ordered coffee and leaned back, eyes briefly closed.

Both she and Gaspar had been right about Reacher this time. He was getting sentimental in his old age. Developing normal feelings, finally.

Finlay's involvement confirmed it.

When Reacher left Chicago, he'd gone to Columbia, South Carolina. Because his brother's son graduated.

Jake had become a soldier. Reacher wanted to be there for that because Jake's father couldn't be there.

Just like Gaspar would have done.

Which could mean Reacher was on his way to see Jacqueline, too.

When they reached cruising altitude, she turned her attention to the files Finlay had sent. The situation was not what Kim had guessed. Jake was in real trouble.

CHAPTER 18

Wednesday, May 25
Columbia, SC

KIM STEPPED OFF THE hotel elevator into controlled chaos. Her finely honed sense of smell tracked the deceased instantly with the first shallow whiff.

"Thank God for air conditioning," she murmured, wishing she'd made the time to change into disposable clothes before coming straight from the airport.

The stink began almost at the moment of death. Unmistakable in the early stages of decomposition, the stench became stronger and more overwhelming with time.

From experience, she knew the odor would cling to her skin, her hair, and her clothes. She shrugged. Nothing she could do about that now.

The fifth floor of the Magnolia Hotel in Columbia, South Carolina, functioned according to the unseen rules of a murder scene investigation familiar to any law enforcement officer.

The entire floor had been vacated. Various official personnel milled about the corridor. A quick visual scan was all she needed to identify several surveillance cameras and make a mental note of each location. CCTV could be useful later.

Locating Margaret Reacher's room amid the disorder was simple. All she had to do was follow her nose.

Kim wished she'd packed another suit. She'd need to burn this one. When the stench of decomposition attached itself to fibers, nothing could eliminate the odor. Ever. And even if specialized cleaning would erase most of the smell, she'd never be comfortable wearing this suit again.

A steady stream of uniformed and plain clothes officers moved in and out through the door to Room 504 from the corridor.

Kim approached the closest officer.

He blocked her path. "How can I help you, ma'am?" The name on his uniform said R. Kent.

"Officer Kent." She paused and showed her badge wallet. "I'm looking for Captain Pete Espin."

Kent looked down to stare at the official FBI identification for a moment, unimpressed. "This is an active crime scene, Agent Otto. Which means access is restricted to authorized personnel assigned to the case."

"Check your list. Captain Espin is expecting me," Kim replied as if she knew it for a fact.

She didn't. But her assertion was a safe bet. Finlay had probably fixed things.

But even if he hadn't, The Boss knew she was here, and he usually handled procedural problems, like introductions, in advance. No reason to believe he'd broken his own protocol this time.

Her orders were to find Pete Espin and squeeze all available intel from him. If Jack Reacher wasn't here already, The Boss had reason to believe he'd arrive soon.

He hadn't shared those reasons with her, of course. He never did.

Her job was to find Reacher. And when she found him, to call for backup.

Whether she would follow those orders was another question. So far, she hadn't been faced with the choice.

Finding Reacher had proven more difficult than she'd expected when she first got this assignment back in November.

Espin had been an army warrant officer seven years ago. Somehow, he'd run into Jack Reacher back then. The nature of the encounter, and its ultimate outcome, was murky.

Kim didn't have many details about the prior situation, which meant Espin could be either friendly or not. Could go either way.

Her experience with Reacher's prior contacts had been mixed. Reacher had a strong impact on witnesses. Some were more hostile than others.

Espin had left the army on solid terms. Honorably discharged with a chest full of medals, still young enough to have a successful second career.

He was a Charleston, SC, police department captain and the ranking officer in charge of this homicide. Captains didn't show up at every homicide scene. This one must have been special.

That was all Kim knew about Espin. So far. As soon as she had the chance, she'd be expanding the background check if Espin's intel seemed promising at all.

"Captain Espin?" she said again when it seemed Officer Kent planned to ignore her until she went away.

Kent's level stare held steady for a few more moments before he correctly concluded that she wasn't leaving without what she came for. He said, "Wait here. I'll get him."

She nodded.

Kent frowned and followed another officer into Room 504.

Kim stopped at the doorway to wait where she'd have a better view.

No reason to get sideways with Espin before she even met the guy.

Kim was a lawyer by training and a cop by trade. She wasn't clear on exactly what had happened here, and she had no desire to contaminate the crime scene. Finlay's reports stated there had been a homicide in Margaret Reacher's room. Nothing more.

She was well aware that catching killers was hard enough without unauthorized visitors on the scene destroying the chain of evidence. She had no intention of adding to that problem.

More importantly, Kim didn't want to be stuck with the paperwork. Or, even worse, get forced to testify by some zealous defense attorney. No thanks.

As it turned out, she and Officer Kent had the same goals. The less unique personal knowledge she acquired about the facts inside Room 504, the better.

From her vantage point in the corridor, Kim had a clear view of several technicians working the scene, gathering evidence, shooting photos, and talking quietly among themselves.

The dead man was lying on the carpet near the exterior wall by the window. She saw his shoes extending beyond the foot of the bed, but the rest of his body was obscured from her view.

Other than the gaggle of officials and the dead man on the floor, the hotel room was unremarkable.

Decorated in a traditional style. Lots of emerald green and gold. A bed, two chairs, small desk, private bath. A bedside table with a telephone and a lamp. Usually, hotels put a notepad and a pen near the phone. Kim didn't see one on the table.

A woman's purse lay open on the bed near a royal blue dress and a pair of low-heeled pumps. It seemed as if she'd been preparing for an evening out and was interrupted, maybe by the dead man.

The room was tidy. It hadn't been used much since the last time it was cleaned.

Kim noticed that the TV had internet connectivity. The room was probably equipped with Wi-Fi. Along with the security cameras, the TV could provide promising leads. Espin's team would know that and more facts that Kim didn't know.

Margaret Reacher had been set to check out today at one o'clock. About an hour later, the maid ignored the "Do Not Disturb" sign hanging on the knob, came into the room to clean for the next guest and found the body.

Finlay had learned about the situation quickly afterward, which was why Kim was here now.

Officer Kent stepped around the techs and approached a man wearing an ill-fitting suit who was talking quietly with a woman wearing a jacket emblazoned with the words "Coroner's Office" on the back.

When the man turned to look at Kim, she recognized Espin. Absolutely.

She'd been supplied with his headshot, along with the warning that Espin wasn't the dumbest bunny ever born. Not surprising. Those who survived and thrived after encounters with Reacher were, in her experience, brighter bulbs than most.

Espin looked like a lightweight boxer. Slight and wiry, dark-haired, hard and muscled. His nose was flat, and Kim guessed the nose had been forcibly rearranged after a few too many rounds with bigger opponents.

Which meant Espin didn't back down.

Good thing to know.

She'd bet ten bucks that Espin gave as well as he got in any fight.

That kind of guy usually had a slew of complaints in his military files. She made a mental note to check for that, too.

CHAPTER 19

Wednesday, May 25
Columbia, SC

AFTER A BRIEF EXCHANGE, Espin sent Officer Kent back to his post near the elevator. On his way past her, Kent said, "Wait here. Captain Espin will be right with you."

"Thanks," Kim replied.

Espin finished his conversation with the coroner's staff and headed her way. "Agent Otto. I've been expecting you." He nodded and extended his hand for a friendly shake.

He smelled like he'd been rolling around in a dumpster in the back of a restaurant filled with rotting meat and fish. She gulped to cover her gag reflex.

He handed her a pair of paper booties and glanced around the corridor. "FBI agents generally travel in pairs. Where's your partner?"

"He's on his way," Kim said, which was mostly true.

Burke was still in the hospital, but he'd be released in the morning. No need to get into all that with Espin, though.

Espin nodded. By way of unnecessary caution, he said, "You're familiar with crime scene protocol, I'm sure."

"Right."

Crime techs were still collecting trace evidence. They would put the deceased in a body bag after the initial evidence collection. Once they zipped the body bag, it must remain closed until the autopsy.

She had arrived in time to view the body before it was zipped closed.

She gloved up first, then took the booties and slipped them over her shoes. She might be able to salvage the shoes if she didn't inadvertently step in something that permeated the leather.

She always wore her long, black hair in a tight knot at her neck, but she slipped a paper cap over her head anyway. "I'd like to see the victim."

"He doesn't have any ID on him," Espin said, leading the way. "We'll request a fingerprint match as soon as we can. DNA will take longer. So if you know who he is, I'd like to know, too."

"Of course," Kim replied.

They'd reached the end of the bed, where Kim got a good long look at the deceased. There was nothing remotely unusual about him.

Kim guessed his age at forty, give or take. Dark hair and dark eyes. He was dressed in jeans, a long-sleeved T-shirt, and black sneakers with no socks.

There was a black baseball cap on the carpet near the body, suggesting he might have been wearing it when he was killed. No logos or slogans on the cap.

He was wearing surgical gloves, which explained why they didn't have a fingerprint match yet. Removing the gloves would be done by the medical examiner during the autopsy instead of at the crime scene.

Kim pulled out her phone and snapped a few photos for analysis later.

"So? Do you know this guy?" Espin asked.

"Sorry. Never saw him before. I can't help you with the ID," she said, shaking her head.

He had access to the same facial recognition programs she would use. He'd probably already started his search.

"Any estimate on time of death yet? He smells pretty ripe."

"Based on what the maid says, she last cleaned the room at noon Monday. After that, no hotel personnel entered the room until two o'clock Wednesday," Espin replied. "That's as close as we can put the time of death right now."

"Fifty hours is a broad time window for a homicide to remain undiscovered in a location like this," she said. "No one heard or saw or *smelled* anything?"

Espin shrugged. "We work with what we've got."

Kim nodded toward the victim's hands. "What's with the gloves?"

Espin wagged his head. "Working theory is that he entered the room uninvited and she shot him. No weapon in the room. We don't know if the weapon was hers or his."

"So you're thinking robbery gone bad?"

"The simple answer is usually the best, in my experience," Espin replied.

"Anything missing?"

"Aside from the shooter?" Espin cocked his head.

"The safe could have been empty before this dude came in. Or she might have had more clothes and stuff here," Kim said, frowning.

"When we find her, we'll ask." He continued snidely, "Maybe the FBI has psychics on staff, huh? Here in Columbia, we solve crimes the old-fashioned way."

"Right." Kim glanced at the door to the connecting room. "So the guy breaks in. She shoots him. Twice. And the guest next door in 502 didn't hear anything? That's hard to believe."

"It's impossible to believe," Espin said, nodding. "Which is why you're here, I assume."

Kim cocked her head, puzzled. "Meaning what?"

Espin leveled an annoyed stare in her direction. "Meaning the woman who occupied this room was Margaret Reacher. And the guest booked into the room next door was Jake Reacher. Don't pretend you didn't already know that."

Kim said nothing.

"Just so we're clear, we know the kid is Jack Reacher's nephew," Espin said as if there was a world of data contained in that one connection.

Which there was.

Kim replied, "I'd like a look at the adjoining room."

Espin waved her through with an exasperated smirk. "Be my guest."

As she walked past, she quickly scanned Margaret's bathroom. Two techs were still working, but Kim saw nothing unusual. It looked like the rest of the room. Clean. Tidy. Unoccupied.

She elbowed the connecting door and walked through to the adjoining Room 502. The room reserved for Jake Reacher.

Jake's room looked like it hadn't been used at all since the last time it was cleaned. Whenever that was. Housekeeping would know.

For Kim's purposes, it made sense to assume the room hadn't been cleaned after the homicide. Which probably meant Jake had never stayed here at all.

But the questions just piled on top of each other. Was he present when the shooting occurred? Did he shoot the guy? Did he hustle Margaret out of the room and run with her?

Nothing could be ruled out at this point. It was just too early in the investigation.

Crime techs were working Jake's room like it was part of the crime scene as if they expected to find evidence to tie Jake to the homicide.

After a brief look around, Kim returned to Margaret's room where Espin was waiting.

Kim asked, "Can I buy you lunch? There's a coffee shop around the corner."

He wagged his head. "Sorry. I can't leave for a while yet. I can call you when I'm done here. We can connect later."

"Works for me." Kim crossed the threshold into the corridor, pulled off the booties and the gloves and the paper shower cap, and stuffed them into the disposal containers.

She rode the elevator down alone. Kim took note of the surveillance cameras inside the elevator car and various other locations as she passed through the hotel lobby.

The place was well covered by video feeds. Kim was satisfied there would be CCTV footage to prove when Jake and Margaret Reacher were and were not inside the hotel.

The same footage might also show the dead man entering Room 504.

Surely Espin's team was checking that already. But it gave her another lead to pursue, too. She'd put Gaspar on it right away.

Running on nothing but instinct borne of experience, she pushed the front door open and hustled down the stairs to the sidewalk.

Kim knew Jake Reacher. Margaret, too. And she'd spent thousands of hours hunting Jack Reacher, obsessively immersed in his world over the past seven months.

At this point, she knew more about the Reachers than anyone else, dead or alive.

What she didn't know was exactly what was going on here. The whole situation was odd.

But she'd bet her pension that Espin's theories were nowhere close. Not even remotely.

Standing on the sidewalk in front of the Magnolia Hotel, Kim kept a watchful eye, scanning everything within sight distance. Looking for someone or something that didn't belong.

After a few minutes, she found it.

An unnatural flash of light in her periphery caught her attention.

She slipped her sunglasses on and turned her head to look directly at the flash point.

Yes. Just as she'd thought.

The bright sun bounced oddly from a rooftop a few buildings east and on the opposite side of the street. She peered in that direction to be sure what she'd seen wasn't simply a trick of the mind.

No. The light was there. It barely flickered. But she hadn't imagined it.

While she watched, the odd flash happened again.

As if a watcher was focused on her exact location.

CHAPTER 20

Wednesday, May 25
Fort Meade, MD

HUGH SULLIVAN APPROACHED THE entrance to his headquarters laden with supplies. After the failure at the Magnolia Hotel and the walk and talk with Dover when he'd learned about the mole, he'd decided to hunker down for as long as it took to regain control.

With a practiced eye, he quickly scanned the exterior premises. Satisfied that his security measures were intact, he activated the biometric security device and applied each measure precisely in the correct order.

First, his ten fingerprints and palm print were read simultaneously, right hand first. Followed by two retina scans, left then right. And finally, both ear prints, right and then left.

As expected, he heard the click of the electronic lock release. He lowered the lever handle with an elbow and pushed the heavy steel door open with his shoulder.

Only after the door snugged closed behind him with a solid, sturdy thunk did Sullivan relax his vigilance.

Sullivan was a careful man and his supplies reflected as much.

The Jake Reacher mission had gone sideways from the outset. He'd instructed Sanz to prepare three graves in the poppy field. Each would be ready and waiting for Jake and his mother and Jack Reacher, too.

With his expert guidance and diligence from Jones, the Jack Reacher situation could be completed. The timing was unpredictable. It could happen today or a year from now.

If the Four Knights Club problem broke wider, Sullivan could be sequestered here longer. Which was why he'd stocked up for several days.

He carried his supplies into the situation room and dumped half of them onto the worktable. Then he carried the rest into the kitchen and started the coffee maker.

He drank his java hot, black, and often. If there was a way to mainline the stuff without sticking a needle in his arm, he'd have done it.

While the coffee brewed, he stored his rations. He intended to remain inside with his hands on the controls until the mole and the Reacher situations were resolved.

Ankles crossed, he leaned against the counter and considered the facts.

Fortune had smiled upon the Reacher mission in the hours after Jones's frantic 10-16 "trouble" message from the Magnolia Hotel parking lot on Tuesday.

Jones had proven his worth once again. He'd made the correct tactical decisions at the scene and advanced the mission instead of aborting.

Specifically, he'd left Smith's body in place and stifled his understandable reaction to eliminate the woman. Removing the hostage retained her usefulness as bait for Jake. She was now securely stashed at the Palace.

Jones had been lucky, too. Smitty's body had remained undiscovered in the hotel room far longer than expected. First responders usually arrived on the scene much earlier.

The delay had allowed Sullivan more time to alter the CCTV at the hotel and cameras in the surrounding area. When the locals finally viewed the video, they'd find no trace of Jones, Smith, or young Jake Reacher.

Sullivan had also spent the delay metabolizing every piece of intel he could find on Jack Reacher. He'd covered some of it before, but now he had a more complete picture of the man. Forewarned is forearmed.

His tactical advantage was that Sullivan knew everything possible to know about Reacher while Reacher didn't know Sullivan existed.

He punched the playback of his earlier notes on the Reacher situation, listening for gaps, mistakes, opportunities.

"Jack Reacher could have easily hitchhiked from Chicago to South Carolina in twenty-four hours," Sullivan's voice said from the recording. "But he didn't need to stick his thumb out. He already had a ride."

Sullivan nodded. Solid intel on that. He'd confirmed with his own eyes.

"Reacher is traveling with Petey Burns, the escaped inmate. A professional car thief. Reacher or Burns or both could be on scene in South Carolina by now."

Sullivan shook his head slowly. Reacher was one lucky bastard.

He wasn't worried that Reacher would come after him here.

The nondescript bunker near Fort Meade was the one and only place in the world Sullivan knew for certain was completely secure. Defeating Reacher from the snow den would be a cakewalk.

His recorded notes continued. "Reacher is all too comfortable conducting operations in and around government installations of various types. He was employed by the US Army for thirteen years. He served as a military cop. He knows his way over, around, and under every weak point in the security."

Sullivan pushed the pause button for a moment to let that point sink in. Then he pressed play again.

"Reacher's files were buried too deep." He smirked.

With enough bribes and dark web hackers on the hunt, Sullivan had finally managed to dig up some of those files. He would find more. Reacher was like a dog in the road. Just a matter of time.

"Tanking those old files like that was a mistake on two levels. Only a handful of men are powerful enough to make it so. Which one was responsible here?" Sullivan's voice mused from the audio.

"The first level was that the records themselves were whitewashed at the time the events occurred," he'd continued. He cocked his head. "Which is a good thing because even the scrubbed versions contain enough crimes to put Reacher away for ten lifetimes. Reacher was never charged with these crimes."

Again, he paused the audio to consider. The obvious question was, who could have made that happen?

The list of suspects was short, and each was an unlikely candidate, above reproach. Which was probably why the cover-ups continued effectively to the present day.

"Reacher once busted an army major charged with corruption out of Fort Dyer in broad daylight. He also killed a corrupt general in his office inside the Pentagon. He was suspected of killing several other miscreants who probably didn't deserve to breathe free air, according to Reacher." Sullivan's voice recited, like a kid in school given a list to memorize.

When his recorded voice finally stopped listing Reacher's transgressions, he punched the pause button again.

The one about killing a general in his office was mildly amusing. *Murder in the Pentagon* sounded like a farcical movie title. But of course, it wasn't.

Sullivan had often wondered why more crimes weren't committed inside those walls.

The Pentagon was not a fortress. That idea had been debunked many times over. These days, just the opposite was true.

Splashy government buildings were terrorist magnets. Osama bin Laden had proven that to the entire world.

Visibility was one reason Sullivan wanted nothing to do with the pomp and circumstance. At his insistence, Sullivan had never been officially assigned a plush office at NSA Headquarters in Fort Meade, Maryland, which would have flagged his importance to spies and crusaders alike.

After his in-depth examination of all available data, Sullivan understood Jack Reacher at the cellular level.

Under different circumstances, the two men might have been friends, he'd thought more than once.

Sullivan had precious few friends.

Reacher possessed fewer.

In Sullivan's world, only friends and enemies existed.

Since Reacher wasn't Sullivan's friend, his status automatically defaulted to enemy.

If Reacher had avoided Sullivan's world completely, they might have coexisted for decades in a state of wary détente.

Like the Soviet Union and the United States during the Cold War. Détente was a total fiction and temporary under the best of circumstances. Sooner or later, one party oversteps. Crosses the line.

Long term, peaceful coexistence was not possible between enemies.

CHAPTER 21

Wednesday, May 25
Fort Meade, MD

SULLIVAN'S NOSE TWITCHED AS the rich aroma of brewing coffee filled the kitchen and interrupted his study. A bold, dark roasted blend of the finest Central and South American coffees contained caffeine and plenty of it.

He pulled a stainless steel mug from the cabinet and filled it with hot water to pre-heat. When the brewing finished, he filled the mug.

Still thinking about Reacher, he slipped the recorder into his pocket. He was satisfied he hadn't missed anything important in his thorough perusal of Reacher's files and confident Reacher couldn't touch him here, even if he was somehow able to find this place.

"He won't. The guy's an army grunt. A smart and well-trained grunt with a questionable conscience, but he's not a superhero," Sullivan said. "Besides, he's not going to be looking for me. Not now. Reacher will be too busy trying to rescue his nephew."

Sullivan grinned and headed into the situation room to immerse himself in the known data again.

As the ancient Chinese general Sun Tzu famously said, and the best warriors had absorbed over time, "Know thy enemy and know yourself; in a hundred battles, you will never be defeated."

Good advice then and now. The art of war had not changed for centuries.

Reacher had been a solid practitioner of the art himself.

Sullivan smiled and sipped the scalding coffee. He loved a challenge.

The more he learned about Reacher, the more worthy his enemy became. This felt almost like playing a game against himself.

"In Vegas, they'd give Reacher a few points, though," he said, somewhat amused about the similarities between them.

Unfettered freedom to move was one of the inherent traits they both prized.

Both he and Reacher had achieved nearly absolute anonymity in all the ways that mattered.

Both men were non-identifiable, unreachable, untraceable.

On that point, neither seemed capable of compromise.

When Sullivan was first recruited, the NSA Director offered him a proper office. Sullivan had declined.

"Give a man a physical office, and he exists on a paper trail somewhere," Sullivan had explained. "Organizational charts, payroll records, pension accounts. All the bureaucratic nonsense that goes along with that office is traceable. No thanks."

The argument had continued for days. The Director pressed the issue. But Sullivan resisted.

"Put me on the payroll, list me at the top of the charts, and sooner or later, some jackwagon gets it into his head that I should be accountable," Sullivan said. "Which, in my line of work, can cost way too many warriors fighting the good fight. We can't have that, can we?"

The Director had talked about accountability, oversight, regulations, and other such irrelevant concepts.

Sullivan shook his head. "What you mean are handcuffs, straight jackets, restrictions, limits. Can't do it. Sorry."

Reacher seemed to feel the same. At least with respect to his life after the army.

Sullivan had identified a few important differences between them as well.

Unlike Reacher, Sullivan had served his country for a long time. His methods were his own and he refused to be questioned.

"It's the only way I'll do the work. And you know there's no one else you can find to do it better than me," Sullivan had paused when listing his demands. "But feel free to try."

The Director finally gave up and hired Sullivan anyway.

That was four presidential administrations ago. Sullivan expected to serve at least another four at the helm of his operations.

National security, as defined by Hugh Sullivan, was the first, last, and only goal. The rest of Washington's political theater didn't interest him.

During his army career, at least, Reacher would have agreed.

Sullivan worked in the shadows behind what the world considered the thrones of power. Which didn't mean he was unknown to those who moved in the limelight. Quite the opposite.

Like the air they all breathed, world leaders simply expected Sullivan and his teams to be there when needed.

Which he was.

Always.

The ultimate fixer.

Sullivan existed, worked, moved, arrived, departed, and operated on his own terms. Simple as that.

Another trait he shared with Reacher.

Sullivan answered to himself and no one else.

Independence was a wonderful thing.

Not that Sullivan expected Reacher to come looking for him. But his plans to eliminate Reacher from Cooper's list of potential disruptors would be executed much easier if Reacher made the effort.

After another quick run-through of known facts, Sullivan felt confident he could profitably mine the similarities between himself and Reacher because he was now intimately familiar with him.

If Reacher didn't come to liberate his nephew as planned, Sullivan could locate him when others had failed.

He nodded once, decisively.

Then he settled deeper into his chair in the situation room and powered up the array of monitors and computers.

A burner phone danced around on the desktop, vibrating as the call came in. Sullivan picked it up. "Yeah."

"We've got a new issue with our whistleblower," Dover replied.

"Whistleblower my ass," Sullivan said angrily. "We're not glorifying him. Let's call this guy what he is. A traitorous bastard. He can't possibly believe he'll survive this. If he does, he's too stupid to live. Are we sure he's acting alone?"

"What do you mean?" Dover asked. "Like someone installed him here? Who would do that? And what the hell for?"

"We'll know that when you answer my question. Look into it. Now." Sullivan growled before he hung up.

Right off the top of his head, he named two possibles. Cooper. Finlay.

Then he added a third. Turner.

CHAPTER 22

Wednesday, May 25
Columbia, SC

KIM DARTED ACROSS GERVAIS Street, dodging traffic and ignoring the angry drivers as they laid on their horns. Once she reached the opposite sidewalk, her viewing angle had changed and she could no longer see the glinting flash on the rooftop that had lured her.

The building was newer and taller than the historic brick structures beside it. The rooftop façade angled oddly, like a scalene triangle tapering toward the west end of the building but stopping in the center of the roof. The façade was taller and wider and the slope was sharper than the retaining wall around the rooftop.

The creative scalene façade was clever but, like many things designed by architects, probably functional as well. Kim assumed it was meant to conceal unsightly but necessary building functions.

Perhaps the rooftop was a parking lot. Which would make sense. The scalene façade could have been the designer's way of improving a utilitarian parking deck's appearance and concealing parked cars from view.

The strange glint she'd seen from the hotel sidewalk could have been the sun's rays bouncing off a vehicle mirror. The vehicle could be gone already. She might be wasting her time.

Or not.

Someone could be watching the hotel entrance from that point on the roof across the street. The angle was good enough. He'd have a clear view of comings and goings.

What was he looking for?

One way to find out came to mind.

Her instincts had saved her way too many times in the past. She wouldn't ignore them now.

Worst-case scenario here was that she'd get to the rooftop and find nothing. But since she was alone at the moment, the risk of embarrassing herself was minuscule.

The reward, if her instincts panned out, could be considerable. She'd find one important thing that Espin didn't have yet. A witness.

Kim hustled along the sidewalk toward the tall building. As she came closer, she saw the ground floor was occupied by a retail department store. The lights were still on inside, and a few browsers milled around.

Store hours were posted on the door. Kim glanced at her watch. Not much time before the store would be closing. If she went inside now, how would she leave?

She looked for an alternative exit. Most fire codes required multiple exits, and this building was new enough to be subject to modern codes.

The building's exterior walls tightly abutted the historic buildings on either side. If the rooftop was a parking deck, the entrance ramp must have been on the back street. Surely there was a back entrance to the store, too. But she had no time to confirm.

If the rooftop wasn't a parking deck, she could get stuck up there. But it was a small risk, in the scope of things. She could call Espin to find a janitor or something to let her out if it came to that.

No time to dawdle.

Kim pushed through the revolving door and entered the cosmetics department. The perfumed air assaulted her senses like a physical force. Her eyes watered and her nose wrinkled. She felt a cough forming in her throat.

A smiling woman stood near the entrance with a small tray and a spritzer bottle in her hand.

"Would you like to try our new signature fragrance?" she asked pleasantly enough but with a sense of urgency. She held the spritz toward Kim, preparing to push the plunger.

"No thanks. Allergic." She held her palm out to reinforce the message, dodged the spray and kept going, clearing her throat as she moved.

She noticed the woman cover her nose when she got a stronger whiff of the decomp odor emanating from Kim as she hurried past.

She considered stopping to buy a new suit and dismissed the idea as soon as it popped into her head. No time for that now. But she made a mental note to deal with the stench as soon as possible.

Kim headed deeper into the store because the restrooms and elevators were probably located in the center of the building for structural reasons.

If patrons and employees parked on the roof, the store's customer elevators must travel all the way up there. If the rooftop was not a parking deck, she'd be hiking up at least one flight of service stairs to get there.

As she reached the elevator lobby on the first floor, management broadcast over the intercom system that the store would be closing in fifteen minutes.

Briefly, Kim wondered whether and how long the elevators would run after closing time. The stairway doors would most certainly be locked at some point.

She punched the call button. The elevator car had been waiting on the first floor, so the doors opened when she pushed the button, but they opened slower than a strolling sloth.

Eventually, the gap between the heavy doors was wide enough.

Kim slipped inside the unoccupied car and grinned when she saw the button for the parking deck. She punched it, and the light came on to indicate the electronics had registered her order.

There must have been a time delay programmed into the elevator's system for relaxed shoppers or parents with toddlers and strollers or nervous elevator riders or something. Kim shifted her weight to control her impatience.

After another long wait while the doors continued to open fully and pause, they finally closed, and the elevator began its leisurely rise.

The car bypassed the second, third, and fourth floors of the store and opened onto a small covered area surrounding the enclosed elevator shaft in the center of the roof.

Kim stepped out of the elevator car and peered into the twilight.

From her vantage point, she could only see half of the roof. The rectangular stucco enclosure around the elevator blocked her view of the other half.

The parking deck consumed the entire rooftop. Light poles dotted the lanes, but the lights weren't on yet.

The sun had dipped behind the buildings in the distance, and not even a small slice of the orange orb rested above now. The deck was bathed in weak sunset afterglow, casting shadows deep enough to conceal.

As she oriented herself, Kim realized she faced the back side of the parking deck. On the far end of the rooftop, in the southeast corner, a small cluster of single-spaced vehicles dotted the parking lanes. Probably employee parking for the late shift. At the end of the workday, most employees had already departed.

She counted eleven trucks, SUVs, and sedans in the employee lot, all of which appeared to be unoccupied with their engines off. If she hustled over there and touched the hoods, they'd probably be cold.

Nothing about those vehicles in that location could have caused the strange flashing lights she'd seen from the sidewalk in front of the hotel.

She walked around the stucco structure in the center of the roof, careful to stay covered by the lengthening shadows. The sun had dropped below the horizon now, and the pole lights had not yet illuminated.

As she rounded the corner, she saw the Gervais Street side of the rooftop. The oddly shaped façade she'd noticed from below poked up like a wedge at the center of the building and tapered toward the southwest corner.

What was left of the sunlight protected much of the rooftop from view. She raised her left hand to shield her eyes and waited for her pupils to adjust.

She scanned the area quickly. She counted six vehicles neatly parked in the lot. Late shoppers, probably.

The seventh vehicle was seriously out of place.

CHAPTER 23

Wednesday, May 25
Columbia, SC

THE SEVENTH WAS A silver panel van parked in the travel lane, parallel to the wedged façade, as if placed there to block the view of the roof's edge. Anyone exiting the store by using the elevator would not have a clear sight line along the north side of the store.

The van had no windows on the sides or rear doors. The engine was running.

The left side mirror was angled toward the driver's seat. By changing her position slightly, Kim could use the mirror to see that no one was sitting there. She couldn't see the passenger seat or the north side of the van.

The sunlight reflected off the silver metallic paint like a big mirror, unnaturally brightening the south side of the vehicle and the pavement surrounding it.

But on the other side, the van blocked the light and produced a darker shadow between the boxy vehicle and the façade. She assessed the geometry quickly.

The strange bright glints she had seen from the street below might possibly have been low sunlight colliding with the van's exterior side mirror on the right.

Kim narrowed her eyes and peered into the oblong shadow between the van and the north façade. After a long moment, she saw him.

A darker shadow hunched over something. Kim couldn't see it well, but the object appeared to be a rifle mounted on a tripod.

She blinked to clear her vision.

She squinted at it again to be sure.

Was he preparing to shoot? Or was he still waiting for his target to appear?

From her vantage point, looking into the shadows, she wasn't sure.

The department store was closing. Any moment now, the remaining shoppers who had parked on the roof would be exiting from the elevator in the center of the building. Employees would follow shortly thereafter.

When the shoppers made their way to the roof, what would the man do? Someone else was bound to see him and the rifle. Then what?

She had a small window of opportunity to disarm him right now.

No time to call for backup, even if she had Espin on speed dial.

Kim ran toward the back of the van as quietly as possible. When she reached the back doors, she flattened her back against them and, controlling her breathing, inched toward the corner.

She drew her weapon.

She turtled her head for quick confirmation.

From this vantage point, the man was no longer backlit. He stood close to the rifle and bent forward, with his eye close to the scope. Both arms were straight down in front of his body.

She guessed that he hadn't identified his target yet. Or, that the target wasn't in the right location at the moment. His finger wasn't on the trigger.

She had a window of opportunity to stop him.

Kim took two steps around the back corner of the van and stood in a solid shooter's stance, her weapon pointed directly at him.

He might have heard her run up or heard the steps she took to position herself. He might have smelled the stench of decomp on her.

Or he might have already finished his observations and had planned to turn before she noticed him.

She couldn't be sure exactly what triggered him to do what he did next.

He whipped around to face her. He had a pistol in his right hand.

"Stop! FBI!" she yelled. "Drop your weapon!"

She could have removed the threat with two rounds to the chest and a third to the head. Right then. Right there. No cop in the world would have faulted her. Hell, she might have even been awarded a medal.

But then she wouldn't have a chance to find out what the hell he'd been planning. Because it made no sense to assume this guy wasn't watching the Marigold Hotel for a reason unrelated to the earlier murder.

She wanted him alive. He was of no use to her dead.

Without a moment's hesitation, he fired two rounds from the handgun in her general direction. The bullets went way wide. She didn't hear where they stopped.

Either he was a spectacularly sloppy shooter or he hadn't meant to kill her.

Not that she wanted to give him another chance.

Before he could fire again, she ducked behind the van for cover. Jake and Margaret Reacher's lives could depend on what she did next.

He jumped inside the van and slammed the transmission into reverse.

Half a moment before he stomped the accelerator, Kim dropped to the pavement out of his line of sight in the big mirror and rolled off to one side.

The van's tires squealed, speeding in reverse, in a desperate attempt to mow her down. He used the van as a weapon. Unlike the handgun he'd fired, he was now making every effort to kill her with the van.

The van weighed more than four thousand pounds. If he hit her with it at any speed, his chances of success were high.

But the van had blind spots. Reversing its momentum wasn't instant. As a weapon, it left a lot to be desired.

Kim couldn't outrun him. But she was outside. She was agile. She could move rapidly in any direction.

And she was a much better shot than he was.

She zigzagged out of the path of the oncoming vehicle. He steered around obstacles and came at her again.

Kim maneuvered herself into position in front of the van. She saw the driver's face.

He had grabbed the steering wheel with both hands at ten and two. He was leaning forward, watching the side mirrors as the boxy van traveled in reverse.

He must have realized he'd become confused. He'd been speeding backward in the wrong direction.

She heard the transmission protest as he shifted into drive while the van was still running backward. The back end of the van fishtailed wildly until the wheels gained traction, and he headed toward the front side of the parking deck.

He had been making every effort to kill her with the van, but now he seemed like he planned to escape down the exit.

Kim positioned herself between the van and the down ramp, standing between him and freedom.

He floored the accelerator and headed straight toward her.

The distance between Kim and the van narrowed as he sped toward the exit.

She felt the moment when her body's consciousness shifted into the mental state she knew was only a trick of perception when time seemed to slow even as her body moved at normal speed.

The scene unfolded in slow motion. The racing van seemed to be barely inching forward. The driver was determined and fierce and moving at the same slow speed as the vehicle.

Kim stood in a shooting stance, feet firmly planted, weapon raised, waiting, waiting.

He came ever closer.

He saw her. His eyes widened and he smiled.

He knew what she meant to do.

He had room to veer away.

He could swerve, drive around her, and still make it to the ramp.

He could escape.

Instead, he kept coming straight ahead, gaining speed, barreling right toward her.

He had a wild, maniacal look about him. Eyes rounded, hair flying in the wind from the open window, mouth wide open, screaming like a kid on a rollercoaster.

She imagined she could hear him. But adrenaline filled her ears with a louder roar than Niagara Falls.

"Stop! FBI!" she yelled again, although she knew he probably couldn't hear her either.

And even if he heard, he was too far gone now.

He didn't stop. Didn't even slow down.

It was as if he was determined to commit suicide by cop.

Or force her to let him go.

For an instant, she considered the choice. She could let him go. She would find him again. She'd wanted him alive. Jake and Margaret's lives might depend on it.

And then he lifted the handgun and aimed straight at her.

The options were no longer open.

One choice, right choice.

She fired four times through the windshield.

All four shots hit her target leaving holes in the windshield.

Three in the chest, one in the head.

He slumped over the steering wheel.

His foot fell off the accelerator.

The van slowed but continued its forward momentum.

Kim jumped out of the way and hit the pavement again, landing harder than she'd intended, and rolled. She barely felt the impact.

A long, slow moment after the van passed Kim's position on the pavement, the front wheels hit the retaining wall and climbed halfway over, where it finally stopped.

The boxy silver van, paint reflecting the twilight now, landed on its belly on the edge of the retaining wall, held aloft, front wheels still spinning, rear wheels straining to push more than two tons over the wall.

The engine was still running when Kim heard the elevator ding, and a group of four giggling girls walked out onto the parking deck and screamed.

CHAPTER 24

Wednesday, May 25
White Kings Palace

JAKE HAD BEEN TAKEN to see his mother, as requested.
They'd shoved him into her cell located in the basement of one of
the white mansions he'd seen through the fence.

Margaret's eyes widened, and she jumped from her bunk to
embrace him. "Jake, Jake," she repeatedly murmured as tears fell
from her eyes.

"It's okay, Mom. I promise. Everything will be fine." He
forced the words past the lump in his throat and held her tightly
until she managed to get her emotions somewhat under control.

He assured himself that she wasn't physically harmed. And
she told him what little she knew about the dead man in her hotel
room and how she came to be imprisoned here.

Her story infuriated him, but he shoved his anger aside. He'd
deal with her attackers later. After they escaped.

Jake pointed to the 360-degree camera mounted in the
ceiling and then placed a finger over his lips. She nodded her

understanding. After that, they spoke only when necessary, unwilling to expose information the kidnappers could exploit.

The forced silence was no hardship for Jake. He could play chess in his head. Poker, too. Or play music. He'd learned long ago that the best stereo in the world is free, inside your head. It sounds as good as you want it to. Loud as you want it to be.

But his mother must have been bored out of her mind. Not even a window to see out of, to watch the birds as she did back home. Nothing he could do about any of that at the moment.

He familiarized himself with their prison.

The footprint for the house itself was at least four times larger than this section of the basement, which had been walled off from the rest. The ceiling was eight feet high.

Jake guessed the room had been built for something else and repurposed as a cell block.

Ventilation was good and the temperature was warm enough. The space wasn't humid or musty like some basements were. A pleasant citrus scent lingered in the air.

The block foundation had been insulated and covered with drywall and painted white to match the opposite walls. Recessed lighting placed in the ceiling at regular intervals illuminated the interior.

The flooring was covered by a beige epoxy of some sort with a rubberized feel. Floor drains had been placed at regular intervals.

The layout also suggested the jail had been added to the space.

A long, wide corridor ran from the stairs to the end of the room, bounded on one side by the exterior wall. The camera was mounted on the corridor ceiling near the middle.

The camera looked like a giant bulging eyeball with a black pupil. It protruded from the ceiling about six inches. The black pupil rotated inside a clear plastic cover to give the remote viewer a constant image of the entire room without blank spots or missed spaces.

Opposite the exterior wall were three modern cells, all identically pristine. The cells resembled cages, not rooms. Each was nine feet wide and twelve feet deep.

All three cages contained the same furnishings. Only the one Jake and Margaret shared was occupied.

The cells contained two cots stacked up like bunk beds in a kid's bedroom or on a ship. A small wooden table rested near the cell door.

There was a toilet and a sink in each cell. No privacy of any kind. Which Jake supposed was as understandable as it was offensive.

The entire room was surprisingly quiet like it had been soundproofed. He could hear no noises from activity that might be going on upstairs or outside or on the remaining basement spaces.

Jake had slept most of the day. He'd awakened for breakfast and lunch simply to familiarize himself with the procedure.

Each meal had been delivered on two trays by a single, unarmed male. Jake had seen many waiters deliver food on trays in his lifetime. These guys seemed inexperienced and awkward. They had difficulty balancing the metal dishes on the trays. Both times, food had been slopped.

Each man had stepped carefully down the stairs, holding a tray in each hand.

As he approached their cell door, an electronic lock clicked open. He pushed the door into the cell with his forearm and set the trays on the small table. When he stepped out, he pulled the door closed, and the electronic lock clicked into place again.

Neither man spoke or hung around to watch them eat. The server strode along the corridor in the opposite direction and took the stairs two at a time until, presumably, he reached the first floor.

The breakfast and lunch deliveries had been made by two different men. If a third man delivered dinner, there was probably a rotation system in place. Making friendly conversation with a variety of servers to develop trust would take way too long.

Jake wondered how many men were housed on the premises and how many were assigned to handle the prisoners. When one delivered the food, was another watching on CCTV somewhere?

There was no television or music in the cells. They had not been offered an exercise period or anything to pass the time. Not even a chess board or a deck of cards.

He found that if he leaned up in the far front corner of the cell, he could see the full length of the corridor leading to the stairs that leading up to the first floor and outside.

He knew that's where the stairs led because they'd removed the bag from his head at the top of the stairs when they brought him down to the cells.

Something unusual was happening tonight. Jake could feel the vibe.

Their evening meal had been due to be delivered an hour ago. Matching the big clock on the wall to the clock in his head, he waited for the minute hand to move.

When the door at the top of the stairs opened, a man's heavy weight pounded down. He emerged from the doorway awkwardly balancing two trays of food, one in each hand.

He was just under six feet tall. His black T-shirt was tight, revealing broad shoulders and a flat belly.

He was unarmed, just as the others had been. Which was smart. Someone had thought this through. If they didn't have weapons, prisoners wouldn't be able to take the guns away from them.

As he came closer, Jake said, "How long do you plan to keep us here? It's getting boring, sitting around with nothing to do."

"You're likely to be here awhile. I can bring you something to read if that would help," he offered, keeping his eyes on the plates and glasses balanced on the trays.

Margaret glanced nervously toward Jake and replied, "Yes, thank you. I'd love to read. I like mysteries and thrillers best. Do you have anything like that?"

"Guys here tend to like sci-fi or military stuff. But I'll see what I can do."

He had reached the middle cell. He waited briefly until the electronic lock clicked open. Still holding the trays, he pushed the door into the cell with his hip.

Jake darted from the corner where he'd been standing and yanked the cell door open.

Margaret gasped. Her hands flew to cover her mouth, her eyes wide.

The man turned his head toward her as he struggled to hold the trays flat.

For a brief moment, he lost his balancing act.

Jake gave him a hearty shove and knocked him to the floor.

The metal trays landed with a series of loud clangs and bounced off the hard floor. The food flew everywhere.

Before the jailer could scramble to his feet, Jake kicked him hard in the kidneys.

Jake reached back and grabbed Margaret's hand and jerked her forward, and she made a little leap over the man squirming and moaning on the floor.

The jailer raised himself up on one hand, struggling to rise.

Jake kicked him again.

He went down, but he yelled out this time as if someone might be watching or listening on the CCTV. Jake hoped they were.

Jake kneed the jailer in the face, busting his nose. Blood spewed as his head bounced on the hard concrete, and he lay still.

Jake bent and patted the guy down, looking for weapons or keys or anything useful. Nothing.

Jake closed the cell door and heard the electronic lock click into place.

Margaret stood in the corridor, hands over her mouth, staring at the bloody jailer, horrified.

"Come on. Let's get out of here before they come after us," Jake said. "Watch your step. There's food everywhere. The floor is slippery."

She didn't move.

Jake gave her shoulder a little push and he shook her bicep.

She turned to stare at him.

"Mom, we have to go."

She nodded.

He grabbed her hand and headed for the stairs.

CHAPTER 25

Wednesday, May 25
Fort Meade, MD

SULLIVAN HAD CYNICALLY DUBBED his bunker the "snow den" to remind himself that traitors lurked and walked even among friends. The damned mole who was trying to take down the Four Knights Club was proving his point.

He pushed his chair back, stood, and stretched. He felt stiff after sitting in front of the screens for too long. He had more work to do before he could hit the treadmill for a hard run to pound out the anger.

He'd planned a simple smash-and-grab at a hotel resulting in two valuable hostages. Instead, he had two men down in Columbia and a traitorous mole to deal with in DC.

He also needed a replacement partner for Jones. Coda was the obvious choice. At least until different arrangements could be made.

He picked up the burner phone that connected him to Sanz. The chemist answered promptly. "Yes?"

"Two things. First, tell Coda and Jones that they're now partners."

Dr. Sanz paused. "For how long?"

"Until further notice," Sullivan snapped. "And second, relocate half our stock to the Texas location by jet."

"Half? We can barely meet our current orders as it is, sir," Dr. Sanz protested. "Can this wait? We can ramp up production. Send it out in a couple days, perhaps."

"Half. Now. Tonight," Sullivan demanded.

He knew the order was unreasonable. But he didn't like having all his product in one warehouse as it was. And given what he'd learned about the mole, it was prudent to have product in two locations.

"Yes, of course, sir," Sanz said. "We'll get it done before daylight."

"Tell Coda to call me." Sullivan discontinued the call and turned his attention to Jack Reacher.

The snow den was the center of his shadow operations, and the place was so obscure that it could have existed on the other side of the world as far as security teams, both foreign and domestic, were aware.

The brick building was located in a warehouse district. It had no windows and a single door, which could only be opened with Sullivan's biometrics. Three touch points, presented in a specific order, were required.

Sullivan was more secure in the snow den than anywhere else on the planet, including every government installation in the world.

Reacher wouldn't show up here. Nor would the mole.

After a few laps around the room, he returned to his seat, making a conscious effort to focus.

The point of the Magnolia Hotel operation was to lure Reacher into a trap and remove him from the chess board to leave Cooper without that particular chess piece, which he was no doubt planning to use to thwart Sullivan's efforts.

First up: Find Reacher.

"First things first," Sullivan said aloud as he settled with his coffee to review the videos again, eyeing the indistinct images taken in Chicago on Navy Pier Sunday night at the end of a recent string of ATM robberies Sullivan had orchestrated.

A big man moved in the shadows.

That man he now realized was absolutely Jack Reacher.

No doubt about it.

He flipped through the videos again and again, watching Reacher move. Observing his body language. Noticing how others reacted to him.

"Why are they looking for you, Reacher?" Sullivan murmured aloud. "Why do they want to find you? We're not so different, you and I. Which means that whatever they want you to do, it's gotta be as illegal as hell."

Reacher's name had first alerted Sullivan's radar as a potential problem back in November through his low-level surveillance of Charles Cooper.

It had come to Sullivan's attention that Cooper had secretly assigned two completely expendable FBI agents to conduct a background check on a man who had left the army fifteen years ago. Ostensibly, the agents needed the background check because Reacher was being considered for a highly classified assignment.

That alone was too odd to be authentically official.

The FBI did many things that the rest of the government and the world were blindly unaware of, certainly. All the three-letter agencies did. Sullivan's entire existence was a testament to that.

But the Reacher assignment was a bridge too far, even for a classified clandestine operation.

The more Sullivan dug into the job, the stranger the situation became.

He'd learned that the Reacher mission was unauthorized, off the books, and buried so far below the usual bureaucratic radar that no one should have noticed.

Sullivan only heard about it because he had his tentacles everywhere.

As things progressed, mission creep had expanded Cooper's original objectives, of course. As always.

Now, the FBI black op wasn't merely doing the background check on Reacher, the agents were actively hunting Reacher as well.

Why?

No one had blinked an official eye, even as Agent Otto's mission had gone off the rails. Several times. The bodies were piling up, and yet, she was still on the hunt.

Hell, with all the lethal resistance they'd run into, Otto and her partners should have all been dead by now.

Yet, they seemed to have an uncanny knack for survival, assisted by inexplicable supporters.

Which meant it was a fluke that Sullivan had discovered Agent Otto and her assignment at all.

The discovery was one of those lucky things that can't be planned or orchestrated.

The sort of serendipity Sullivan had learned to revere and then exploit.

Otto had come to Sullivan's attention because her assignment was a curiosity where Cooper was concerned. But she had captured and held Sullivan's interest for other reasons.

For starters, Otto had powerful contacts in high places. The kind of contacts a regular FBI agent shouldn't have.

Two such contacts, specifically.

Men Sullivan had been watching closely for way too long.

Men with big titles, scores of minions, and the kind of visibility both Sullivan and Reacher avoided like the plague.

The first was Charles Cooper, the commanding officer for Otto's mission. Sullivan was well aware of Cooper. They'd crossed swords in the shadows many times.

Sullivan pulled several snapshots and video clips of Cooper's activities over the past few years onto the monitors for another look.

Cooper had moved from his career as an army general to the unofficial top of the food chain at the FBI. He wasn't the director. But he was the man in charge, the one who got things done.

Cooper was also a psycho. He had no conscience at all. Coupled with an uncompromising survival instinct. The combination made him both a lethal adversary to his enemies and a comforting ally to the like-minded.

His enemies whispered that Cooper had killed his own mother.

The woman had died under suspicious circumstances long ago, and the case remained unsolved. Sullivan couldn't disprove the story, although he'd tried.

Reacher had crossed Cooper's path somehow. Cooper had sent Otto to find Reacher for some private purpose. Which was completely illegal, of course.

Anyone who believed that elements inside the FBI were above such illegal and immoral activity never read a newspaper or watched a congressional hearing. Men were men. All had weaknesses that could be exploited.

Believers in truth, justice, and the American Way had their heads in the sand and their hands in someone's pocket where the government was concerned.

These were very dangerous places to keep one's head and hands, in Sullivan's experience. He should know. He was an insider, too.

Cooper's setup here was brilliant. He was a superb tactician. Under different circumstances, Sullivan would have invited him to join the Four Knights Club.

On the hunt for Reacher, Cooper had insured plausible deniability all around if Otto succeeded. The strategy was flawless.

If she failed, everyone except Cooper went down. Cooper would make it so.

Sullivan nodded with approval. "Brilliantly done, sir."

On that score alone, Otto was playing with an exceptionally hot fire. Did she know that? Or not?

Sullivan turned his attention to video and images of the second of Otto's curiously high profile contacts. Another man Sullivan knew well enough.

Lamont Finlay, Ph.D., was Special Assistant to the President for Strategy, whatever that meant.

He'd been selected by the highest-ranking civilian responsible for Homeland Security and Counterterrorism and placed one heartbeat away from the United States Commander in Chief.

No watchdog kept tabs on him. He reported seldom and only through a verbal briefing. No paper trail so much as named the missions he'd undertaken. Mission processes, performance, results, were also absent from the record.

In short, Finlay's position at DHS was uncomfortably close to Sullivan's position at NSA and Cooper's position at FBI.

Sullivan cocked his head and narrowed his eyes as he stared at Finlay's photo, committing the likeness to indelible memory.

"Exactly how good are you?" he mused.

Like nuclear power, when properly harnessed, Finlay might be useful. But was such control over Finlay even possible? Unlikely.

Exceptional leverage would be required, for sure.

Sullivan had already begun the quest to find that leverage. No luck yet.

Based on the data he'd located so far, Sullivan's already rock-solid opinion on the two men had been re-confirmed.

As bad as Cooper was, Finlay was worse.

Exactly the kind of men Sullivan appreciated and preferred. It was satisfying to defeat worthy adversaries.

Finlay's patina of suave respectability cloaked the heart of a jackal, a cold and calculating killer, like the vicious thugs of the animal world.

Sullivan had begun to wonder if both Cooper and Finlay were toying with Otto, like lions tossing a mouse. She should have been no match for them, physically or otherwise.

Yet, Otto had been remarkably difficult to thwart in pursuit of her objectives.

She'd been assigned to find Reacher, and she'd attacked the problem like a piranha, tiny but impressively determined, ferocious, and deadly in her own way.

Perhaps both Cooper and Finlay had underestimated her. But to what end?

The situation was beyond perplexing.

Sullivan had seen small mistakes bring down giants before. History and myth were filled with examples. David brought down Goliath with a rock, after all.

Powerful men ignored and discarded such threats at their own peril.

All of this left Sullivan with a puzzling conundrum.

He narrowed his eyes and gazed at the screens as if he might peer deeper into the truth of the perplexing players on the two-dimensional board like chess pieces during a high-stakes tournament.

Cooper and Finlay, two untrustworthy giants of US government, were both wild cards.

Reacher, a mammoth and uncontrollable soldier gone rogue.

And the enigma that was tiny Kim Otto. She had turned up at the Magnolia Hotel. Then she'd killed Manny, one of his operatives, on a Columbia rooftop.

Did Otto's presence in Columbia mean Reacher was there, too? Or on his way?

What was this hunt for Reacher really about?

Sullivan wasn't certain, but since he first discovered the situation, his instincts had kicked into high alert and hadn't backed off.

Whatever was going on here was something he needed to decipher. It felt like an operation that could interfere with his plans on multiple levels.

Which was unacceptable.

He stood and paced with his coffee, speaking aloud to the empty room.

"Moving Reacher off the board is the goal. It seems he can't be bought or persuaded. He's proven more difficult to kill than expected," Sullivan said, running through the usual options.

"Only one choice." Sullivan shook his head and plopped the stainless steel mug down on the granite tabletop. "My inside operative hasn't done the job. Perhaps it's time for more opposition."

CHAPTER 26

Wednesday, May 25
White Kings Palace

JAKE AND MARGARET, HAVING escaped their cell in the basement, rushed to the top of the stairs leading to the first floor.

Their escape was abruptly halted by the heavy steel door with an electronic lock, closed tighter than a submarine hatch.

Jake's vague improvised plan had been to rush whoever opened the door, overpower them, and force his way out of the stairwell. Which should have worked well enough. He was a big guy. He'd played enough football and won enough fights off the field to take down a man.

Except no one came to help the jailer who was busted up and waiting on the floor of their cell.

Jake remained in position for a while, ready to bust heads if that's what it took to get his mother out of there. After five minutes, he concluded no one was sitting in the room on the other side of the door watching the camera feed.

After thirty minutes, he concluded that the jailer's backup must have gone on a dinner break or something.

After the first hour, Jake realized he would need a new plan.

There was no doorknob on the basement side. The door opened out onto the first floor.

Whatever activity might be happening on the other side of the door, the noise didn't carry through.

He examined every inch of the door and its frame and the walls around it. He found no way to go over, around, or through.

On the plus side, there were no CCTV cameras in the stairwell, and the camera probably couldn't see in there. The jailers couldn't see what Jake and Margaret might be doing as long as they stayed on the stairs.

He wondered if the night shift had been just the one sentry.

The clock in his head told Jake they'd been sitting here almost two hours. There was no clock in the stairwell to confirm, and neither he nor Margaret wore a watch.

The jailer he'd subdued and locked in their cell must have awakened long ago. But he'd made no sound, which was odd. He could have simply asked for help. The camera would have transmitted his request instantly.

The fact that he hadn't demanded to be released probably meant there was no one monitoring the cells. He'd been working solo.

It was strange.

If that guy was the only person on duty for the two prisoners, who had killed one of theirs, Jake wondered how many men were stationed here at the compound.

What were they doing that was more important than aiding their man or recapturing their hostages?

Margaret stood up to stretch her cramped muscles again. She'd done that several times before. Had they hurt her in some way before he arrived?

She whispered, "Jake, I need to pee."

"Me, too."

"You still think someone is coming to rescue that guy?" Margaret asked.

"Eventually, they'll have to. He's not going to leave on his own," Jake replied. "Something else has them occupied now. It could be morning before they get around to him."

"Are we just going to sit here and wait?"

Good question. He'd been wondering that himself.

"No. We're not," Jake said as he moved past her on the stairs, "Come with me, but stay back."

When he stepped into the corridor at the base of the stairs, the jailer who had delivered their dinner was stretched out on one of the cots in the cell. His forearm covered his eyes and most of his face.

His mouth was open. Jake could hear the guy struggling to breathe through his busted nose.

Jake reached out to bang along the metal bars as he approached the cell.

"It's obvious I'm sleeping," the guy said in a nasal whine without moving. "What do you want?"

"How do we open the door?" Jake replied.

"The lock release is in the control room. Somebody presses that button, and the door opens," he said. "Until then, it stays closed."

"When will that happen?"

"Shift changes at midnight." He yawned with combined nonchalance and insolence. "I'd offer you a comfy cot to take a nap, but all the cell doors are electronically locked, too."

"So you can't open the doors to the cells or at the top of the stairs from down here," Jake replied flatly.

"That's right. Sorry about that."

Which was nonsense. He wasn't the least bit sorry. And he was probably lying.

"Where's your backup?"

"Working. We're short-handed tonight."

"Why aren't you out there working, too?"

"I was. I should be. But you gave me the night off," he said, with more insolence this time.

"I have to pee," Margaret said again.

The jailer removed his arm from his eyes and squinted toward her. His nose was a mess. Smeared dried blood covered most of his face.

"Too bad you can't get into the cells to use the toilets. There's floor drains on each end of that corridor." He plopped his arm over his face again. "The camera will still see you, though."

Maybe Jake could disable the camera. While they were locked in the cell, he couldn't reach the camera. Now he could.

The camera was mounted directly to the ceiling in the center of the corridor and hardwired to the control center.

The hard plastic casing was meant to withstand vandals. Too bad he wasn't wearing the boots he'd been issued in basic training. Striking the camera with the soles of his sneakers to destroy it wouldn't work.

Nor could he bust the camera off the ceiling without tools of some kind, which he didn't have.

The jailer's statements replayed in Jake's head. The watchers could see their man bleeding and locked in the cell, yet no one had come to his aid. Which meant they either hadn't noticed or they weren't worried.

If they hadn't noticed, then there was nothing Jake could do but wait until they realized what was happening down here.

But if they had seen the situation and simply weren't worried enough to rush, the backup might come faster if they couldn't see what was happening in the cells.

Jake took another look around. Except for the jailer in the cell and the crap he'd dropped on the floor, nothing about the room had changed.

He looked at the food spilled and strewn. Tonight's meal was mashed potatoes and gravy, two pieces of fried chicken, canned green peas, and a dinner roll with a butter pat.

A paper cup with a lid on it contained a drink. The lid fit pretty tightly, because it hadn't come off when the tray hit the floor. The utensils were flimsy plastic, sealed into a clear plastic envelope along with a cheap napkin.

He couldn't destroy the camera. But he could disable it. Sort of.

Jake reached down to scoop the mashed potatoes and gravy off the floor. He grabbed both of the plastic envelopes with his left hand and stuffed them into his back pocket.

He stood on his toes and extended his right arm. He couldn't quite reach the eyeball, so he repeatedly jumped to smear the mashed potatoes and gravy over the clear plastic.

When he was satisfied the images from the camera feed were sufficiently degraded, he pulled the plastic envelopes from his back pocket, opened them with his teeth, and used the thin napkin inside to wipe his hands.

"Go ahead, Mom. No one can see you now," Jake said, turning his back to offer her a bit more privacy.

"Just one problem, kid." The jailer must have opened an eyelid to check things out. "There's nobody up there to notice your handiwork."

Jake said nothing.

The jailer was right.

But this was the best he could do with the tools at hand.

When she'd finished, he gestured his mother toward the stairs where she'd have a place to sit while they waited, at least.

They didn't wait long.

CHAPTER 27

Wednesday, May 25
White Kings Palace

JAKE HEARD THE HEAVY steel door's electronic lock click open. He rushed to the top of the stairs, arriving just as the door swung away from the stairs. He leaned into the door and shoved with his right shoulder, propelling himself with the strength of both legs.

The door opened fast and smooth on excessively lubricated hinges. He stumbled like a charging bull into the room, struggling to regain his balance quickly. He swiveled his head to scan the space.

The control room was smaller than he'd expected. According to the monitors, not all the compound's operations were directed from here. There must be a larger control room somewhere. Maybe other smaller ones, too.

This control room seemed dedicated to the jail itself.

The room was roughly ten feet by ten feet. It had no windows. A small desk abutted the wall to the left of the open door. An elaborate keyboard rested on the desk. Mounted on the wall above it was a large TV screen reflecting an image that looked like a three-year-old had smeared it with mashed potatoes and gravy.

Jake grinned. The scene in the basement was impossibly blurred. Even the jailer wasn't visible on the cot in the center cell. Nor could his mother be seen waiting on the stairs.

Opposite the door Jake had busted through stood a man with a pistol aimed squarely at Jake's torso.

He recognized the weapon he'd surrendered at the front gate. The gun still had the stripe of yellow tape across the handle put there by Jake's dad.

Jake's high school and college football skills had been honed well during his ten weeks of basic training. He'd excelled at exercises involving close-quarters combat. His size was a definite advantage against all opponents.

But confidence was his most effective tool. Put simply, Jake expected to win.

Before the guy had a chance to get off a shot, Jake rushed ahead, hard and steady like a freight train. He grabbed the gun and twisted it sharply, bending the guy's wrist backward at the same time.

The sickening snap of wrist and arm bones inside the skin came first. Then the guy's screams sounded. Followed by the sharp edges of the broken bones gouging through the skin.

One of the bones must have snagged an artery. Blood spurted out with the guy's rapid heartbeat.

He reached to grab Jake's neck with his left arm. Jake jabbed him hard and fast with an elbow, straight to the solar plexus.

The guy gasped and released his hold. He bent over, howling in pain, and sunk to the floor. Jake kicked him in the head to make him quiet.

A few moments of silence followed while Jake reached down for the gun and turned to grab Margaret's arm.

"Run!" he said, pulling her through the exit.

He dashed out the same way he'd arrived. With the bag over his head, he hadn't been able to see the area between the front gate and the basement cells.

But he'd spent his basement time reconstructing the route in his head. He remembered the distances and the turns that led outside, through the front gate, and to the place where he'd hidden his Jeep.

Margaret followed along, grasping his hand, without a single complaint. When they reached the exit to the verandah, Jake didn't waste time with the biometric panels. He raised the pistol and shot the lock.

The blast of gunshots was deafening in the corridor, but the lock surrendered. Jake pushed the door open with his shoulder and pulled Margaret into the cool night air.

To him, the fresh air filling his lungs felt like freedom and victory and all good things.

Margaret was gasping and limping, too. She needed a break.

Jake held her hand tightly and rushed down the steps onto the gravel driveway and ran toward the front gate, looking for a place to hide where Margaret could catch her breath.

When they rounded the corner of the house, he heard a loud thwapping noise coming from the back of the property. A helicopter spooled up, preparing for lift-off.

Whatever they were working on back there, it involved a helicopter. Which meant there was a way to get over the fence.

He stopped running and turned to Margaret. "We need to get on that helicopter."

Her eyes grew wider, and her mouth opened into an O. "Are you crazy? There's woods all around us. Let's run until we find a road."

He looked into her face. "Mom, there's an electrified fence surrounding this property. I saw it fry a rabbit. We can't get through it. We can't climb over it."

She looked at him, shaking her head as if she thought he was crazy.

"The helicopter can get us out. See?" The rotors were gaining speed and the noise was deafening. "It'll be okay. I promise. Trust me."

She shook her head. He grabbed her hand again and pulled her toward the helipad. She resisted until she had to move because he refused to let go of her hand.

They jogged as quickly as they could while darting from one source of cover to another, attempting to stay out of sight as much as possible. Although Jake was certain the entire compound was fully covered by security cameras, just as the basement had been.

The closer they came to the helo, the louder the noise and the more impossible conversation became.

Margaret was struggling to breathe, struggling to run, terrified by everything.

Jake kept going.

When they reached the back of the huge mansion at the base of the U-shaped cluster of homes, he stopped in the shadows of the building to assess.

Jake flattened his back against the wall and gestured to Margaret to do the same. He peered around the corner where he expected to find the helipad.

But it wasn't there.

Immediately behind the big house was a series of outbuildings and another gravel drive.

The helipad had to be on the other side of the outbuildings.

Jake wasn't sure Margaret could make it that far. He could carry her the rest of the way. But that would mean he couldn't defend them or remove obstacles as they appeared.

The noise blasted loudly through the quiet night. The helicopter was there. They still had a chance.

He pulled his head back and turned to talk to his mother.

He saw two men with her.

One immobilized her with his big arm circling her waist.

The other stood beside her pointing a gun to her head.

"Drop your weapon and raise your hands," one of them shouted into the helo noise. "You might be able to kill us, but we'll kill her first. Count on it."

The helo was ready for takeoff. It rose into the air behind Jake. Too late. They'd lost their chance to escape.

These two might not kill them. Live hostages were better than dead ones. But Margaret couldn't run anymore. She was already exhausted. And the helo was gone now, anyway.

He dropped his dad's pistol to the ground and raised his hands, palms out. As the helo lifted higher, the rotor noise diminished, and Jake could finally be heard.

"Let her go," he said, scanning the area, memorizing everything he could see, already planning how to get on that helo the next time it flew out.

CHAPTER 28

Wednesday, May 25
Columbia, SC

KIM HAD CHECKED INTO a hotel near the airport to shower and change into clothes which didn't reek of the decomposing murder victim at the Magnolia Hotel. She'd hoped the clingy stench would dissipate, but it hadn't.

The offensive odor announced her presence to one and all long before she actually appeared.

The desk clerk's eyes widened, and he gagged and almost vomited when Kim checked in. The scene might have been funny to observers, but she felt like a walking pig pen. Although she grew up on a farm, and the analogy did pig pens a disservice.

She rode the elevator alone to her room.

Kicking herself for failing to change clothes into something disposable before she entered Margaret Reacher's hotel room, she stuffed her pricey Armani suit and every item of clothing on her body into a plastic laundry bag and tied it as tightly as possible.

There was a small air hole in the top of the bag, which was enough to let faint traces of ripe rotting meat waft into the room. She stuffed the bag, top-down, into a stainless steel trash container and covered the bin with a towel. It was the best she could do at the moment.

Kim had saved a good chunk of her paychecks for a while to buy that suit a few years ago in San Francisco at a store that catered to Asian women. The tailor had done a remarkable job with the alterations. The suit fit her petite shape perfectly.

Beyond that, she knew intellectually that her instincts were silly, but she'd always felt lucky when she wore that suit. She imagined it had extraordinary powers of some sort.

After all, the maniac on the roof hadn't managed to kill her. And he wasn't the only one who had tried and failed to harm her while she was wearing the suit.

It had served her well. She hated to lose it. But from experience, she knew she could fumigate the thing, and the dead man stench would never, ever be extracted from its fibers.

Her plan was to drop the bag and its stinking contents in the nearest dumpster as soon as she had a chance and never look back.

The problem was, she couldn't walk around naked, and she hadn't packed a second suit when she left home. But she'd packed respectable workout clothes and running shoes, which would serve well enough until she could find something better.

She shrugged, pumped up the fan on the air handler to suck the stink out of her room, and stepped into the shower. The hotel's hot water flowed warm and hard over her body. She stood under the spray for a while, allowing the water pressure to do the job.

Then she used an entire bottle of scented shampoo and another bottle of scented body wash. After thirty minutes of scouring every inch as well as she could, she stepped out of the shower and wrapped herself in a big towel.

After using a hand towel to blot the excess water from her hair, she twisted it onto her head and walked into the bedroom.

Her primary cell phone was dancing around on the bed. The caller ID said simply, Burke. Which was curious.

He rarely called on that number because just about anybody could hack it at any time. The phone company recorded the numbers of all incoming and outgoing calls, too.

No normal commercial cell phone was suitable for clandestine conversation. Period.

So why was he using it?

She picked up and asked, "Did the docs cut you loose?"

"Yeah. I was about to bust out anyway. Hospitals are not great places to spend time. Too much stuff going on," her partner replied with a smile in his voice. "I hear you've had a busy day."

She frowned. "Who'd you hear that from?"

"Three guesses," he replied sardonically, implying he'd talked to their boss, Charles Cooper. "He's been trying to reach you. Something wrong with your phone. It turns out the service was terminated."

He meant the specialized burner phone that tethered her to The Boss.

Kim had removed all her possessions from the pockets of her suit before she'd stuffed it into the laundry bag. The Boss's burner phone wasn't in there. Which meant she didn't have it.

Now that the service had been terminated, there was no reason to worry about the phone itself. She hadn't used it since she'd arrived in Columbia anyway. If the phone were a security threat, The Boss would find and destroy it.

"I guess I must have lost it," she said, not explaining the probability that the phone fell out of her pocket when she was rolling around on the parking deck, dodging a psycho van driver.

"He figured you threw it into the Congaree River," Burke said with a laugh.

"Not this time." She pulled the towel from her head and combed her hair. "What did he want?"

Before Burke had a chance to answer, she heard a firm knock on her door followed by a female voice. "Ms. Otto. Delivery."

Burke overheard. He said, "I'll call you back."

She tossed her phone onto the bed, walked to the door, and peered through the peep hole. A young woman stood in the corridor holding a familiar-looking manila envelope.

Nothing sinister about the envelope. The US Government stocked them everywhere by the gross.

"Just leave it there," Kim called out.

The woman knelt and deposited the envelope on the carpet in the alcove. Kim waited a few moments before she opened the door, kicked the envelope inside, and closed and locked the door again.

Kim had seen enough of these envelopes by now to identify them on sight. The contents were predictable, too.

She bent and picked it up, noticing this one felt heavier than usual. There was more than a single replacement burner cell phone inside.

She tossed the envelope onto the bed and went into the bathroom to dress.

Her workout gear hugged her body snuggly. Which meant it would be challenging to conceal much of anything in the pockets. If she unzipped the jacket, she could wear her shoulder holster, but she couldn't hide it very well.

As soon as she had a chance, she'd find better alternatives. Now that her entire being didn't smell like a dead body, she could slip over into the Columbia Metro Airport terminal and find something more serviceable.

Even a loose-fitting hoodie would be better. Airport gift shops usually had plenty of those for traveling parents to buy at the last minute and take home. She could find something serviceable in the kids' department.

Like most hotel rooms these days, this one was equipped with a small coffee pot. She set up a single cup to brew. While waiting for the coffee, she tore open the envelope and dumped the contents onto the bed.

There were two specialty burner phones and a thumb drive. One of the burners would connect her directly to The Boss. The other, no doubt, would connect her directly to Burke.

All three items were protected by the most sophisticated encryption available to the US Government.

Which did not mean they were impenetrable to hackers.

The pricey encryption could slow the less sophisticated hackers down a bit, although even that much was uncertain. Gaspar's hardware and software were better. The Boss should upgrade his suppliers.

When the coffee finished, one of the phones rang. She made a mental bet and picked up the call. "Otto."

Burke was at the other end of the line. "Did you win?"

He had only been her partner for thirteen days, but he was already too familiar with her quirks. In this instance, she'd adopted one of Reacher's eccentricities.

Reacher liked numbers. She liked numbers. Witnesses had told her he sometimes flipped an imaginary coin in his head when he was thinking things through.

Since the coin was imaginary, it was a silly system.

Because the coin was imaginary, the odds were fifty-fifty. Every time.

With a real coin flipped by a real human, the results trended closer to 51-49 in favor of whichever side was up at the outset.

Where things got complicated was flipping the imaginary coin multiple times.

For instance, the chances of flipping four heads in a row were about ninety-four to six against. Meaning an improbable chance of six in one hundred. Simple math.

Kim loved math. It amused her to know Reacher loved math as well.

Working his coin-flipping system brought her one step closer to understanding how Reacher thinks. Which would give her an advantage when it came to finding him.

Or so she hoped.

"The coin toss is imaginary, Burke. I always win," she replied pleasantly enough.

"How so?"

"Simple math. Would one of the two phones be assigned to you? Yes or no. Fifty-fifty. Would you call me before Cooper did? Again, yes or no, fifty-fifty," she explained. "Would our orders go against my better judgment? Again, yes or no, fifty-fifty. And if Cooper called himself, instead of making you do it, would the outcome be different?"

"Let me guess," Burke said dryly. "Yes or no, fifty-fifty?"

"Actually no. He never wants to argue the point with me. He wants to bigfoot me because he can." Kim replied sourly. "If The Boss had wanted to talk to me, he'd have delivered his new burner hours ago. It's not like he doesn't know where I am every moment of every day."

"Can't argue with that," Burke said, chuckling. "You're an odd little woman. You know that?"

"Says the freakishly trigger-happy dude who can't seem to keep his ass out of trouble long enough to accomplish anything," she replied lightly, pleased to hear him in good humor again.

Joking released tension. She'd been worried about Burke. He'd lost a fight on Sunday night and was beaten badly. Although she remained wary of him, she was relieved that he'd recovered enough to be released from the hospital and return to work.

After all, he was the only partner she had at the moment. If he'd been with her on that rooftop tonight, things could have gone a lot better.

The two of them together could have captured the psycho, and they'd be that much closer to finding Jake and Margaret Reacher right now. Maybe that much closer to finding Jack Reacher, too.

With the van driver dead, they were back to square one.

She shook off the failure when she realized he was talking.

"I said, are you packed?" he asked.

"For what?"

"So you're lucky in a coin toss and good at playing the odds, but you're not clairvoyant, eh?" Burke teased.

"What are you talking about?"

"Like I said, your flight's departing in sixty-five minutes. It's the last nonstop tonight. You don't want to miss it," Burke repeated what he'd said when she wasn't listening.

She heard noises in the background from his call she hadn't noticed before. Sounds that seemed to be emitting from a cavernous space.

Burke was sitting in an airport somewhere.

"Flight to where?" she asked.

"DC. I'm texting you the flight details and your boarding pass. He's already set things up," Burke said.

He meant The Boss, Charles Cooper, whose every word was her command. Or so he pretended to believe.

"Nope. Sorry. I'm in the middle of something here that could pan out. Still stuff left to do tonight. Reacher could be on his way here. Or he might be here already. All we need to do is wait for him." Kim sipped the coffee and shook her head. She grinned and teased, "Besides, I've got nothing to wear."

"You're *such* a woman." Burke burst out laughing. And then he sobered quickly. "They just called my flight."

"Have you forgotten that I'm lead on this assignment? I'm the one calling the shots," she said. "You come here."

He paused a moment and then replied, "I'll meet you at Reagan National in a few hours."

"I'm not joking, Burke. I can't leave here now," she said sternly. "I won't be there."

"It's a ninety-minute flight from Columbia to DC. We can go back there later if you want. But for now, it's important we get to DC," Burke insisted.

"I've got a meeting with Espin tonight."

"You want to disobey these orders, call and tell Cooper yourself. Otherwise, he's greased all the wheels. He always knows things we don't. If he's sending us to DC, there's a good reason for it," Burke replied. "Trust me on this. I've read the files on that thumb drive he sent you, and you haven't."

Kim said nothing.

"At the security checkpoint, look for a woman named Wagner. Tall, blond, attractive, fifty," Burke continued. "She'll pass your weapon through and whatever else you've got with you, no questions asked."

"I seriously can't do that," Otto said through gritted teeth.

"Review those files during the flight. You'll see why we're going."

"Are you even listening to me?"

The last thing he said before he hung up was, "Get your butt on that plane, Otto. I can interview this witness alone, but you don't want me to do that. Trust me."

And then she was holding dead air. She had no idea who the witness was and no chance to ask him what was so damned important.

When Finlay sent her here, he'd said it was essential. A matter of life and death, he'd said.

Which turned out to be true.

For the dead guy in Margaret's hotel room, certainly. But probably for Margaret Reacher and her son, Jake, too.

The Boss could have countermanded Finlay's request. He hadn't. Which she took to mean that he agreed with Finlay's plan.

This morning, Columbia was vitally important. Now, it wasn't, and DC was the important place.

She was tired of being bounced around like a ping-pong ball.

But Cooper was quite literally The Boss.

Burke was right. Cooper had better intel, more data, and a helluva lot more rank than she did.

The hunt for Jack Reacher was his operation. Like Burke had said, if Cooper wanted her in DC tonight, he had good reasons.

Even if she had no idea what those reasons might be.

Even if it pissed her off to admit it.

Chances were six in a hundred that she was right. and he was wrong. But it was her imaginary coin. She had the advantage.

And like Burke said, she could come back tomorrow.

When there's only one choice, it's the right choice.

She gathered her few remaining possessions and stuffed them in her travel bag. She holstered her weapon and her backup

Kim didn't want to dwell on how Finlay was able to retrieve her backup weapon from the gun safe in her Detroit apartment.

For the moment, she was just glad to have the second gun.

But soon enough, she'd need to deal with how he broke through her apartment's airtight security.

She completed a quick checkout on her television screen, tossed the door key onto the desk, grabbed the plastic laundry bag containing her disgusting suit from the trash can, and headed out.

First chance she got, she dropped the laundry bag into a dumpster.

One good thing. There were decent clothing stores in a city where more business suits were sold every year than the entire population of some small American towns.

When she lived in DC, she had a tailor who could work magic in short order.

She could see her tailor and get a new suit in the morning before they interviewed the witness. Whoever he was.

While she walked, she placed a call to Espin's cell. His voicemail picked up. "This is Agent Otto. I need a rain check on our meeting tonight. Sorry. I'll call you later."

Twenty minutes after Burke's second phone call, she approached the gate for her flight to Reagan National, grumbling under her breath the entire time.

Her personal cell phone vibrated in her pocket. She fished it out. The text came from a number she didn't recognize. She opened the text. Which began with two initials: CG. Carlos Gaspar. The rest consisted of two images.

The first had been snapped by a camera at a traffic light. The photo was enlarged. The two men sitting in the front seat were plainly visible.

The driver was Petey Burns. The passenger was Jack Reacher. No question.

The photo was time-stamped fifty-six minutes ago.

The second image was a map with a red locator pinned onto it, showing the location of the traffic cam.

Bethesda, Maryland.

Thirty minutes from downtown Washington, DC.

She texted back a thumbs-up and walked onto the plane.

CHAPTER 29

Wednesday, May 25
Washington, DC

SULLIVAN'S ANGER BUBBLED LIKE a rancid sausage in his gut. He should have been one hundred percent focused on the Reacher problem.

Instead, the promised appearance of the mole had lured him to the Four Knights Club tonight.

A fully vetted legacy member of the Club turned by hard experience into a traitorous menace.

Unthinkable.

And yet true.

Sullivan's resentment was compounded by the sheer gall the little twerp exhibited. Nothing worse than a little man with a little power turned loose on the world.

The idiot seemed to believe he could take on the man he knew as Patton and survive.

He'd learn otherwise soon enough.

Sullivan took a satisfied look in the mirror. He'd transformed himself into Patton, a titan of power befitting the position of every member of the Club.

Only one glance was required to recognize him as an insider worthy of the exclusive tribe to which he actually belonged.

From the thousand dollar gray wig and well-trimmed false goatee to his bench-made footwear, he was attired in expensive charcoal gray. A cashmere blazer over a silk polo, a pair of fine woolen trousers, and calf-length silk socks. The supple brown loafers which felt like bedroom slippers completed his sophisticated attire.

He secured the snow den's monitoring systems and let himself out. He pulled on the tightly fitting latex gloves embedded with Patton's biometrics and tucked them well into his sleeves. He walked a mile away to a coffee shop, where he contacted his usual car service.

The driver arrived promptly and asked no questions along the route.

Traffic was light. The driver pulled up in front of the historic Federal-style brick building in Georgetown without mishap.

From the backseat, Sullivan lowered the window. He scanned the historic old home and the surrounding area.

The four-story building rested twenty-five yards from the street, surrounded by majestic old trees, lush green lawns, and well-tended English flower gardens befitting its history.

A decorative brick retaining wall outlined the property and attached to the building's front façade at the corners by two ornate wrought iron gates.

The clear message was that only invited guests were to enter and only through the front door.

Should they be so bold as to approach, uninvited visitors were turned away.

Surveillance cameras were posted throughout the property. Some were visible and others were not. Only a fool would assume the grand old place was without adequate security.

The visible security cameras were intended to reinforce the message that unauthorized visitors were not admitted here. The hidden cameras did the bulk of the work.

From here, Sullivan saw nothing suspicious and heard only the usual evening noises. Thus assured, he climbed out of the car at the curb.

When the driver rolled away into traffic, Sullivan mounted three short brick steps to the brick-paved walkway leading to the front entrance.

Three more steps led up to the fine old door painted shiny black with a shiny brass lantern perched above it. The door had a gleaming brass letter slot and a street number just above the brightly polished brass door knocker.

The door did not have a handle. Instead, a matching shiny brass orb had been affixed where a handle would have been.

The orb did not turn. It collected fingerprints instantly and surreptitiously from everyone who touched it. The prints were electronically matched to databases and stored in secure servers in the Club's operations room.

One could never be too careful.

A small brass plaque affixed to the brick on the right side of the door, much newer than all the other hardware, said *Four Knights Club*.

There were hundreds of clubs in the Washington, DC area. On the outside, this one seemed no different from the rest.

Sullivan flipped the name plaque open and placed Patton's palm on the biometric reader. When his identity was confirmed, he heard the door unlock. So far, everything was as it should be.

Sullivan closed the cover on the biometric panel and pushed the door into the foyer with his elbow. He stepped across the threshold into what had been built as an exceptionally affluent single-family home two hundred years ago.

The Club's designers had been handsomely compensated to re-create the authentic period décor. He stepped into a wide, cool hallway decorated in pale yellow. The décor was Colonial style with brass candlesticks and clocks and richly polished mahogany wood and oil portraits of famous American patriots from centuries ago.

Members were milling about in the common areas. No women. The club was men only.

Men came here to enjoy themselves. Sometimes they stayed all night. Politicians and military and media and businessmen. Masters of the universe.

Well dressed, well-groomed, well behaved, well satisfied. Relaxed and unconcerned, serenity shed off them in waves of contentment only the privileged possessed.

Precisely as the Four Knights Club should have been.

Sullivan wandered toward the bar where he received a glass of warm whiskey in a crystal glass. He scanned the room, seeking the mole.

Dover approached from his left. "There's an impromptu tournament playing in the blue room," he said, gesturing toward the back of the house with his drink.

Sullivan followed Dover past antiques and paintings and museum-quality furniture.

When they reached the blue room, four chess tables were occupied in total silence. He recognized the older players as longstanding Club members.

The fourth board displayed a close game between two younger men.

Dover lowered his voice to avoid disturbing the players' concentration. "You recognize Major Milton, I'm sure."

"Of course," Sullivan replied politely.

"His opponent is playing especially well tonight. Perhaps you know him?" Dover said, inclining his head toward the mole, speaking as if his words might be overheard. "Rupert Adams. A relatively new member. He's been with us about three years. His father was with us, too, before he passed."

"Milton is an excellent chess master. Adams has a challenge ahead," Sullivan said.

Dover nodded. "He's relatively new to the game, but Adams is playing well enough."

They stood watching until the current game was finished. The others continued to play with the intensity of great competitors, but Milton and Adams were free to take a break.

Dover waved Adams over and put a hand on his shoulder and murmured, "Congratulations. So far, so good."

Sullivan nodded. "Milton is difficult to beat. I've lost to him many times myself."

Adams smiled with satisfied humility. "The tournament isn't over yet. I've got a long way to go if I hope to win."

"Is there a wager involved?" Dover asked.

Adams blushed. He had the calmly satisfied look of a man who had spent an hour or so upstairs in his room with an opium pipe before the games began. "I'm hoping Milton will do me a favor if I win."

"What sort of favor?" Dover asked, eyebrows raised.

"I'd rather not say. If I lose, it'll seem presumptuous," Adams replied.

Two of the other games had ended, and the players were milling about quietly while the last game continued.

Sullivan nodded toward Adams and said, "I recently heard about your friend. My deepest condolences."

A flash of anger brightened Adams's eyes and widened his nostrils before he stifled it. "Thank you. The grief is still a bit fresh."

"I'm sure. Perfectly understandable," Sullivan said as if he sympathetic. He might have been, if Adams weren't trying to destroy the Club. "Any leads on where the product came from?"

Adams set his mouth into a grim line and swallowed hard. "Not yet."

"It's a shame there's so much adulterated heroin on our streets. Well, do let me know if there's anything I can do to help," Dover said smoothly, nodding toward the tables. "Looks like your game is about to start."

Adams nodded and returned to his table, his serenity now disturbed. Another member sat across from him, and the next game began.

"Do you think that was wise?" Dover asked quietly. "Letting him know you were aware of his efforts to expose the Club?"

"Pushing his buttons. We need him to make a public mistake. We need witnesses who will testify that he was distraught and irrational," Sullivan replied. "Be certain any footage of our conversation is deleted before the evening's records go into storage."

Dover held up a finger and listened to a message transmitted through his earpiece from the operations room.

He spoke quietly, leaning toward Sullivan's ear, "We've got an intruder on the grounds."

"I'll come with you," Sullivan replied, following Dover toward the threat.

CHAPTER 30

Wednesday, May 25
White Kings Palace

JONES HAD MARCHED THE two hostages back to the basement cells. The woman was a mess, crying, stumbling, making things more difficult than they needed to be.

The kid was trying to help his mother, but Jones could see he wanted to make a run for it. Jones shook his head. An escape was impossible. The kid was just wearing himself out for no good reason.

Jones was dead on his feet. He needed at least a few hours of sleep. The Palace was understaffed even before Smitty, Rudy, and Manny died. They needed reinforcements and soon.

When they reached the control room, Jones pushed the lock release button on the cell doors and called down. "Get your ass up here, Harvey."

Harvey had the sense to look embarrassed when he climbed the steps two at a time and burst into the control room at the top of the stairs. He looked like he'd taken a good long nap, which just pissed Jones off. "Sorry, Jones."

"I don't want to hear your excuses right now, Harvey. Get these two back in their cell. And since you've had time to sleep more than any of the rest of us, you can stay on watch here for another shift," Jones snarled.

Harvey gave Jake a little push. "Take your mom downstairs. Get her into bed. And get some sleep yourself. You won't get another chance to break outta here tonight."

Jake threw him a fierce look and escorted his mother down the stairs. When they had entered the cell and taken their places on the beds as before, Harvey pressed the electronic cell door locks. They were secure once again.

Jones gave Harvey a shove. "Get down there and clean up that mess. Be quick about it. I'll wait 'til you're done."

Harvey picked up a spray bottle and a cleaning rag. He grabbed a trash bag, too. Jones watched as he cleaned the smeared food off the camera and picked up the food and service items which had been flung everywhere.

Jones stood, kneading his sore neck with one hand as he watched. The kid was the spitting image of Jack Reacher. But he didn't have the destructive streak. Or, if he did, the reactions were less violent, less immediate, than Reacher's reputation.

Jones had never met the kid's father. Maybe Joe Reacher had been a different breed. Rumor and gossip said otherwise. That Joe was just as much a badass as his brother.

But with young Jake here, it seemed like this particular apple might have fallen a long way from the Reacher tree.

When Harvey returned to the control room, lugging the garbage, Jones pressed the lock button to secure the cells. Then he flipped the night switch for the basement, dimming the lights and activating the night vision in the 360 camera.

Maybe the kid and his mom would sleep awhile. She was exhausted, and they'd punched some of the vinegar out of the kid, too. Maybe.

Harvey said, "Okay. I've got it. You can go now."

Jones gave him a steely stare. "Patton hears about you letting them get out, and your ass is done. You know that, right?"

"Yeah." Harvey nodded, shoving his hands into his jeans.

"So do your job. No harm, no foul this time. I'll cover for you. But don't screw up again," Jones said as he turned to leave.

"What's going on outside?" Harvey asked.

"Helo just lifted off for DC and a quick turnaround. The jet's already on the way back from Texas. We're gonna grab some shuteye and then get back to it," Jones said just before he ducked out into the corridor and trudged up the stairs to his room.

CHAPTER 31

Thursday, May 26
Washington, DC

THE TWO MEN WALKED abreast down the long hallway to the back of the Club. The operations room was located in the north wing near the kitchen. Dover placed his palm on the biometric reader and the door lock clicked open.

Dover strode into the room and Sullivan followed, noting that the security door had remained open long enough for him to do so. Sloppy.

"Show me the intruder, Zed," Dover ordered the man monitoring the screens that filled the walls.

Every room inside the building was monitored and recorded at all times. Sullivan glanced across the screens for a quick look to confirm that all was as it should be. So far.

Zed clacked a few keys and brought up the correct video feed on the large center screen.

The first images were recorded ten minutes ago under natural light. An intruder had scaled the brick wall at the back of the property and dropped into the garden.

Zed highlighted the dark figure with a bright yellow circle on the screen.

"Let's see it with the night vision cameras," Sullivan said.

Zed glanced at his boss for approval and Dover nodded. Zed clacked again and the rear gardens immediately popped into a brighter black and white view.

He increased the speed of the video. The intruder's stealthy trek around the perimeter, hugging the retaining wall, staying in the shadows, seemed to finish quickly. But the recorded real elapsed time was eleven minutes, thirty-four seconds.

"Where is he now?" Dover asked.

"Near the garages," Zed replied, clacking again to enhance the images from cameras aimed at what had once been the carriage house at the base of the driveway.

Zed brought the intruder into sharp focus.

He was shedding his concealing clothes, under which he wore a dark blazer, crisply pressed dress shirt, slacks, and dress shoes. The standard casual dress code at the Club.

He pulled the stocking cap off his head and organized his short brown hair with his fingers.

He collected the shed clothes and dropped them into one of the dumpsters behind the garage. He stepped onto the paved path along the edge of the grass and advanced toward the rear entrance to the house.

One of the cameras caught his face full-on.

Zed froze the image and snapped a screenshot.

"Do either of you recognize him?" Sullivan cocked his head. The face was familiar but not identifiable.

Zed shook his head in reply.

"Run his image against our facial recognition software, Zed. Do the member database first. It includes known associates of all members. This guy seems to have familiarity with our property, which suggests he may have been here before," Dover said. "If you don't find him in our databases, run all the databases we have access to, official and unofficial. I want to know who this threat is. Pronto."

Sullivan said, "Enlarge the image, Zed. Let's see what he does next."

The intruder pushed both hands into the pockets of his trousers and strolled nonchalantly toward the entrance to the mud room at the back of the kitchen. He climbed the stairs and reached for the doorknob.

Up until this point, the intruder had made the invasion seem effortless. He was a pro. Sullivan was mildly impressed with his craft.

Attempting to simply walk inside the building through the mudroom adjacent to the kitchen was the intruder's first mistake.

"Isn't that door secured by a biometric lock?" Sullivan asked, frowning.

"Absolutely," Dover replied. "He'll be denied access to the premises. Unless he's a member in good standing or authorized staff."

"Not likely he fits in either box," Zed replied. "He could simply have come inside through the front door if he was authorized. No sneaking required."

As they watched the feed, the mudroom door opened from the inside, and the intruder slipped into the house.

Zed located a clear headshot of the man and pulled it up on the screen. "We have a positive identification. His name is John Templar. Son of Walter Templar, who is a Club member in good standing."

Sullivan nodded as comprehension dawned. No wonder the intruder looked familiar. Walter Templar was a United States senator. Chairman of the recently established Veterans Assistance Committee.

His ridiculous mug was splashed across television screens everywhere several times a week as he tried to make himself famous before he became infamous. He was a lion in the Senate, but his popularity could take a fast nosedive very shortly.

Senator Templar was in debt up to his eyebrows due to his unfortunate gambling addiction.

More specifically, Senator Templar owed Patton thirty million dollars, which Patton had asked him to repay last week.

Fully aware Templar couldn't acquire enough money to pay his debts, Sullivan intended to pressure him further. And to keep squeezing until Templar knuckled under.

They all did, sooner or later.

Templar had been incensed. "You're nothing but a shakedown artist, Patton," he'd spewed through an outraged snarl.

Sullivan had simply shrugged and waved Templar's anger aside. He'd come around. What choice did he have?

Now, Sullivan cocked his head as he watched the screen. Perhaps Templar possessed more innate fortitude than Sullivan expected. Stronger measures might be necessary. And young Templar had just handed Sullivan all the leverage he'd ever need.

"Is Walter Templar in the Club tonight?" Sullivan scowled.

Zed ran through the list of members present. "Yes, sir. He arrived two hours ago. He has the Lincoln Bedroom tonight."

"Is he in his room at the moment?" Dover asked, eyebrows raised.

Zed flipped over to the screen showing the Lincoln Bedroom. After checking all the cameras, he replied, "No, sir, he is not."

Sullivan turned and left. Dover quickly instructed Zed to kill the surveillance of the exterior grounds and the mud room until further notice.

Zed flipped a few switches and the screens for those cameras went black.

"Stay alert and await further instructions," Dover ordered before he followed close behind.

Sullivan strode through the kitchen to the mud room. The entry door to the space where the staff kept gardening boots and other supplies was secured.

He pressed his palm to the biometric lock. The door clicked open. He walked boldly across the threshold.

Senator Templar was standing near the door with his son John. Both men looked up when Sullivan walked in, wearing expressions worthy of cartoon villains caught in the act.

They had been talking quietly but stepped apart, momentarily gobsmacked and more than a little afraid.

Dover entered and closed the door to the kitchen, his weapon equipped with a suppressor, drawn and pointed at the pair.

"Walter," Sullivan said snidely, nodding toward the old man. "And this is your son, John. I don't believe we've met, sailor."

Old man Templar cleared his throat and nodded. He put all his considerable authority into the curt greeting. "Patton. Dover."

"John, you are a Navy SEAL, I believe. SEALs are men of honor, are they not?" Sullivan asked.

"Yes, sir," he replied with a somewhat sheepish glance toward his father.

"And no doubt fully aware of the law. Yet here you are, invading our premises," Dover said with a sharp edge, still brandishing his handgun. "Give me your weapon. Slowly. I'm a good marksman, but a one-eyed dog could hit the senator from this short distance."

"Okay. No need to start shooting," Young Templar said as he pulled the gun from his waist and carefully held it out.

204 | DIANE CAPRI

Sullivan took the pistol from young Templar in one swift move.

"Raise your hands. Keep them where I can see them," Dover said.

Both Templars complied.

Sullivan pointed Templar's pistol at the senator. "Dover, take the sailor outside while I have a chat with the senator."

Dover nodded. He gestured young Templar toward the still-open doorway.

"Don't worry, Dad." Templar raised his hands and backed out, never taking his eyes off Dover. "I can take care of myself."

When the door closed solidly behind them, Senator Templar's legendary belligerence pushed through his fear. He dropped his hands to his sides. "What the hell do you think you're doing, Patton?"

"We have every inch of this place under constant surveillance. Which means we have recorded video of everything that's happened here tonight and every night," Sullivan replied, his angry tone unwavering. "Do you understand what I'm telling you, Walter?"

Templar's jowls slapped back and forth as he shook his head, a deep scowl darkening his features. "Spell it out for me. We don't want me to be the least bit confused."

"You have made your situation worse for yourself and better for me," Sullivan replied smoothly. "In the next few days, we will be asking for your assistance on important matters. You will be more than happy to assist us, I am sure."

"Why in the hell would I do that?" Templar demanded with his chin thrust forward.

Sullivan raised the weapon and placed the barrel a few inches from Templar's eyes.

While he held the weapon aimed at Templar's face, he said, "This pistol belongs to your son. He seemed somewhat distraught to me. Some veterans, like your boy, can suffer from terrible depression. PTSD, even. Suicide rates are higher than we'd like. Sometimes, veteran suicides follow homicides of close family members. Surely you know that already."

Templar's eyes widened. His mouth opened and closed like a fish. Drool moistened the corner of his mouth and dribbled down to his chin like a sloppy mastiff.

"You're crazy," he croaked.

"Quite possibly," Sullivan replied. "The thing to remember is that we have hours and hours of video featuring your ugly mug. You're really quite disgusting when you're high on opium. You know that? We recorded your son's escapades tonight, too. Shooting intruders is a time-honored American tradition. If both of you failed to survive this experience...."

"If you hurt my boy, you'll pay the price," Templar growled.

The impossible threat sparked fury. Sullivan's finger itched to shoot the bastard. Right here. Right now.

With supreme effort, Sullivan stifled the impulse. For now.

That time would come when the senator least expected it.

Sullivan lifted his knee quickly, without warning, and jabbed the old fool hard in the groin with the full force of his anger.

Templar cried out and doubled over and slumped to the ground, moaning. Before he had a chance to shield himself, Sullivan gave him two more solid kicks to the balls.

Tears rolled down the old man's face as he brought his hands forward, holding his crotch.

Templar's eyes closed and he lowered his head to his chin for a couple of moments as if he might be praying. When he lifted his eyes to glare at Sullivan again, he was a man defeated but no less enraged and defiant.

Sullivan waited until Templar managed to pull himself together enough to hear the message. "Wait here at least half an hour. Pick yourself up. Straighten your clothes. You can stay the night upstairs as you'd planned or let yourself out the front door. Your choice."

Templar nodded, still writhing on the floor, holding his groin.

"Meanwhile, I'm on my way to deal with your son. Get in my way again, and you'll both regret it. Understand?"

Templar nodded. Barely.

"We'll be in touch." Sullivan slipped young Templar's weapon into his pocket. "We'll have eyes on you twenty-four-seven now, Walter. Don't do anything stupid."

Sullivan opened the door to the mud room and closed it behind him. He made his way swiftly across the kitchen to the operations room.

Inside, behind the keyboards, Zed remained at his post. Sullivan glanced at the still dark screens to confirm that Zed had been smart enough not to witness or record events in the mud room or the garden.

Zed seemed like a smart man. He would remain in place for now.

Sullivan left the operations room to join Dover and the young Templar.

On the way, he called Sanz. "Send the helo to Four Knights."

Sanz replied, "Already on the way with tonight's shipment."

"ETA?"

Sanz covered the microphone and asked someone nearby. When he returned, he said, "Forty-five minutes."

CHAPTER 32

Thursday, May 26
Washington, DC

WHEN KIM DEPLANED AT Reagan National in Washington, DC, shortly after midnight, Burke was waiting, stretched out on a chair in the gate area. His legs were extended and crossed at the ankles, and his hands were folded over his flat stomach. His eyes were closed.

A brief wave of nostalgia washed over Kim. She had observed Gaspar in that precise position many times.

"Eat when you can and sleep when you can, Suzy Wong," Gaspar often said. "You never know when you'll get another chance."

Gaspar claimed he'd learned those habits in the army. Kim assumed Reacher would have similar habits.

Gaspar had always been her secret weapon where Reacher was concerned, for the very reason that he instinctively understood how Reacher thinks.

But Burke was a navy man, so maybe this eating and sleeping whenever, wherever issue wasn't an army thing. Maybe it was a military thing.

Burke didn't stir as passengers filed off the flight and walked past him, which gave Kim a chance to check him out.

He looked gaunt with sunken cheeks and eyes rimmed with dark circles as if he'd slept very little since Sunday. Hospitals were not places where one should expect to rest.

She suspected his body was covered with bruises under the long sleeves and slacks.

Kim tapped the sole of his shoe to nudge him awake. "Checking your eyelids for holes, sailor?"

"I knew you'd come." Burke stretched and yawned. "I flipped an imaginary coin."

"Chances were fifty-fifty," Kim replied cheekily.

He grinned and got to his feet. "Nice outfit," he said, after giving her running clothes and the slouchy black hoodie a pointed once-over.

Kim ignored the sarcasm. She owed him no explanation.

They set off, walking the near-empty terminal toward the exit. All the shops were closed at this hour. Eateries, too.

"I didn't have any dinner. Did you?" Burke asked as they made their way outside. She shook her head. "Let's find our hotel and check in and then get a bite to eat."

"Sounds like a plan," Kim replied. DC wasn't the city that never sleeps, but the whole town didn't roll up the sidewalks at midnight, either.

She flagged down a taxi and gave the hotel's address. The driver wandered to offer a scenic view of Washington, DC's best known tourist attractions on the way.

The Lincoln Memorial, Washington Monument, and National Mall were beautifully lit, as always. The skies were clear enough to see the Capitol building in the distance. The images might have been snapped by the Chamber of Commerce for the annual calendar.

"This city is really impressive at night," Burke said quietly.

Silently, Kim agreed. She had mixed feelings about the place, and for good reasons which dated back to her law school days at Georgetown and her failed marriage. Reasons she didn't plan to share with Burke. Not tonight, anyway. And not in a taxi or any kind of vehicle where conversations could be monitored by almost anyone.

Burke must have felt the same because he asked no further questions.

Later today, their appointment with the witness was scheduled to take place in her office, located in a sturdy building near the Department of Defense in Rock Creek, Virginia.

The witness was Lieutenant Colonel Susan Turner. She was still the CO of the 110th MP Special Unit. The building was still its headquarters.

Kim had reviewed files from The Boss on her flight from South Carolina. As usual, the files were much thinner than they should have been.

Reacher had moved across the country from South Dakota to DC seven years ago. Apparently, the siren call from then-Major Susan Turner had lured him back to his old haunts. As usual, wherever Reacher went, trouble turned up soon afterward.

From what Kim could glean from the Boss's files, both Turner and Reacher had been arrested on vague charges. Eventually, the charges were dropped. Reacher was also named in a paternity suit, which the army took a dim view of. The suit had been dismissed. None of the reasons were spelled out with the usual level of government specificity.

Whatever issues Turner experienced during Reacher's time here hadn't derailed her career completely, which was okay. But those events had stalled her upward mobility, which wasn't okay.

By now, Susan Turner should have been a full colonel.

But she'd been cooling her heels as a lieutenant colonel for a bit too long.

Kim wondered if that pissed off Turner.

The army didn't exactly have an up or out policy. But Turner's career path had clearly hit some bumps. She'd been busted back to captain after the Reacher incident. That lasted two years. And she'd spent more time as a major when she was eventually promoted the second time.

Maybe it was the job itself that led to career problems. When Reacher was the CO of the 110th MP, he'd experienced failure to advance issues, too.

Of course, Reacher's problems with authority were often due to his bad behavior.

Was that Turner's issue, too?

Competent COs weren't that easy to find. Maybe Turner was stuck here because she handled the job too well, and her bosses didn't want to replace her. Stranger things had happened.

Regardless of the reason for her uneven career trajectory, Turner had agreed to meet and was expecting them at eleven o'clock in the morning.

Which was the excuse Cooper had offered to require them to fly into DC tonight, airline schedules being what they were.

But the truth was that Cooper gave the order because he knew the same thing Gaspar had discovered. That Reacher was almost there already.

The taxi driver completed his impromptu downtown DC tour and deposited them in front of their hotel near Turner's office. They registered, picked up room keys, dropped off bags, and washed up.

Kim made it downstairs to the lobby again before Burke.

"You're fast, for a girl," Burke said with a smile as he approached. He held himself stiffly and moved with a certain lack of grace that Kim hadn't noticed before.

"So I've been told," Kim replied. "The concierge says there's a place down the block where we can get a decent hamburger and a beer at this time of night. That okay with you?"

"Yeah. Fine."

"You're okay to walk that far? It's been a long day for me, and I wasn't in the hospital this morning," Kim said.

"I'm fine. I'll let you know when and if I'm not," Burke said curtly as he strode toward the exit like he had something to prove. Which he did.

Kim followed him through the front door and out onto the sidewalk. A cool breeze blew across from the river. She shivered, glad to have the sweatshirt hugging her body.

"This way?" Burke asked and then set off at a solid clip. He was probably trying to emphasize how fit he was for the job. Like she'd insulted him with her concern or something.

Kim hurried to catch up. "I need to spend an hour buying new clothes in the morning before we see Turner."

"There's no time. Our appointment is at eleven. You won't find a store open in this town before nine or ten o'clock," Burke replied.

"I'm not shopping for a prom dress," she said. "I don't plan on loitering."

They reached the restaurant in record time. Burke held the door open and Kim went inside. He followed her.

The hostess stand and the entire diner were deserted at this hour.

A waitress came out from the back wearing a food-stained white apron tied at her waist. She probably doubled as the night cook. "Table for two?"

"Yes, please," Kim replied, pointing toward the spot she wanted. "How about that one?"

The waitress shrugged and collected two setups from the hostess stand. She led them to the table in the corner where they could both sit with their backs to the wall while watching the entrance.

"We have a limited menu after midnight. Grilled cheese, grilled ham and cheese, or burgers. With or without fries. What's your poison?" She smiled when she said it, but the words, like the smile, were flat and tired.

"Got any fresh coffee?" Kim asked.

The woman cocked her head and stared at Kim as if she were a freak of nature. "At this hour? Do you work the graveyard shift or something?"

"I just like coffee. It's okay if you have to brew it first. I can wait. I'll take a cheeseburger," Kim replied. "If the fries are already made, no thanks. But I'll pay extra if you can make them fresh."

Burke ordered the cheeseburger and fries, and water. "No special cooking required for me. I'm happy however it comes."

Without another word, the waitress turned and walked back to the kitchen, shaking her head the whole trip.

CHAPTER 33

Thursday, May 26
Washington, DC

"WHAT DO YOU THINK the chances are that we'll get fresh coffee *and* fresh French fries?" Burke mused with a grin. "Fifty-fifty?"

Kim shook her head. "You really don't understand simple math, do you?"

"I understand more than you think I do. For example, I'd say your chances on the freshly brewed coffee are one hundred percent," Burke said, making a show of sniffing the aroma of brewing java wafting from the station behind Kim.

"And it's the same on the french fries. Because it's not really a coin toss, imaginary or otherwise." Kim smiled. "You know why?"

"This place closes in less than an hour. The dining room was squared away when we walked in, so she'd already cleaned up for the night out here. She was probably almost done cleaning up in the back, too," Burke said, like a kid answering the teacher's questions in school. "She's tired, and she's been here a long time, and she wants to go home as soon as she can. So she probably tossed out the old french fries laying around back there. And she didn't say there were no fries to be had. Which means there's a one hundred percent chance you'll get your fresh, hot fries."

Kim cocked her head and smiled. "Seems logical."

"Yep. Simple deduction." He tapped his temple with two fingers as if one finger wouldn't be enough to emphasize his mental gymnastics.

The waitress used her hip to push open the double door from the kitchen. She juggled the order, all piled onto a big tray, so she'd only need to make one trip. Two coffee cups and a thermos. Two plates piled high with burgers and fries.

As soon as she set the plates on the table, it was obvious the fries were cold and limp.

Kim gave Burke a side-eye and said nothing.

When the waitress retired to the kitchen, Burke pointed a limp french fry without apology. "Tell me about South Carolina."

She shrugged. "Not much to tell at this point. There's a dead guy in a hotel room. And two people missing."

"No ID on the dead guy?"

Kim wiped grease off her fingers and retrieved her phone. She flipped through the photos until she found the ones she'd snapped of the corpse in the hotel room and the guy in the van. She passed the phone across to Burke.

He studied the photos, enlarging the images for a closer look.

"Do you know either one of these guys?" Kim asked.

"Both, actually." Burke nodded and returned her phone. "The guy in the hotel's name is Norman Smith. They called him Smitty. The other guy is Manuel Rosa, Manny. Both Army Rangers, I think. Served in Afghanistan when I was in and out over there. I didn't know them well. What happened?"

"Locals aren't sure yet. But Smitty died in Margaret Reacher's room. The other one tried to run me down with a van," she explained. "I wasn't sure he was connected to the first guy at the time. But he was positioned on a rooftop with a rifle and a scope aimed at the hotel entrance. When I confronted him, he had no interest in explaining himself."

Burke's eyes widened, and he digested the news one piece at a time. "How is Margaret related to Jack Reacher?"

"She's not. Strictly speaking."

"What does that mean?" Burke frowned. He'd almost finished his burger and the cold fries on his plate. He pointed toward hers. "Are you going to eat those?"

"Not a chance," she replied, pushing the plate toward him.

He raked the fries from her plate to his and squirted a blanket of catsup over the revolting mess. He then proceeded to inhale them like a man just returned from a long famine.

She shook her head, nauseated by the display. "You can have the burger, too, if you want."

"Great," he said, grabbing the burger and stacking the plates.

"Margaret Preston Reacher." Kim freshened her coffee. "Married to David Reacher. Margaret's son is Jake. His father was Joe Reacher."

"Joe? As in Jack Reacher's brother?" Burke's eyes widened as if he didn't already know.

Perhaps he didn't.

But he should have.

She'd reported the relationship weeks ago, and Burke should have reviewed all those files. One of the things she didn't love about the guy was his failure to bring himself up to speed on the case. He wasn't thorough enough to suit her.

"Joe Reacher's kid." She nodded. "Exactly."

"You talked to the locals. What did Margaret and young Jake have to say about how Smitty died?" Burke asked after swallowing the last of the burger and washing it down with the remainder of his coffee. He refilled his cup from the pot.

"Nothing so far. We can't find Jake," Kim replied. "Can't find Margaret, either. At least, not before I left Columbia. I wasn't too worried about it until you told me the dead guy was an Army Ranger."

"Why is that a problem?"

"Because I don't see Margaret Reacher as the kind of woman who could take down a Ranger with two bullets. She might have gotten off one shot, maybe. But two? Unlikely," Kim replied slowly.

Burke nodded as comprehension dawned. "So you think Jake killed him. And you're worried the locals will come to the same conclusions. So both Jake and Margaret are suspects and fugitives. And now we've got three Reachers on the run instead of just one."

"Kind of. Although, strictly speaking, none of that is our problem," Kim murmured, sipping the coffee. "I was more worried that Jack Reacher was in Columbia or on his way, and we wouldn't be there."

"How would he even know any of this is going on?" Burke said. "It's not like the kid can just call up his uncle and get him down there, is it?"

Kim shrugged. Gaspar's all-purpose gesture.

"What you think is that we're wasting time here, messing around with Susan Turner, when Reacher is more likely to be in South Carolina," Burke said slowly. "But you know that's not true."

"I do? How so?"

"Because The Boss is always several steps ahead of us. He sent us here. Which means he has good reason to believe that

Reacher's here, or soon will be," Burke replied, draining his coffee.

Kim nodded and took a breath before she admitted the truth. "Yeah. Well, turns out, The Boss was right. Again."

"And you know this how?" Burke's eyebrows popped up, followed quickly by a frown. "Wait. Let me guess. Gaspar told you."

Burke didn't like Kim keeping Gaspar on standby or sharing intel with her prior partner. Burke had made that very clear several times. But until Burke proved she could trust him, Kim planned to keep the Gaspar channel open.

"He found Reacher and Burns heading into Bethesda a few hours ago. Just before I flew out of Columbia," Kim admitted.

"Isn't that just terrific," Burke snarked.

She reached into her pocket for more than enough cash to cover the meals and a generous tip. She tossed them on the table. "Let's go."

"Smitty wasn't much of a soldier," Burke said, changing the subject as they headed out the door. "In Kabul, he was shot once by a kid. About six years old. Smitty didn't think the kid would shoot him. He let his personal views get in the way of his training."

"So you're saying he could have let his guard down with Margaret. Meaning she could have shot him twice before he'd dodged the second bullet," Kim said.

"It's possible," Burke nodded. After a moment's reflection, he added, "But it's a lot more likely that Jake Reacher killed Smitty with that second shot."

"You say that only because you don't know Jake," Kim replied flatly.

Unwilling to give Kim the last word, Burke said, "But I know Jack. Better than you do. If the kid is anything like his uncle, he'd have killed the guy without a second's hesitation."

Kim said nothing.

The air was cold and a little damp. In the middle of the night, in the middle of spring, in the northeastern corner of Virginia. A north wind whipped down, cutting through her workout clothes. She hustled along and Burke's long strides struggled to keep pace.

The lazy Potomac was not far away. Beyond it, DC's glow lit up the clouds. The nation's capital was where all kinds of things were going on. Some more legal than others.

"Tell me about your service weapon," Burke said.

"What about it?" Kim replied, eyes straight ahead, hustling along the empty sidewalk.

"I heard you lost it. Is that true?"

"Who'd you hear that from?"

"Doesn't matter. Do you have your weapon or not?" He paused for a breath. "Because if you don't, I can get yours replaced in the morning while you're shopping for clothes."

"I'm good. Thanks for the offer, though." She shook her head slowly, still worried about how he acquired that particular piece of information.

At the next intersection, they were stopped by a traffic light. While they waited for the light to change, a green sedan pulled up to block the sidewalk. The window lowered.

From her position on the sidewalk, Kim saw the driver and recognized her from the official head shots she'd reviewed in The Boss's files on the plane.

Susan Turner, well-groomed, fresh, and alert, leaned across the console, all business. "Otto and Burke, right? I've been looking for you. Hop in."

She had a great voice. Warm. Slightly husky. A little breathy. Men would probably call it intimate.

CHAPTER 34

Thursday, May 26
Washington, DC

SULLIVAN HUSTLED THROUGH TO the Four Knights Club kitchen and into the mudroom again. He supplied Patton's biometric palm and fingerprints to unlock the exterior door. He pulled on a pair of leather gloves, palmed his gun, and stepped out into the cool night air.

He glanced around the back gardens and noticed nothing amiss.

Dover would have muscled Templar into the garage closest to the house and closest to the exit gate. The garage was originally a carriage house and later converted for vehicles. Since the Club didn't require or possess any vehicles, the garage had been expanded and converted to store food supplies.

Inside, the space resembled a small grocery store complete with walk-in coolers, a generously sized meat locker, and aisles with stacks of shelving. Supplies were sorted, repackaged, and stored as they were delivered.

A separate room outfitted as a butcher shop had been installed across the back of the building to prevent cross-contamination while the meats were cut and packaged.

Sullivan hustled along the sidewalk from the kitchen's mudroom door to the garage's side entrance.

He turned the knob, slipped into the building, and closed the door silently behind him.

He paused a moment to allow his eyes to adjust to the darkness.

If Dover or Templar were talking, their voices didn't carry to Sullivan's ears. A weak light escaped from beneath the door in the back leading to the butcher's work station. Sullivan walked silently along the packaged food aisles toward them.

At the door, he paused to listen. He heard nothing but the hum of condensers keeping the chill inside the coolers.

He readied his pistol and shoved the door open, pushing it back hard against the wall. Bright light flooded the darkness, but Sullivan didn't blink. His pupils reacted quickly enough.

Dover was leaning against the stainless steel table. Templar was seated in a straight- backed chair, chin resting on his chest, hands cuffed behind. His ankles were bound together with duct tape. A slab of duct tape covered his mouth. He was unconscious.

"How long has he been out?" Sullivan asked, tilting his head toward the prisoner.

"Twenty minutes or so," Dover replied.

"What did he say before you dosed him?"

"Nothing. That's why I dosed him." Dover shrugged. "He's a SEAL. Takes a lot to break those guys. What did you think he'd say?"

"Right," Sullivan said, returning his pistol to his pocket. "Helo's on the way already. After they deliver the product, we'll send Templar on the return trip back to the Palace."

"The senator won't like that much," Dover said with a smirk.

"I don't like it much, either. I'd rather dispose of him now. But that won't get me what I want from his father," Sullivan replied.

"We could solve both problems tonight. Adams is still inside. The tournament he's playing isn't over yet," Dover suggested.

Sullivan nodded again, considering. The plan appealed.

Eliminating Templar and Adams at the same time could raise eyebrows here in DC. Inquisitive minds didn't accept coincidence as a reasonable explanation for such things.

But if he moved them to the Palace now, the exact time of death would be vague, and disposing of the bodies would be exponentially easier.

He heard helo blades whapping in the distance. It could be the bird flying in from the Palace. Helicopters were not uncommon around DC. Public and private helipads abounded.

Sullivan never worried about helo deliveries causing undue alarm among the Club's neighbors. They were used to the noise now, too, and tuned it out.

He glanced at his watch. The timing was right. The helo he heard could be close to landing here.

"Okay. Go pick him up. We'll send both Adams and this one out tonight."

"Copy that," Dover said, unfolding his long legs and standing to stretch. He was so thin that if he turned sideways, he'd be a hard target to hit. "You'll be okay here until I get back?"

Sullivan pulled his silenced pistol from his pocket again. If Templar stirred while Dover was gone, the problem was easily solved.

"I'll be fine. Don't dawdle," Sullivan replied, tilting his head toward the ceiling.

Dover nodded. "Be right back."

The helicopter was coming closer. With a practiced ear, Sullivan estimated the bird would touch down soon. Unloading the cargo and refueling would be done quickly, too.

Whatever drug Dover had used to inject Templar was beginning to wear off. The helo's noise seemed to have roused him.

He raised his head and stared at Sullivan, uncomprehending. The duct tape over his mouth kept him silent. But Sullivan saw the questions in his eyes. "Who are you? Where am I?"

"All in good time," Sullivan replied as if the younger Templar had asked.

CHAPTER 35

Thursday, May 26
Washington, DC

KIM AND BURKE CLIMBED into Susan Turner's sedan for
the quick drive back to 110th HQ. Turner paused at the sentry hut
to show her ID. When the young guy waved them through, she
parked the sedan next to a snazzy red two-seater and led the way
up the short flight of stone steps.

Kim wondered whether the little red car belonged to Turner.
She figured it might. Turner seemed like the kind of woman who
would own a car like that.

The building was classic 1950s Department of Defense
architecture. Long and low, two stories, brick, stone, slate,
featuring green metal window frames.

Kim grabbed the green tubular handrail and trudged up to the
doors. Burke followed behind.

Inside the doors was a lobby. A stone staircase on the right
led to the second floor. A reception desk on the left. The lobby
narrowed to a corridor with offices on each side. The lights were
on, providing blinding brightness after the dark outside.

There was a sergeant seated at the desk. Turner nodded toward him and marched up the worn stone stairs to the second floor like she'd been up and down those stairs a thousand times. She probably had.

On the second floor, which was laid out exactly like the first floor, they walked the linoleum along another corridor and ended up at the third door from the left of center.

The door was exactly like all the others. Painted. Several times. Wood below, reeded glass above split the dull glow into distorted vertical slices.

On the wall near the handle was a name plate. *Lt. Colonel S.R. Turner, CO.*

"Home sweet home," Turner said in her breathy voice as she pushed the door open. "We're not fancy-like here. The army is short on luxury, long on durability."

The room looked like it had been furnished shortly after it was built. The same murky linoleum as the corridors and the lobbies, polished to a subtle sheen. Metal file cabinets. A light fixture hung from the ceiling burning green and sickly with a fluorescent bulb.

A current world map was affixed to the wall like it was the only furnishing that had been replaced in the office since the Eisenhower administration.

Four chairs, one behind the desk and three in front. The desk was steel, painted battleship gray, but worn to a sheen here and there.

Technology had advanced since 1950. So now there was a phone, desktop computer, and a laptop sitting on the desk.

"This was once Jack Reacher's office back when he was CO of the 110th. Not much has changed." Turner took her seat and waved them to the visitor chairs. She grinned and pointed to the dented side of the desk. "Story goes that he made that dent there with some guy's head."

"Ouch," Burke said, grinning back. "So you knew Reacher back then?"

"Not exactly. He taught a class his last year in the service about integrating federal and military investigations. I took the class. But that's the only contact I had with him before he moved on," Turner replied. She really did have an awesome voice.

"Sounds like some bullshit title for public consumption," Burke said. "The class was probably about screwing the feds, not cooperating with them."

"Fortunately for you, I didn't learn much." Turner smiled. "You passed the test."

"We know you connected with Reacher again, seven years ago," Kim said. "And you've seen him recently. Here in DC. We need to find him."

"We can cover all of that. But right now, what we really need to deal with is Jake and Margaret," Turner said.

"You know Jake and Margaret?" Burke asked, frowning.

Turner shook her head. "No. But Kim does, don't you?"

"Did Jack Reacher tell you that?" Kim asked.

"Let's not waste time," Turner replied. "Jake and Margaret are in serious trouble. We need to find them and help them out before this situation goes even further sideways than it already has."

Burke said, "Jake isn't AWOL at the moment. He's on leave until next week. His whereabouts are his own business, don't you think?"

"Jake is a soldier. And an officer. He's on leave after basic training, yes. But you were a SEAL, Burke. You know how the military works. Jake is one of ours. He shows a lot of promise, and he's our responsibility. We don't want him to screw up his entire career before he even gets started. We need to find him," Turner said, leaning back in her chair.

"I'm guessing you talked to Espin," Kim said. "Did he tell you about the situation at the Magnolia Hotel, or did you see it for yourself?"

"Yes, I talked to Espin. Yes, I went to the hotel. So did you. We're on the same page, as far as the known facts go," Turner replied. "Jake and Margaret are missing. Frankly, they're both suspects, although Espin isn't releasing that yet. At my request. Because, like I said, we're trying to save Jake's career here, as well as his life."

"That's not all it is, though. You don't protect all the soldiers who get themselves in trouble, I'm sure," Kim said, following her instincts. "You're interested in Jake because Jack Reacher is in DC. You've talked to him. Did he know his nephew was in trouble? Or did you give him that intel?"

"Either way, we need to find Jake while we still can," Turner said flatly.

"That's not quite true," Burke said. "Our assignment is to find Jack. Margaret and Jake and two dead citizens are Espin's problem. Beyond that, the two victims were vets, not active duty. Technically, I don't see where the army has a legitimate interest in this."

Kim picked up the thread. "Which, again, means this is personal to you. Because of your relationship with Jake's uncle."

Turner didn't bother to deny the relationship. Why would she? There was nothing illegal or immoral about Turner having sex with Jack Reacher, whether it was seven years ago or seven minutes ago.

Still, it was good to have the request on the record. Even though she knew Turner wouldn't tell her. The Boss was listening, same as always. He'd want the official version.

Kim said, "Maybe we can all work together to sort this out. Where is Jack Reacher?"

"He said he had plans to play chess," Turner replied with a grin as she glanced toward the monitor on her desk. Instantly, a serious expression replaced her good humor.

"What's that message about? Reacher?" Burke asked.

"A local issue." Turner shook her head. "Sorry. I've got to cut this short. I need to read you into the events that happened seven years ago for any of this to make sense. But I can't do it now. Let's meet back here later this morning, as scheduled."

"You think Jake and Margaret will be okay until then?" Kim asked, all her senses on red alert.

She craned her neck to get a look at the message on the monitor, but she couldn't read it.

Turner, focused on the situation, whatever it was, replied, "Tomorrow. We'll pick up where we left off."

She punched keys to lock up her system, stood, and left the office.

Burke and Kim exchanged frowns.

"Guess there's more than one way to give visitors the bum's rush, eh?" Burke said.

"Let's go," Kim replied as she left with Burke walking abreast.

When they were outside again, making their way back to the hotel, Burke said, "Was that message from Reacher?"

"Unlikely. He wouldn't have access to Turner's secure communications inside the DoD."

"What, then?"

"Could have been anything, really. She does have a day job, after all," Kim replied, stuffing her hands into the pocket of the sweatshirt. Damn, it was cold out here.

Burke wasn't ready to let it go. "So you're saying whatever that message was about, it had nothing to do with Reacher?"

"Odds are fifty-fifty."

"Very funny," Burke said snidely.

The hotel, with the promise of a few hours' sleep, was a block away. She quickened her pace.

Half a block later, The Boss's cell phone vibrated in her pocket.

"Otto," she said when she picked up.

"Turner's on her way to The Four Knights Club, a private chess club downtown," he replied. "The message she got while you were in her office said a helo was on its way. Landing shortly, which caused her to cut your meeting short."

"You think Reacher might be there or headed there?" Kim asked. "Why?"

"We can discuss my reasons later. Get over there as quickly as you can. I've texted the address."

And just like that, she was holding dead air. Again.

"What did he want?" Burke asked as they approached the entrance to the hotel. "Has he located Reacher?"

"Possibly." She opened his text and read the address. Traffic was light at the moment, which meant getting there was doable if they had a car. They didn't.

Kim fished her personal phone out of her pocket and called the car service she used whenever she was in the city. She gave a pickup location at a coffee shop two blocks away.

"This way," she said to Burke, jerking a thumb in the opposite direction of the hotel's entrance. "You're armed, right?"

"Always." Burke followed her lead. "Where are we going?"

"The Boss hacked into Turner's system. She's on her way to a chess club. He thinks Reacher could be there," Kim replied with a shrug.

"Is this new intel or stuff he conveniently didn't mention before?" Burke asked.

She gave him a side-eye. "He always knows more than he tells. Never forget that."

They had almost reached the coffee shop. She saw the limo sitting at the curb, engine running, so she picked up her pace. Burke stepped it up, too.

They climbed into the back of the vehicle with Kim behind the passenger seat and Burke behind the driver. She recited the address for the Four Knights club from memory.

Burke yawned and closed his eyes. "What are the chances we'll get some sleep before dawn? Fifty-fifty?"

She snorted. "No chance at all."

CHAPTER 36

Thursday, May 26
Washington, DC

WHEN THE LIMO ROLLED past the front entrance of the Four Knights Club, Kim realized the digits she'd received from The Boss were actually the delivery address, located in the alley behind the historic brick building. The limo driver turned right at the corner and turned right again into the one-way alley.

Up ahead, deeper into the alley, Turner's green sedan was parked along a fence. Kim pointed toward it, and Burke nodded. "Yeah, I see it."

The car was unoccupied. Where was Turner?

From this vantage point as the limo approached, Kim couldn't see over the brick wall surrounding the Club's back gardens. But the overwhelming noise of the rotor blades on the helo as it idled on the other side of the wall was unmistakable.

The limo driver slowed to a stop. "Shall I wait?"

"No. But the alley is blocked farther up. Reverse out of here and go back the way you came in," Kim replied.

She didn't want the limo driving past the club, announcing their arrival.

They climbed out of the backseat and crouched low as they moved along the brick wall. Kim watched until the driver sped backward to the street, which gave Burke time for a head start.

He ran toward the open rear gate on the other side of the property and ducked inside, with Kim chasing to catch up. She flattened her back against the brick and scanned the scene. The area was dimly lit, but she could see well enough.

The helo was a Bell 222, a light utility vehicle, perhaps the best looking civil helicopter ever made, until they stopped producing them. Kim hated helos more than she hated airplanes. She had been ferried here and there in this same model more times than she wanted to remember.

At least it wasn't tiny. A small helo was the kiss of death as far as Kim was concerned. The crash reports confirmed her views on that, too. Whenever she was required to fly, she wanted the biggest jet with the most experienced crew she could find.

The Bell 222 was a roomy twin-engine craft with a seven-passenger capacity. The rear doors were as big as a panel van's, and they were opened wide.

From her vantage point, Kim saw the middle row of seats had been removed, leaving plenty of room for cargo.

The pilot remained in his seat.

Kim reached Burke's spot in the shadows along the brick wall. "Looks like a quick stop to drop off cargo. What do you think is in those boxes?"

Three men were working at the back of the helo. Two were speedily unloading lightweight boxes and placing them onto a dolly until the last one was stacked atop the rest.

"Whatever it is, they're working fast and not very hard to hump it out of there," Kim replied.

"Maybe they're empty," Burke said.

Kim ignored the snark. "And they're almost done. Where's Turner? Have you seen her?"

One of the men signed for the delivery and returned the electronic tablet. Then the two men wheeled the dolly swiftly toward the back of the house and up the ramp from the sidewalk.

"Not yet. There's a lot of shadows out here. She could be anywhere," Burke said. "But she'd be crazy if she's alone. And she didn't strike me as crazy."

When the dolly reached the exit door, one of the men placed his palm on a small flat square beside the doorknob. Then he reached down and opened the door, and the two men wheeled the dolly inside.

"That's sophisticated security for a bunch of empty boxes," Kim said.

Burke replied, "Yeah. Look at that third guy. Does he look familiar to you?"

The third man stood aside, waiting near the back of the helo as if he was expecting return cargo. He was big and bulky and carried himself ramrod straight, in the way military men do.

"I've seen hundreds of guys like that. The FBI is full of them," Kim said. "You're thinking that could be Reacher?"

"He's supposed to be skulking around here somewhere. Could be him." Burke shrugged. "Turner knows things she didn't tell us about this place. Didn't she say Reacher was playing chess tonight? And isn't this a chess club?"

Minutes later, a side door opened from one of the outbuildings near the back gate.

The third man hustled over to help when two hostages stumbled forward through the door as if they'd been shoved outside from behind. The shorter one fell to the ground and struggled to rise again.

"Over there," Kim said, drawing Burke's attention to the action on the ground.

Both men wore bags over their heads. Their hands were cuffed behind them. A tall, slender man followed, shoving both hostages ahead of him, jabbing them in the back with a handgun. His words were lost in the helo's noise.

Oddly, both hostages were dressed in fine casual wear, complete with once highly polished shoes, now scuffed, shirts askew and bloody, jackets torn and mangled, trousers ripped and dirty.

"What the hell is going on here?" Burke whispered urgently. "Where's Reacher? Are you sure he's not that big guy? Looks like him to me."

When the big man reached the trio, the odds were evened up. Now two on two, the hostages were prodded and moved along faster.

They reached the open back doors of the helo and both hostages were shoved inside.

"Who are those guys and where are they going?" Burke said.

In the outdoor lighting, it was difficult to see the skinny man's features. He reached into his pocket and pulled out what looked like syringes.

He bent into the helo, his torso temporarily out of sight, and then backed out. He dropped the syringes into his pocket.

The pilot goosed the turbines, and the idling blades ramped up in speed and volume. Whatever the two men were saying to each other was covered by the helo's rotor noise.

The skinny man stepped back. The big guy closed one of the doors and reached to close the other.

Turner emerged from the shadows. She stood in a classic shooter's stance and fired toward the helo.

Both men seemed surprised but hesitated for only a moment.

The skinny man dropped to one knee, aimed his weapon, and returned fire in Turner's direction.

Turner was in trouble and outmanned.

If Reacher were here, now would be a damned good time for him to get into the game.

"Come on!" Kim yelled to Burke in an attempt to be heard over the deafening helicopter's whine. She waved him forward out of the shadows and toward the helo.

The skinny man adjusted his stance and squeezed off two shots aimed toward Kim. She ducked into the shadows for cover and returned fire.

Her rounds hit the mark.

The skinny man fell onto the grass and stayed there.

Turner yelled, "Hold your fire!"

Kim stared at the big man at the helo. Was that Reacher? Could Turner be protecting him?

The big man closed the second cargo door, drew his gun, and fired toward Turner as he hustled around to the passenger door of the helo. She zigzagged toward cover.

Which told Kim everything she needed to know.

Reacher wouldn't shoot Turner. Never happen. Not even in some sort of improbable role-playing exercise.

Odds were way better than fifty-fifty. Whoever that guy was, it wasn't Reacher.

Burke must have reached the opposite conclusion.

He aimed his service weapon at the big man and fired. His timing was off. The first shot hit the helo's skin and deflected.

The big man reached the passenger door. He shot back as he pulled the door open and lifted one leg into the cabin.

Burke aimed and fired twice this time. Both bullets hit his intended target. One in the leg and one in his left side.

The combined pistol, bullets, and distance was a losing combination, though. But Burke's rounds failed to stop the brute.

The big man howled angrily, louder than the whapping blades and helo's twin engines.

Instantly, he shot back, aiming directly for Burke.

One. Two. Three.

But he was juggling too many distractions at once.

Somehow, all three shots missed their mark. The big man struggled his body into the cabin of the helo as it lifted straight up from the ground.

The back cargo door fell open and flapped in the wind.

In his haste to get aboard and away, he had failed to secure both doors properly.

Nothing he could do about that now.

He dragged his wounded leg inside and closed the passenger door as the helo lifted higher into the night.

It climbed a thousand feet before it hammered west, high and fast.

Turner ran up to Kim and Burke. All three were breathing hard.

Burke had raised his gun to fire again.

"Hold your fire!" Turner yelled to be heard over the retreating helo, knocking Burke's arm wide with a sharp jab to his kidney and doubling him over. "Hold your fire!"

Burke turned and glared. "What the hell is wrong with you?"

"You can't bring the bird down with a pistol at that distance. You'd have to hit the engine inlet, which is on top of the cabin. Your angle's wrong. Your weapon's wrong. Your ammo's wrong. All you're doing is making too much noise," Turner replied.

Burke didn't argue, but he didn't shoot again, either.

"Let's go find that helo," Kim said, holstering her weapon.

"Not yet," Turner said.

"Why the hell not?" Burke snapped.

"No rush. It'll be in the air a while. And there's a lot you don't know," Turner replied.

Kim pulled the phone that connected her directly to The Boss from her pocket. He answered on the first ring. "We've got a helo in the air with two hostages. Solid FBI jurisdiction."

"Right. I'll take care of it."

"There's something more going on inside this chess club. We go in there and bust it up, and everyone in DC will know the FBI is on top of crime. It'll make you look good," Kim argued, although making him look good was never her top priority.

"No. The threat is neutralized for the moment. I'll handle this. Keep your eye on the ball. Stick with Turner," he snapped before he disconnected.

Burke said, "Let's get in there. If that wasn't Reacher in the helo, he could be inside."

Kim dropped the phone into her pocket, shaking her head. "The Boss says he'll handle this."

"Cooper knows what he's doing. And I'll call the locals. They'll get the right teams on the job," Turner nodded. "Come with me. I'll bring you up to speed. Then we'll go after Jake and Margaret."

"Let's hear what she has to say," Kim told Burke as she followed Turner toward the back gate. "The range on that bird is no more than four hundred miles. He'll stop to refuel at some point, too. We can find the helo if and when we need to."

Burke shrugged and did as he was told, for once.

Which ramped up Kim's internal threat level into the red zone and held it there.

CHAPTER 37

Thursday, May 26
Washington, DC

SULLIVAN HAD WAITED INSIDE the storage building while Dover and Coda marched the two hostages to the helo. He'd watched until Dover had injected the sedatives to keep them unconscious during the return flight to the White Kings Palace.

When the gunfire broke out, Sullivan ducked back into the building to avoid being discovered. He wasn't concerned. Coda could take care of himself and Dover was there for backup. All they had to do was hold off the attack until Coda got inside and the helo took off.

Sullivan remained ready to assist only if necessary.

The situation went south. Fast.

They had come in from the back gate, which Sullivan couldn't see from inside the building. The back gate should have been closed and secured. Why wasn't it?

When the shots rang out, Sullivan realized there were three attackers against Coda and Dover.

238 | DIANE CAPRI

He couldn't see the shooters or provide cover. He couldn't call out and be heard over the noise of the helo.

The shooting was over almost as quickly as it began.

Dover went down. He was dead. No other possible outcome there. Fine. Dover had made too many mistakes of late. The outcome for him was inevitable. It came a little earlier than planned was all.

Coda was wounded but alive. When they returned to the White Kings compound, he'd get adequate medical care. Sullivan wasn't concerned.

The helo finally lifted off, and Coda managed to close the door before the pilot sped away.

Afterward, the three remaining shooters had huddled together at the back of the property near the open gate. Shadows hid their faces, but from his viewpoint, he could see them well enough to know who they were.

The tiny one was Otto. The man was Burke. And the other female was Turner. They didn't loiter after the helo departed.

Reacher could have been close by. So why didn't Sullivan hear four shooters instead of three?

And what about Petey Burns? Where was he and what had he witnessed?

Sullivan waited, ears cocked, listening for approaching sirens. A nosy neighbor might have heard and reported the gunshots. In a normal residential neighborhood, police would be called under such circumstances.

But it was possible the shots had not been heard. One of the reasons he'd chosen this particular historic house was its relative isolation. The neighbors were sealed into their own lives and well secured, just like the Four Knights Club.

The helo's noise could have covered the pistol fire. Possibly.

Sullivan continued to shelter in place while he listened and watched the three huddled near the back gate. Burke and Turner appeared to be arguing, although he couldn't hear their words. Perhaps the issue between them was whether to call the local authorities.

He wondered how they planned to explain the dead man and the gunfire.

Otto left the other two and approached Dover's body. She knelt and checked his non-existent pulse.

She patted his pockets for ID. Finding none, she pulled out her phone and took several photos of the body.

Then she picked up his left hand and collected his fingerprints on an app on the phone's screen. His right hand still held his pistol, and she left that intact. Probably unwilling to tamper with the evidence more than she already had.

After she finished, she stood and captured a video of the grounds, careful not to include Burke and Turner in her sweep.

Next, she pushed a few buttons on the phone before she slipped it into her pocket and returned to her group. She sent the evidence she'd gathered somewhere.

Whatever the argument had been, the three then left the garden together through the back gate. Turner's sedan started up and ran along the alley to the street on the corner.

For a moment, Sullivan considered dealing with Dover's body. Before Otto had documented the death, Sullivan had planned to move the body into a freezer until it could be disposed.

But for now, he decided to leave Dover in place. If a busybody did report the shots, Dover's weapon would answer those questions. If the shots went unnoticed, Sullivan could deal with Dover's body later.

Sooner or later, the body would be discovered. At that point, the locals would be called in to the crime scene.

"The back gate was open. Someone came inside and killed him," Sullivan imagined one of the cooks stating for the record to a local detective.

Should the need arise.

Sullivan intended to prevent it, if possible. At least for tonight.

After all, the neighborhood wasn't Chicago, but DC wasn't all that safe these days, either.

During the renovations, the old residence had been soundproofed as well. Members were involved in other pursuits, and the Club itself was impenetrable. Young Templar had proven that earlier in the evening.

Dover could have been shot by an intruder and no one in the Club would have been aware of the crime.

In fact, that's exactly what happened.

All in all, the night had been a success.

New product had been delivered, and it would be consumed before tomorrow. If police searched the premises, they'd find nothing illegal or immoral going on.

Dover was dead, but no one at Four Knights was responsible.

The Judas and young Templar had disappeared. They were adult males. They could go where they pleased.

They would be dead soon enough and buried at the White Kings compound.

The only open issue at the moment was Senator Templar, which couldn't be helped. His situation would be resolved shortly as well. Perhaps the senator would like to visit his son's grave and join him there.

The suggestion brought a slight curve of amusement to Sullivan's mouth.

He turned off the lights in the storage garage, slipped outside, and hung in the shadows as he made his way to the rear exit.

At the open gate, he crept into the alley, which was now abandoned.

Keeping alert for sirens, he walked in the opposite direction of Turner's route, just in case they might still be lingering out there.

When he reached the street, he turned the corner and walked away.

He pulled a fresh encrypted burner phone from his pocket and called his car service to pick him up at a nearby bar.

When Sullivan returned to the snow den, all would be revealed. His personal cameras placed around the gardens had captured images of tonight's events.

Secure government satellites would supply moment-by-moment videos of everything beyond the immediate grounds.

It was premature to declare the entire mission accomplished. But Sullivan was pleased with the night's work.

The Judas and Templar were as good as dead.

And finding Reacher would be simple enough.

CHAPTER 38

Thursday, May 26
White Kings Palace

JONES HEARD THE HELO returning from DC when it was still ten minutes away. "Man, I'm getting too old for this crap."

He groaned, climbed out of bed, and showered before dressing in black jeans and a clean black T-shirt. He shoved his feet into work boots, grabbed his pistol, and headed toward the helipad.

Elapsed time, he noticed on his way out the door, was eight minutes. He was getting slow.

Jones hurried down the stairs and out the back verandah door just as the helo set down. The early morning sky had lightened some, but the sun was well below the horizon.

Dense forest on all sides kept the compound almost as black as midnight. The big diesel generators kept enough electricity flowing to light the grounds until well after sunrise.

As he moved toward the helo, Jones noticed that the back cargo door was jacked. As if the handles were tied together on the inside instead of secured flush with the back of the bird as they should have been.

The door definitely wasn't like that when the helo left the compound. What the hell had happened in DC?

The helo settled onto the helipad and the rotors slowed. The passenger door opened. Coda slid out, landing on one leg.

The other leg sported a bloody bandage secured around his thigh.

Coda leaned against the helo and then pushed himself upright.

The White Kings were gathering, but Jones was closest. He hustled toward Coda. "What's up?" Jones shouted over the slowing rotor noise.

"The jackass shot me, that's what. When I find him, I'm planning to return the favor," Coda said.

"Who shot you?" Jones asked.

Coda ignored the question. "Get the cargo out, will you? I'm on my way to the infirmary."

"Cargo? I thought you were coming back empty to be reloaded," Jones said.

"Yeah, me, too." Coda winced as he walked, making his way with difficulty.

Jones hurried around to the back of the helo. He couldn't force the doors open from the outside.

Dr. Sanz approached one of the other guys, instructing Kenyon to get inside the helo and cut the restraints to open the cargo doors. When the doors opened, Jones got a good look at the cargo.

Two men. Hands and feet bound. Canvas bags covered their heads.

The rotors had continued to slow, making conversation easier.

"Great. More hostages. Just what we need." Jones pulled a knife from his back pocket and sliced through the duct tape binding their feet. "Get them out of there," he ordered.

244 | DIANE CAPRI

A second man, Mack, climbed aboard the helo. The two men shoved both hostages from the cargo compartment onto the helipad. They landed hard, like bags of dirt, and didn't move.

"How long before they're conscious?" Jones asked.

"I'm a chemist, not a doctor," Sanz replied with a shrug. "Depends on what drugs were used. Could be a while. Or not."

Jones nodded and swiped an exasperated palm over his face. Then he turned to Mack. "Go get the quad ATV and trailer. You and Kenyon load these guys up and haul them to the cells."

"I'm not lugging that dead weight down those stairs," Mack replied. "Let 'em sleep it off right there on the ground. We can move them later. When they can walk."

"Drop them down the steps on their heads for all I care," Jones growled. "But get them locked up."

"It's not like they're gonna give us any trouble," Mack continued to argue. "Even if they could get past the fence, where the hell would they go? It's miles to the nearest neighbor you know."

Jones's patience had been exhausted long ago. He glared and fisted his hands, tempted to give Mack a quick, hard jab to the gut to improve his attitude. And remind him of the chain of command.

Lucky for Mack, he was down too many men already.

"Harvey's there. He'll help," Jones said sternly. "When Patton gets here, I'll gladly hand over my job if you'd like to be the one giving the orders."

Mack shook his head and sauntered toward one of the barns to collect the quad.

Jones pulled a phone from his pocket and knelt beside the hostages. He lifted the canvas bags and snapped photos of their faces. Then he used an app on his phone to collect full palm prints.

He didn't recognize either of them. He wondered why the hell Patton had sent them here.

"Kenyon, keep an eye on these two until Mack gets back with transport," Jones said on his way to the front of the helo where Sanz and the pilot were arguing.

Sanz wanted to send another load of product to Texas tonight. The pilot objected to flying the helo with the damaged cargo doors.

Jones caught movement in his periphery as if one of the hostages were climbing out of the helo. But they were both lying on the ground where he'd left them.

He turned his head but the shadow was gone. He closed his eyes hard for a few seconds and looked again. Nothing.

When he had a chance, he'd review the CCTV. If someone were sneaking around out here, he'd find out about it soon enough.

By the time he turned his attention to the argument again, Sanz had prevailed. The pilot headed toward the fuel depot on the far end of the property. He'd said the helo's fuel supply needed to be topped off for the longer flight to Texas.

Jones asked, "Did Patton tell you those two hostages were coming? Or what we're supposed to do with them?"

"Haven't talked to him. I have no idea," Sanz shook his head. "Get someone out here to secure the cargo doors for the flight. They'll get repaired in Texas. We'll need to keep the product inside the helo until it lands again."

"You got the product ready?" Jones asked. "Let's get this bird loaded and off the ground."

"You know we're shorthanded. Almost finished. We'll bring the last of it out as soon as it's done," Sanz said, with a sharp glance toward the warehouse. "You can get your guys to secure those helo doors while we finish up."

Jones scowled at him, but Sanz didn't see it. He'd already hurried away.

Sanz was an annoyingly prissy little man. Jones and the others put up with him because he possessed essential chemistry skills and raw material contacts in Spain that the rest of them didn't have.

But just because Sanz was useful didn't make him one of the guys. Nor did he seem to care.

Sanz kept to himself. He had his own private chef in the big Palace and took all his meals alone. Every few months, he'd fly home to Spain to visit his wife. When he came back, he always brought better raw materials from his poppy farmer contacts there.

Jones shook his head and turned his attention back to business.

He ordered guys to get to work on the helo doors. Refabricating wasn't an option due to the time constraints. The helo didn't move around much during flights through good weather. If they hit turbulence or storms, the doors needed to be as tight as possible.

Refueling was already underway. Fuel supplies for the big diesel generators which supplied power to the entire compound were kept beside one of the outbuildings near the rear gate. Gasoline for the backup generators and the emergency fuel for the helo and the jet were stored in the same area.

Managing fuel supplies for the compound was a full-time job in itself. There was enough fuel stored on-site to keep everything humming along nicely for two months. Refueling was on the schedule for next week, but there should be plenty in the tanks to carry them through.

Once Sanz delivered the product, they'd get it loaded and get the helo off the ground. Then he'd call for orders from Patton to deal with the hostages. Which would probably mean digging two more graves in the poppy patch.

And there was still the matter of the kid and his mother.

The point of having the kid here was to lure his uncle to the compound for disposal. Those three graves had already been prepared.

Jones and Coda were in charge of the operation. They had developed a solid strategy for handling Jack Reacher's assault.

The first line of defense was the electrified boundary fence. Even as big as he was, Reacher couldn't get over or around that fence without getting fried.

Jones hoped Reacher would try to breach the fence. The operation would be quick and done.

Patton was a careful man. He'd required contingency plans, which Jones and Coda had dutifully created.

But those plans relied on a full staff of well-trained soldiers. Which they no longer had. Without a full staff, Reacher might stand a chance if he could breach the fence. Which meant adjustments to the plans were required.

Jones glanced up to see Sanz and his minions advancing with the product. Good.

The helo had been refueled and the pilot had conducted the pre-flight inspection. The bird was ready to go.

The cargo doors were closed and secured well enough for the flight to Texas. Which meant the product had to be loaded through the side doors.

They set up a relay line and made quick work of the loading. When the last box was in place, Jones closed and secured the side doors. He gave an extra tug on all the door handles to be sure they wouldn't pop open during flight.

The pilot had begun to warm up the engines.

Sanz opened the passenger door and climbed aboard. Jones secured the last door while Sanz fastened his harness in place.

He waved Jones away from the bird and Jones stepped back to observe the helo lift straight up and head west.

"Okay," Jones said to the remaining men on the ground. "Get some shuteye. Report for duty at zero nine hundred."

They groused and plodded toward the barracks in one of the mansions, and Jones headed to the infirmary to check on Coda.

CHAPTER 39

Thursday, May 26
White Kings Palace

JAKE LAY AWAKE ON his cot in the near-total darkness, listening to his mother's soft snore. He couldn't see the clock on the wall because it was not illuminated.

The clock in his head advised that the sun had been up for a while, but no one had turned on the lights in the basement cells to announce the new day.

It was long past breakfast time, and his stomach was complaining. Worse, he'd had no coffee, which he was sure must be a violation of the Geneva Conventions, or at least the law of the urban jungle. No sane human could function under such circumstances.

He considered making a complaint about the lack of coffee. The camera was operational again and equipped with night vision as well as listening devices.

The guards could see the cells and should hear him if he demanded room service.

For two reasons, he waited.

First, his mother appeared to be resting after their botched escape attempt. He didn't want to disturb her. The ordeal was wearing her down. She seemed to age before his eyes when they returned to the cells.

He'd tried to reassure her, but she wasn't stupid. The situation was dire, and they both knew it.

The second reason he waited to demand his breakfast was more complicated.

He'd been awakened hours earlier when two guards had manhandled a pair of men down the stairs.

The new prisoners were wearing canvas bags on their heads. They had mumbled and stumbled several times, suggesting they'd been drugged.

Both guards were armed and neither of the new hostages tried to break free. Which was another indication they'd been jabbed with some sort of chemical agent.

The guards dumped them onto the cots, turned, and marched up the stairs.

Jake heard the door click shut before they extinguished the overhead lights. Dim LED night lights provided just enough illumination in each cell to see the toilet, should the need arise in the middle of the night.

The prisoners remained still and silent and prone on their cots for hours.

Jake heard a rustling noise accompanied by the kind of whining a puppy makes from the cell on his left, the one closest to the stairs that led to the equipment room on the first floor. The scrawny guy had been dumped there.

The second man was locked in the cell on Jake's right, next to the far wall. He was taller, fitter, and better on his feet than the scrawny one, even with a bag on his head.

He imagined they were coming out of their drug-induced stupors. Very soon, they'd have all kinds of questions. Which was okay because Jake had a few questions, too.

He'd had plenty of time to think since he and Margaret had been recaptured and returned to their cell. He'd considered several potential scenarios. None of them quite fit the facts on the ground.

Except one.

He'd been turning that one over in his head for several hours when the two new prisoners arrived. At which point, he factored the prisoners into his escape strategies.

The canvas bags over their heads suggested that neither one had seen anything on the way in. Such as the exterior of the compound. They'd be no help with navigating the grounds once they all escaped.

The biggest obstacle was the electrified fence. Before Jake had surrendered at the gate, he'd examined the perimeter. Aside from the front and back gates, there was no way through the fence. Touching it was out of the question.

The fence was too high to climb over, and there were no trees or other structures to jump from to clear the barrier.

When he drove toward the compound that first night, he'd passed the last municipality fifty miles before he reached the fence and the big gate. There were no overhead power lines. Underground cables were not likely, either.

Which ruled out an electrical supply from a public or private power grid. Leaving only one viable option.

The power source for the electricity on the compound must be private generators. Jake had limited experience with generators. Back in New Hampshire, electricity was supplied by the power company. Heat was natural gas. They had gasoline backup generators at home, but they'd rarely used them.

Perhaps the compound had more than one primary diesel generator. Smaller gasoline backups could be in place for when the diesels went off-line for various reasons.

The power system had to be complicated as hell. Or at least, too complicated for Jake to figure out on the fly.

Producing power necessary to support the residences, the vehicles, the fence, and whatever operations were going on in those outbuildings back there required some expertise and a lot of fuel.

The obvious solution to the fence problem was to cut the power source for its electric supply.

Which meant identifying the generator locations and destroying the connection. Somehow.

In an operation like this, Jake figured the connection was designed to be severed manually or remotely. Which gave him three options. He ticked them off in his head.

He could find the control room and disable the generators remotely. That would be the simplest, fastest, and least dangerous solution.

The problem was locating the control room. This was a huge compound. There were at least a dozen buildings, including the residences. He could eat up too much time trying to find the central control panel.

He could locate the generator that powered the fence and flip whatever manual switch was required to shut it down in case of emergency.

A generator that size shouldn't be too hard to find. Most likely, it was installed inside or near one of those outbuildings behind the big mansion.

Problem was, he'd also need to disable the generator somehow, or they'd simply turn it back on pretty quick.

The third option was to destroy the generator. There were ways to do that. Maybe drain the oil or contaminate the fuel and let the engine burn up, which could take too long.

Or he could ignite the fumes in the fuel tank and burn up the fuel, which seemed like the most dangerous option.

A big explosion followed by a hot fire would also be the most likely way to keep all the personnel on the compound occupied and distracted long enough for the prisoners to escape.

He shook his head in the dark. He had no idea what he'd do to disable the generators when he found them. He'd have to figure it out when he got there.

Once outside the fence, his Jeep would get them the hell out of here.

Before any of that could happen, they had to escape the basement. Again.

The guards wouldn't repeat the mistake of leaving one jailer alone on duty. The backup would be in place before he came down alone.

So he'd have to neutralize two guards before he could execute plans to disable the generators.

"Where the hell am I?" the guy in the cell to Jake's right shouted. "Turn on the damned lights!"

Jake grinned. Not because the words were funny, but because he'd felt the same way the first time he'd awakened here in the dark.

"You're imprisoned in a basement cell. There are three cells. No windows. We're locked in," Jake replied, keeping his voice level and his tone as reasonable as possible. "They can see us and hear everything we say."

The guy was quiet for a moment. Then he said, "I'm John Templar. What's your name?"

"Jake Reacher. My mother's here, too. Margaret Reacher."

"And the third cell's occupant?"

A phlegmy and timid high-pitched voice emerged from the darkness. "Rupert Adams. How do we get the lights on?"

"Someone has to flip the switch," Margaret said from her cot as if she was only half awake.

"Nobody has a phone with a flashlight?" Templar said. "It's black as pitch in here. The last thing I need to do is bumble around in the dark."

Jake explained. "Your cell consists of sturdy bars, nine by twelve. Your cot is placed along the far side, opposite my voice. There's an electronic lock on the door which is near your feet. You have a small table near the door. Opposite the door is a toilet, a sink, and the bars between your cell and mine."

Adams replied shakily as if on the verge of hyperventilating, "And my cell is the same?"

"Exactly," Jake said.

"Why aren't they turning the lights on?" Adams sounded like a whiny child terrified of the dark.

"There are two men posted in a control room at the top of the stairs, which are at Adams's end of the corridor in front of our cells. Normally, they turn on the lights around six-thirty in the morning. They're running late," Jake replied. "I'm guessing they don't want to turn on the lights, or they're not there."

"AAAAHHHH!!!" Adams let out a bloodcurdling scream and shouted repeatedly, "Turn on the lights! Turn on the lights! AAAAHHHH!!!"

The noise and the words reverberated off the walls of the basement producing palpable vibrations.

Margaret waited until Adams stopped to breathe and interjected quietly. "Rupert. Can you hear me?"

He sucked air into his lungs and screamed again until he'd exhausted his air supply.

Margaret repeated her calming words again. "Rupert. It's Margaret. Can you hear me?"

Jake heard his ragged breathing wondering how long the screaming could go on before Adams did something harmful to himself.

During the brief respite, while Margaret continued trying to calm Adams, Jake raised his voice and spoke directly toward the microphone in the 360 camera.

"Turn the lights on. Adams is terrified of the dark. You don't want him to kill himself." Jake said. "If your boss wanted him dead, he would be dead already. He dies on your watch and you'll have hell to pay."

Jake had no idea whether what he said was true, but it made sense.

Another round of screaming began. This time, it was punctuated with pounding noises. Adams was hitting the bars of his cage with something harder than his fist. Jake hoped it was a shoe and not his head.

When Adams stopped to breathe, Margaret tried calming him again. She had no more success than before. Adams's screaming was impossible to tune out, but there was no escape from it.

He'd exhausted his lung capacity again and gulped great quantities of air into his mouth and nose when suddenly, the lights came on.

Just as suddenly, Adams stopped screaming.

The quiet was surreal.

Jake blinked a few times to give his eyes a chance to adjust.

He stared at Adams, who looked as freaked out as he'd sounded. His mouth was slack, and drool glistened on his chin. His hair was wildly disarranged. His eyes bulged as if he'd been attacked by an angry grizzly.

But he'd stopped screaming, and Margaret was trying to soothe him with quiet words.

Jake turned to look at Templar. He hadn't attempted to intervene with Adams at all. He was prone on his cot with his forearm covering his eyes.

Templar sat up on the cot, forearms resting on his thighs, and gave Jake a frank stare.

Jake nodded, offering a meaningful look toward the camera in return. Adams would be a liability. But Templar could be a worthy ally.

There was no way to know for sure until they could talk freely, which would be way beyond the point of no return.

Templar tilted his head toward the staircase. "What are the chances we'll get breakfast? I missed dinner and I'm starving."

CHAPTER 40

Thursday, May 26
Washington, DC

AS THEY LEFT THE Four Knights Club, Turner had been ordered to report to her CO in person and get the appropriate agencies to respond.

Which left Kim and Burke on their own.

They'd promised to meet in Turner's office at nine o'clock for a full debrief. After which they would develop a plan for going forward.

In the intervening hours, Kim had slept too little, swallowed a gallon of black coffee, and written and uploaded her reports. One report for The Boss, containing the facts and nothing more. Another longer report for her private server, including her assumptions, opinions, and conclusions.

She also called Gaspar way too early. She needed a few favors.

He yawned as if he hadn't slept at all. He probably hadn't. Whatever his injuries were, they kept him awake well into the wee hours. "How can I help you, Suzy Wong?"

"You traced Jake Reacher's Jeep for me a few weeks ago. Could you find it again now?"

"Are you sure he hasn't sold it?" Gaspar asked.

"Title transfers on motor vehicles aren't centralized. So we can't confirm quickly," Kim said. "Let's just assume he owns it and he drove it near Columbia, South Carolina, recently."

"Anybody else looking for the Jeep?"

He meant The Boss, which was feasible but unknown.

Or Finlay, who had means, motive, and opportunity. Also unknown.

Turner wouldn't have the capacity to track the electronics in Jake's vehicle, even if she wanted to. Which might be one of the things she wanted from Kim. But again, unknown.

"Safer to assume you're not the lone wolf here, Chico. But no, I don't have any direct evidence one way or the other," Kim replied.

"Okay. What else?"

She smiled. "What makes you think there's something else?"

"Hundreds of hours watching the wheels turn in your head, that's what," Gaspar replied.

His voice was louder as if he'd left his warm bed and moved to another room to avoid waking his wife.

Kim gave him a quick report of last night's events. The quick trip to Turner's office. The Four Knights Club, the helo, the two hostages, and the dead man in the back garden.

"Burke shot one of the guys from the helo." And after a long pause and a deep breath, she said, "I want to know who owns that helo. And who the pilot was. And who that passenger was."

"Because you think the passenger might have been Jack Reacher?" Gaspar said.

"Sort of depends on where that helo came from, doesn't it?" she replied. "We know Reacher and Burns were in Bethesda last night. If the helo was local, then it could have been Reacher, I guess. If the helo flew in from somewhere else, then probably not."

"I see why the details on that helo are things you need," Gaspar said. "But what's your gut say? Was it him?"

She cocked her head. She'd had plenty of time to think about the question. She'd visualized the passenger repeatedly until she could probably pick him out of a lineup. "No. Not Reacher."

"Then what's bothering you, exactly?" Gaspar asked. "The guy was armed and dangerous, and Burke did his job."

"I'm pretty sure Burke thought he *was* Reacher."

A long pause followed.

Something beeped in Gaspar's kitchen. She heard pouring noises and then his long, slurpy sip of what was probably the sweet, thick coffee *con leche* he consumed in massive quantities whenever he was awake.

"Talk to me, Suzie Wong," Gaspar said. "What are you worried about?"

"I'm worried that Burke is *trying* to kill Reacher," she replied quietly, surprised she'd mustered the will to say those words aloud, even to Gaspar.

The thought sounded insane, even to her. Burke was an FBI agent. He'd served as a SEAL. His orders were the same as hers: find Reacher and bring him in for a classified assignment. No way Burke would be *trying* to kill Reacher. Right?

But Gaspar didn't brush off the possibility. Which he would have done in a hot Miami moment if she were off base.

She waited.

Gaspar took another long moment and more slurps before he finally replied. "Did you get the NSA report you requested on Burke yet?"

"Not yet. Did you?"

"No. And that's decidedly odd. They're usually quicker," Gaspar said. "I'll ask around. Something's definitely going on here."

Which wasn't what she'd expected or wanted to hear. She'd been hoping Gaspar would say her suspicions about Burke were ridiculously, completely, absolutely, unquestionably unfounded, and she should quit being paranoid and move on.

But he didn't say any of that. He didn't even imply as much.

Her stomach churned like a blender. She pulled an antacid from her pocket, chewed it, and swallowed.

Doubting one antacid would work, she popped another into her mouth.

"Tell me about Susan Turner. Does she know anything useful?" Gaspar moved past the troubling speculation to more practical matters.

"Hard to say. We didn't learn much from her before the Four Knights free-for-all. She was ordered to get back and report when we left there. We're meeting up with her again shortly. So I guess we'll see," Kim replied.

There were dozens of things Turner knew about Reacher. Did she know where he was right this minute? Possibly.

Kim had a feeling about that, too. Her intuition said Gaspar couldn't find Reacher in DC because he was no longer here.

Reacher and Burns were spotted in Bethesda yesterday. There were more cameras around DC than perhaps any other place in the country. If they were still in the vicinity, Gaspar would have found them by now.

He hadn't.

She heard him pounding away on his keyboard. "Finding anything useful?"

"Yeah, kind of. To the extent the absence of something is worth noting," he said, keys still clacking. "Nothing's pinged on Jake's Jeep for more than twenty-four hours."

"Can you see the vehicle?"

"You mean, can I hack into government satellites to get eyes on a vehicle belonging to a private citizen where it sits at this very moment, probably on private property?" he replied flatly as if she had asked him to commit a dozen felonies.

She hadn't. At least, not directly.

"This will take a while. I'll get back to you," Gaspar said.

"Okay. I'm off to meet Burke and Turner. I'll call when I can," Kim replied.

Before he disconnected, Gaspar added one last warning. "Watch your six out there, Kim."

"Yeah," she replied and rang off.

It was the kind of thing guys said. Sort of like a mother would tell her kids to be careful.

She hoped he wasn't confirming she had something new to worry about.

After dawn, she'd called her tailor and acquired a new suit. She'd been lucky. He'd had an order for another client he altered for her quickly. She'd spent an hour with him and then hurried back to the hotel.

After a quick shower, she dressed and packed up. Burke was due any minute.

She took another glance in the mirror. The suit fit her almost as well as the one she'd ruined. She shuddered every time she thought about the price, but she had no other viable options.

"Only one choice," she muttered under her breath.

A hard rap on the door was followed by Burke's voice. "Come on. Let's go."

Kim stuffed her service weapon into its holster and slid the three phones she carried everywhere these days into her pockets.

When she opened the door, Burke gave her a quick up and down visual inspection with a smirky grin. "I kinda liked the running suit and sweatshirt combo, myself."

"Yeah, that's me. Always fashion-forward." She shook her head and pulled the door closed behind her. "Let's go. Turner's waiting."

Burke punched the up button at the elevator. "Change of plans. We're meeting her on the roof."

Kim arched her eyebrows. "Turner didn't say anything to me about a change in plans. Why?"

"She tried to call you. You didn't pick up." Burke continued snidely, "Let me guess. Talking to Gaspar?"

She shrugged but didn't deny the truth.

Burke and The Boss had made it clear that they didn't want her working with Gaspar since he had retired. Kim didn't care what they wanted on that score, and she was done arguing about it.

The elevator car arrived, they stepped inside, and with typical DC efficiency, the car sped up to the roof.

When they stepped out, Turner was waiting. "The helo's on its way. Locals went over to the Four Knights Club last night. The place had not been on their radar, but they went anyway."

"And?" Burke asked.

"No criminal activity taking place on the premises when they arrived. They didn't find anything suspicious, so they left."

Kim shook her head. "What about the dead guy in the back garden?"

"What dead guy?" Turner shook her head as the helo approached. "Someone moved the body. My questions are who moved it and when and why and where is it now?"

Kim nodded again. *And why do we care?*

"So that's the end of it?" Burke said, scowling to make his disapproval even more obvious.

Turner gave him a quick nod and turned her attention to Kim. "You don't seem surprised."

Kim shrugged. A quick clean-up like that on short notice could only have been accomplished by a fixer with the right connections in the right places. Men like that couldn't be stopped by two FBI field agents and a lone army officer.

Kim's money was on Cooper. She had shot and killed a man, and Cooper wouldn't want that intel made known. Even though the shooting was justified. Too many questions would be asked that Cooper didn't want to answer.

But this was DC. Cooper wasn't the only fixer in town. Options were thick on the ground around here.

Instead of sniffing down a dead-end, Kim asked, "Where are we going?"

"Got a solid lead on Jake and Margaret," Turner replied. "You can stay here until I get back. Or we can talk on the ride."

"We're not interested in the kid and his mom unless your lead includes Jack Reacher," Burke demanded angrily.

"That's a fair guess," Turner said, without confirming either way. "But if you have better leads, then you should chase them, of course."

Kim had dozens of unanswered questions and Turner knew a lot more than she was telling. How much of it could she be persuaded to spill?

Even if Turner were willing to share what she knew, would the intel be old and unusable? Or was she on her way to meet up with Reacher now?

The helo set down expertly on the helipad. Burke, still angry, and Turner in a hurry, took the two seats in the back.

Kim made her way to the front on the passenger side. She hated helos. Too many things could go wrong in flight, and too often, they did.

The skill of the pilot made all the difference in these death choppers.

But Turner knew something about Reacher. Unless Kim was prepared to cool her heels hanging around DC all day, she had no choice but to climb aboard.

When she opened the door and looked across at the pilot, she immediately felt better about this whole operation.

Gaspar, the one man she knew for sure she could trust no matter what, had come through for her once more.

She climbed into the passenger seat, closed the door, and secured her harness. When she donned her headset, she grinned and said, "Good to see you again, Flint."

"Heard you needed a ride," Michael Flint replied with a smile.

Briefly, she wondered what had happened to Turner's pilot. Not that she was objecting.

Burke was already peppering Turner with questions before Flint lifted the bird into the air.

Flint flipped a switch to turn off the chatter in the backseat, allowing Kim to talk privately with him. "Gaspar found something. He diverted Turner's request for a helo and sent me instead since I was already in DC."

"I see," Kim said, flashing him a thumbs-up. The instrument panel was a bewildering and intimidating display of dials and gauges. The last thing she wanted was to distract the pilot.

"He'd already located Jake's Jeep. He tracked another beacon. This one moved from the chess club to a location close to the Jeep. Close enough to walk from one to the other. He compared the beacon's trail to satellite imagery. The speed of travel suggested the beacon was generated by the helo's equipment," Flint explained quietly.

"But it wasn't?"

"No. It was inside the helo, though." Flint glanced toward her as if he wanted to be clearly understood. "The beacon wasn't inside the helo when it landed at the chess club. But it was there at takeoff. And it was still there when the helo landed at the other end of the flight."

Kim absorbed the implications.

Cargo had been unloaded from that helo at the Four Knights Club. But the only thing she'd seen loaded into it were the two hostages.

The hostages should have been stripped of all possessions before they were loaded into the helicopter. It was possible but unlikely that either hostage would have been sent out with a beacon in his pocket.

"So Gaspar thinks what, exactly?" Kim asked Flint. "That Jack Reacher climbed aboard that helo and hitched a ride to wherever it was headed?"

Flint shrugged. "It's as plausible as anything else."

"Why would Reacher do that?" Kim asked thoughtfully.

"For the same reason he does everything. Because he can."

She shook her head as if the idea of following a beacon in Reacher's pocket was appealing but too good to be true.

"Plus, Gaspar's been listening to Turner's phone calls. It's her beacon. She's the one who handed it off." Flint grinned and turned his attention to the flight.

CHAPTER 41

Thursday, May 26
White Kings Palace

AFTER THE LIGHTS CAME on, Jake had expected coffee and breakfast to be delivered. That didn't happen.

Margaret had managed to calm Adams, but he was still whimpering and curled into the fetal position on his cot.

He and Templar had been exchanging information they figured was already known to the guards. Names, occupations, and the like. Nothing sensitive.

"Any idea where we are?" Templar asked.

Jake shook his head. "A compound. In the middle of a lot of empty acres. Surrounded by an electrified fence. Nobody around. The nearest town is fifty miles away."

"Did they ever take you out of these cells for exercise or anything? Every prison in the country does that," Templar said after a while.

"Not so far." Jake understood he was turning his attention to escape plans. He jerked a thumb over his shoulder. "What do you know about Adams over there?"

"Nothing. Never saw him before in my life," Templar replied. "They loaded him onto the helo with me. That's all I know."

"Where were you before?" Jake asked.

"A chess club."

Jake cocked his head and raised both eyebrows. Before Templar had a chance to elaborate, Jake heard the electronic lock on the door at the top of the stairs click open, followed by boots on the stairs.

He smelled the coffee before Harvey, the guy Jake had subdued earlier, emerged at the bottom of the staircase. He carried a metal tray with four plastic mugs and three plastic pots.

"About damned time," Jake said loudly.

"You don't like the room service, then pay for a better hotel next time." Harvey shrugged. "And don't get any bright ideas about breaking out of here, either. I've got two backups at the top of the stairs just itching to shoot you all now and get it over with."

The threat was enough to get Adams's freak-out going again. He jumped off the cot and flattened his back against the wall of his cell. The whining noise was bubbling up from his belly.

Harvey didn't flinch. He stopped in front of Adams's cell door. The electronic lock clicked open. He put a mug and a coffee pot on the table and closed the door.

The lock clicked closed and he moved past Jake's cell to Templar's.

Jake looked at Templar, who nodded in return.

Adams's whining had started to reverberate off the metal bars. He'd ramped up into full-scale screaming again.

The noise rattled Harvey. Jake noticed his hands shaking. He set the tray on the floor, grabbed another coffee pot and a plastic mug in one hand, and stood close to Templar's door, waiting for the electronic lock to click.

Adams flung himself onto the cot and began writhing, yanking his hair with both hands. The screaming was nonstop now.

"Shut the hell up!" Harvey turned his head and screamed toward Adams, just as Templar's cell door unlocked.

Templar jumped toward the door, landing on it with his full body weight. The door slammed open and caught Harvey on the side of the head. He went down like a sack of sand, puddled on the floor along with the spilled coffee.

Templar barely paused. He ran toward the staircase and took the steps hard and fast.

Jake listened to Templar's progress as well as possible, given Adams deafening interference. He'd expected Templar to hit the steel door at the top of the stairs.

Instead, what he heard next was the release of the electronic lock on his cell. And then the electronic lock on Adams's cell.

Margaret didn't seem to grasp what had happened. She was attempting to calm Adams again and had no luck at all.

"Mom! I'll get him! Go!" Jake yelled over the noise as he grabbed Margaret and pushed her through the open cell door into the corridor.

She ran toward the stairs.

For a brief moment, Jake considered leaving Adams in the cell. They could come back for him later.

"What the hell," he said as he pulled Adams's door open, dashed inside, and pulled him out before the door could lock again.

Adams continued screaming.

"Shut up!" Jake pushed his chin up to close his mouth and shook him violently until Adams seemed to grasp that he was no longer imprisoned.

"Be quiet," Jake said. "Otherwise, I'm leaving you here. Understand?"

Adams nodded.

"Follow me up those stairs," Jake pointed and headed up.

If he didn't try to save himself, Jake would have no choice but to leave him here.

Jake reached the staircase and looked up. The door at the top was open. He took the steps two at a time and burst into the room.

The scene was surreal.

Two burly guards were down. They weren't dead, but they probably wished they were.

Their faces had been smashed by something hard and solid. Noses were busted and pulpy and bloody. Arms and wrists were broken. Legs were askew at unnatural angles.

Margaret took one look at the revolting carnage and retched.

Jake stared at Templar. "You've only been up here a few seconds."

"Sorry to say it wasn't me, man," Templar shook his head. "The guy who did this had to be huge to overpower these two. And he's a ruthless machine. The damage is massive overkill."

Jake shook his head, perplexed.

Both guards were fully functional when Harvey came downstairs. No question about it. He'd been so smug about his backup in place.

Someone had come in, taken these guys out, and opened the electronic cell door locks. All in the course of what, five minutes?

The mauled guards, the electronic locks released. Seems they had an ally on the premises. Someone who wanted to remain anonymous.

At least, for now.

But why?

"Earth to Jake," Templar said. "There's nothing in these monitors that will help us. Seems like this control room is just for the basement cells."

Jake shook off his questions about the fate of the backup guards. "Mom, you okay?"

She averted her gaze from the bloody bodies on the floor and wiped her mouth with the back of her hand. "Yeah. I'm fine."

Jake turned to Adams. His eyes were wide and his mouth slack. Jake grabbed his arm and got up close. "This place is surrounded by an electrified fence. Looks decorative, but it's one thousand percent business. Don't touch it under any circumstances. You'll die in an instant. You got that?"

Adams nodded, too horrified by the bodies on the floor and his circumstances to speak.

Templar searched the guards. He relieved the bodies of two handguns. Then he dragged them to the door at the top of the stairs and pushed them down. Their broken bodies thumped all the way to the bottom. Not that they felt it as it happened.

Templar pushed a few buttons on the control panel to secure the electronic lock on the steel door at the top of the stairs. "That'll keep them down there for a while."

Jake nodded. "Mom, can you help Adams get to the front gate?"

"Yeah. I can do that," she replied.

"You were with me last time. You know what to do. Cameras are everywhere, so try to stay in the shadows as much as you can."

"Okay."

"When the gate opens, run through it and hide in the woods until I get there. Okay?"

Her eyes widened and she gasped. "Okay."

Adams had begun to whine again. Quieter, but still audible.

"And if Adams starts to freak out or doesn't follow you, leave him. He's on his own. Got it?"

Adams swallowed hard and pursed his lips together.

Margaret nodded as if she understood, but Jake didn't think she'd leave Adams to fend for himself regardless. He had to hope she wouldn't have to.

He couldn't be everywhere at once. And if they couldn't get the electric charge on the fence disabled, they wouldn't be going anywhere anyway.

"Harvey will be stuck down there until someone lets him out," Templar said, handing Jake one of the two pistols he'd retrieved from the guards. "How do we get out of here?"

Jake figured Harvey must have been armed, too, before he came downstairs. He might have left his weapon in the control room.

Jake glanced around the room and spied the third handgun on one of the tables. He handed it to his mother. He already knew she could use it. "If anybody tries to mess with you, shoot to kill. Understand?"

She took the gun and nodded again.

"We need to turn off the fence. Templar and I will handle that. You and Adams get to the front gate and be ready to run. Get out the first time you have the chance. We'll find you as soon as we can," Jake summarized one last time.

Jake gave her a quick squeeze and a kiss on the head.

He'd done all he could for the moment.

He approached the exit door and turned to say, "Follow me as quietly and quickly as you can. When we get outside, Mom and Adams go left toward the gate. Templar, we'll turn right and head to the back of the compound."

All three murmured agreement.

Templar said, "Keep your weapons ready. Fire first, ask questions later."

Jake took a deep breath, turned the doorknob, and said, "Okay. Let's go."

CHAPTER 42

Thursday, May 26
White Kings Palace

THE LOCK ON THE exit door to the verandah had not been repaired. When Jake reached the door, he muscled it open and stood aside to let the others run out and down the stairs to the driveway.

Margaret grabbed Adams by the arm and pulled him toward the front of the compound.

Watching her go filled Jake with dread. He wished he had another option.

Templar came through the door last and hustled down the stairs.

Jake followed quickly behind. At the bottom, he gestured to the visible cameras mounted on the building and the fence across the driveway. Templar nodded.

Jake retraced the route he'd taken before. Templar followed.

When they reached the back of the huge mansion at the base of the U-shaped cluster of homes, he flattened his back against the wall.

Templar did the same.

"This is where they picked us up last time. They can see us standing here. We've got to move," Jake said quickly, pointing across the open space ahead. "There's a series of outbuildings back there. Another gravel drive between here and the outbuildings. And a helipad somewhere close by."

"How many outbuildings?" Templar asked.

"Dunno." Jake shrugged. "We're looking for a commercial-sized diesel generator. Maybe two. Backup generators for each of the residences and the fence. There's also got to be fuel storage tanks of some sort."

"Any idea how many men they have to defend this place?" Templar asked.

Jake grinned. "At least five fewer than they had on Tuesday."

Templar nodded, returning the smile. "There's gotta be a control room somewhere. We could cut the power from there. Destroy the electronics to keep them from restarting quickly."

"Yeah, but where?" Jake replied. "The easiest thing to do is find the big generator and disable it. Generators make a lot of noise. We'll hear it running. There will be backup generators. Probably gasoline or propane engines. But only one of them will power the fence, most likely."

Templar nodded slowly like he was thinking about it. "When we get past the fence, then what?"

"I've got a Jeep. We'll drive away from here like the hounds of Hell were chasing us," Jake replied.

"This building we're leaning against is the largest of the residences. The control room is probably in there," Templar said as if he was getting himself up to speed. "But you're right. We don't have time to search for it. This place must have thirty rooms, at least. Let's find that big generator."

"First, we have to get across that open driveway. I'll go. Cover me," Jake said and ran full out, zigzagging across the open spaces until he reached the first of the outbuildings.

Then he turned and waited for Templar.

"Why didn't they shoot?" Templar asked when he made it safely across. "We were easy targets coming across there."

"Maybe they're taking a nap," Jake replied, pointing. "These first two outbuildings over there are the smallest. Could be used for food supplies."

Templar said, "They probably keep all the fuel in one place. Most likely in a large above-ground tank."

Jake pointed toward the back gate. "We need to get back there, closer to the helipad where they'd refuel the bird."

"Let's go," Templar said, crouching low and taking the lead this time as he ran toward the back of the compound.

Before they reached the cover of the next building, shots rang out. It sounded like one shooter. For now.

Templar ducked around the corner and fired back. He might have hit the shooter because the bullets stopped for the moment.

Jake ran to Templar's position.

From this vantage point, Jake saw pre-engineered gray heavy-duty steel buildings installed on concrete pads between the residences and the back gate.

On one side of the gravel drive were two twenty-by-twenty buildings, each with one with a thirty-six-inch walk-in steel entrance door.

The third building was significantly larger and set apart on the opposite side of the gravel drive. Back home in New Hampshire, Jake had seen similar buildings used for farming equipment. Equipment needed fuel, too.

This one was thirty-by-forty. It had three roll-up doors, each ten-by-ten. There was a walk-in door on the side. One of the roll-up doors was open. From this distance, Jake saw supplies of all sorts piled inside.

Outside the building was a large commercial diesel generator.

The diesel fuel storage tank to feed the generator was probably close by. It could be underground. But above ground was better and newer, and the buildings all looked fairly new back here.

Even from a distance, Jake heard the generator running. For a generator, it was quiet enough. But the noise was unmistakable.

"You're army, right?" Templar jabbed a thumb toward his chest. "Navy. I've had a fair amount of experience with diesel engines. Let me take this one."

Jake nodded. "What are you going to do?"

"I'll figure it out when I get there. There's at least one emergency stop button somewhere on the system. I'll find it and turn the system off," Templar said. "That'll give us an immediate power failure."

"The backups will kick in, and then they'll turn the big unit back on before we can get out of the gate," Jake said, shaking his head. "We need a bigger, longer distraction."

"Yeah. Well, find me enough gas to pour into the fuel tank, and I can give you a monstrous explosion." Templar grinned. "Or a fuel leak could cause it to overheat and flip off on its own. It might generate enough fumes for an ignition source to create an explosion. We'd want to ignite it from a distance, though," Templar said, thinking things through. "Find the gas and something to light it with, if you can. Then leave it to me."

"I'll find the standby systems," Jake said.

"They're probably propane or diesel-powered, too. So they'd be located near smaller fuel tanks similar to this one," Templar replied. "And not too far away, either. Easier to refuel when needed if they're as close together as feasible."

Jake heard shouting around the residences behind them. The shooter Templar had engaged must have called for backup. "They're headed our way. I'll look for ammo while I'm looking for gas and a torch of some kind. But we gotta move."

"This is where it would help to know how many guys they've got here," Templar said. "More than fifty?"

"One of the jailers, Harvey, said they were short-staffed and working around the clock doing whatever they're doing," Jake replied. "No clue what that means. But we need more ammo, for sure."

"Okay," Templar said and checked the magazine in his pistol. "Maybe whoever took out those guards in the control room at the jail is still around and on our side."

"We could use the help, for sure. Anyway, inside that building next to the generator I see four-wheelers and gasoline cans. You get the diesel generator. I'll grab the gas and handle the standbys," Jake replied. "And I'll hold these guys off as long as I can."

"Got it." Templar nodded. "Let's do this now before they're close enough to stop us."

As Templar crouched low and headed forward, Jake said, "Don't blow yourself up."

Templar grinned. "Right back atcha."

CHAPTER 43

Thursday, May 26
White Kings Palace

JONES WAS ON HIS way to the infirmary to check on Coda when he heard the unmistakable report of gunshots from the open space out back.

"What the hell?"

He turned on his heel and dashed down to the first floor, past the chess tournament rooms, and toward the exit.

Unlike a military base where personal weapons are forbidden, White Kings were always armed while on duty. Precautionary measures.

Patton was a careful man.

And every White King appreciated it.

No one had ever come over the fence alive. Patton had insisted that there should never be a first time. But if it ever happened, the White Kings were prepared.

Sanz had a crew of twenty to thirty men and women working to process the product. They were technicians he'd brought from

Spain. They'd be useless in a firefight. They'd been sent to their quarters before Sanz left in the helo for Texas.

Jones hoped they stayed inside until this was over. He didn't need civilians running foolishly into the line of fire. Patton would be pissed for sure.

The compound's standard security forces were a thin crew of fifteen skilled veterans who reported to Jones and Coda. They'd been hand-selected and approved by Patton.

These were not normal times.

In the past few days, they'd lost three men. Rudy to the overdose, Smitty at the hands of Margaret Reacher, and Manny. Jones was still unclear on what had happened there.

Coda and one of the jailers were in the infirmary. Coda was shot in DC and Jake Reacher had attacked the jailer.

This left a functioning ten-man security unit, plus Jones, assuming the three at the jail now, Harvey, Kenyon, and Mack, were all okay. But the short hairs raised on the back of his neck told him they were far from okay.

Which meant the security team could be down to seven, plus Jones.

He'd bet his seven-man crew against anybody, but he'd rather have a full fifteen.

Jones took a breath, readied his handgun, and pushed through the exit door to the grounds. He scanned the area quickly to assess the threat.

One of the White Kings was standing near the gravel driveway with his weapon still drawn. As Jones approached, Davis glanced over his shoulder.

Davis said, "Two men, running toward the back gate."

"Not two of ours, right?"

"Ours wouldn't shoot back, would they?"

The remaining members of the White Kings security team were emerging from their stations. "What good will it do them to reach the back gate? They can't get out. If they touch it, they'll be dead before we find them."

Jones nodded to acknowledge the valid observations and then ordered, "You two, get over to the jail. Make sure everything's secure. Radio when you get there. Confirm the hostages are squared away and then secure the front gate."

"You got it, Boss," one said as the others readied their weapons and headed toward the cells.

To the rest, Jones said, "Fan out. There's two of them and six of us. They're armed and they're shooting back. Shoot first. Don't give them a chance to kill you."

Davis said, "They're hostages. What value do they have if they're dead?"

Jones replied, "You let me worry about that."

Four White Kings acknowledged their orders. Two went left, two went right, moving around the outbuildings between the residences and the back gate.

Jones and Davis followed the same path the fugitives had taken along the driveway toward the back gate. They reached the first of the pre-engineered steel buildings and heard one of the four-wheeled off-road vehicles fire up in the big barn near the helipad.

Davis said, "Guess we know where they are now."

Jones replied, "Yeah. But what the hell do they think they're doing?"

The radio signaled and one of the guards said, "White King One, this is White King Four. We're at the cells. We've got three men down. The hostages have escaped."

Jones swore and pressed the talk key. "How the hell did that happen?"

"Can't say. They are in bad shape."

"How bad?"

"Not sure they'll make it. We need to get them to the infirmary."

"Call Coda. Get him out here. He can relax on that bum leg later. We need the extra firepower," Jones ordered.

The conversation was cut short by gunfire from Jones's left. He counted four shots total. One of the ORVs was revved up and on the move, too.

Davis's radio signaled. "White King Three, this is White King Six. Man down. Hit by a bullet from one of the fugitives."

Davis gave Jones a questioning glance. Jones shook his head. Davis clicked the radio and replied. "We'll pick him up. You stay on mission. Copy that?"

No response.

Davis tried to reach White King Six again for confirmation.

No response.

"Both those guys might be down now," Davis said to Jones.

Jones grabbed the radio and called "White King Two, this is White King One."

"Copy that," Coda had picked up. "I've been listening. On my way."

Above the noise of the ORV, Jones heard the unmistakable sound of a helicopter approaching. The compound's remote location kept it out of the flight path for aircraft of all types, except those owned by the White Kings.

Sanz was still on his way to Texas in the Bell. Repairs to the cargo doors would take a while. The Bell wouldn't be back this soon.

"What the hell is going on here?" Jones swore and glared at Davis.

The ORV roared around the corner, heading toward the second pair of White Kings.

Jones stared. The driver could have been Jack Reacher.

But it was more likely the kid.

Maybe it was Jack Reacher. His presence would explain what happened to three of his best guys at the cells. Reacher surprised them and took all three out before they had a chance.

The more he thought about it, the more likely his guess seemed. He'd seen Reacher fight six guys at once and send four to the hospital and two to the morgue.

Reacher. Inside the compound.

Patton's orders had been clear. Kill Jack Reacher. All collateral damage was acceptable.

Jones had been dubious about the plan to lure Reacher here by kidnapping his nephew. Coda had insisted the plan would never work. Jones had had his doubts.

Patton said the plan was worth trying. It seemed like he'd been right. Again.

But was Jack Reacher really here?

Could Jones possibly be that lucky?

He smirked. Sure. Why not?

Jones and Coda could easily find Reacher inside the fence and blow him away. Jones made the radio call to Coda and headed toward the front gate.

CHAPTER 44

Thursday, May 26
White Kings Palace

KIM WATCHED THE TWO beacons on the small screen in the dash of the helo. The one representing the Jeep was green and stationary. The red beacon moved in bursts and pauses. As if it was darting from one place to the next with a break between spurts.

Briefly, she wondered whether Cooper and Finlay were paying attention at the moment. Cooper watched her constantly, but not always in real-time. If they got into serious trouble out here, would he send reinforcements?

"We're close. Another ten minutes, and we'll be able to see conditions on the ground." Flint's voice came through the headset. "Turner, you still want a flyover before we land?"

"Yes. I'd like to know what we're getting into." Turner's voice came from the backseat. "We have satellite views from this morning. But nothing current."

Flint pointed to another screen, this one above the helo's instrument panel and also visible to passengers in the back. The screen appeared to show current satellite images of a large compound. The likely source was Gaspar, but Kim didn't ask how he'd accessed them.

"Property records list the owner as The White Kings Chess Club. Bought the existing property from a bankruptcy and then made modifications," Turner said. "No permits were pulled, so we're not sure exactly what they've built out there. But the outbuildings and fuel tanks were added by the new owners."

"Who knew chess clubs were so popular?" Kim replied snidely. "I gather this is some sort of drug-running operation connected to the Four Knights Club."

"We think so," Turner said. "Makes sense that the two are related. The helo was probably delivering product in DC and then came back for restocking."

"How many members of the White Kings are down there?" Kim asked.

"We don't know for sure. The operation includes manufacturing and shipping to other locations. So they could have a dozen or more," Turner said. "And they've got a security team of battle-tested vets. All as well trained as Uncle Sam can turn out."

"In which case, there will be plenty of firepower on the ground. In addition to Reacher," Burke replied. "If he's down there."

Turner didn't confirm or deny. Which could mean that she didn't know.

"Sounds like a job for drug enforcement," Kim said. "Did you call DEA?"

"We will. Soon as we rescue Jake and his mother," Turner replied. "DEA would come in with an army of agents. Bullets flying everywhere. Bodies on the ground. No way we'd be able to extricate Jake from all that in time for him to report to Fort Benning, even if he survived the battle."

"What's so special about this kid?" Burke complained. "Nobody acted as my guardian angel when I was in the navy. Hell, the FBI doesn't protect me like that now. Is this some sort of an army thing?"

Turner said nothing. Kim figured rescuing Jake was less an army thing than a Reacher thing. Turner felt obligated to Jake.

Or his uncle.

Or both.

The question was why. And the reason was probably anchored to whatever happened between Turner and Reacher seven years ago.

The images on the screen showed the compound located in a rectangular clearing surrounded by forest. Beyond the clearing was a runway long enough for a private jet. There was a helipad closer to the interior.

Kim identified seven large rooftops near the front and smaller rooftops near the helipad. The entire compound was surrounded by a decorative fence similar to the one surrounding Buckingham Palace.

This fence wasn't as ornate, but the concept was the same.

Twelve-foot vertical spires placed six inches apart were topped with finials. Horizontal members ran along the top and the bottom to anchor the spires. The fence appeared to be wrought iron.

At each end of the rectangle, an elaborate gate crossed the driveway.

The overall effect was regal. Visitors could see between the spires, but the fence operated as an effective barrier to keep trespassers out.

"Getting over that fence won't be easy. And we'll be sitting ducks while we try." Turner's voice came through the headset. "Can we set down inside?"

Flint said. "There's an unoccupied helipad in the back. The Bell you chased out of DC last night came here, but it's gone now."

"I'd rather not be blown out of the sky before we land if you don't mind," Burke said, annoyed. "Plenty of places they can shoot us down from near that helipad. Is there another option?"

"It's not like we're gonna surprise anyone when we arrive in a helo," Turner replied, annoyed. "They can just run to wherever we land and take us down if they want."

"We need clearance of sixty feet on all sides," Flint said. "Do you see anything like that?"

"How about the front lawn inside the residential area?" Burke replied. "Plenty of room."

Kim continued watching the screen with the red beacon, which was hanging near the outbuildings at the back of the property. The red dot seemed to move in quick spurts with long pauses between.

If Reacher had that beacon in his pocket, what the hell was he doing?

Flint began the descent.

Kim leaned over, peering forward. "There. Behind the smaller outbuildings along the driveway. I count four armed men, two on each side."

"Two more armed men near the fuel tanks. One of them is big enough to be Reacher," Burke said, "Let's get this bird on the ground."

Kim looked at the red beacon and then toward the compound. She matched the beacon with its location, but she couldn't see the man or confirm that he had the beacon on him.

Turner had her phone out. She peered at the screen as if she might have located the red beacon, too. "Looks like they're near the fuel tanks. Way in the back."

Flint landed the helo as gently as possible.

Turner opened her door and jumped to the ground before the rotors stopped and ran toward the back gate.

Burke filed out next, weapon drawn, running through the gap in the residences and on toward the outbuildings, making a beeline for the red beacon.

Kim climbed out and turned to shout toward Flint. "Are you coming?"

He nodded, attention focused on his instruments. "I'll be right behind you."

CHAPTER 45

Thursday, May 26
White Kings Palace

JAKE HAD DUCKED INSIDE the biggest of the barns. Quickly, he located three full red plastic gas cans. Five gallons each. He set them into the cargo bed of one of the ORVs.

He ran back and rummaged through two workbenches until he found four long-nosed propane lighters and jammed them into his pocket.

He wasted a few more minutes searching for ammo. He didn't find it.

When he heard the unmistakable noise of a helo landing, followed by gunshots close by, he cut his search short.

He hopped into the ORV, fired it up, and revved in reverse out of the big roll-up door.

As soon as he emerged into the daylight, he became a moving target.

The first shot missed his head by no more than three inches. He raised his pistol and fired back as he floored the gas, speeding forward toward Templar's last known location near the big generator.

He expected more incoming fire but heard none.

When he reached the generator, he turned the steering wheel sharply and curved around to the back of the big yellow power machine.

Templar climbed out from under the generator on the far end. He rolled along the gravel, raised his handgun and fired two shots at a target beyond Jake's seat in the ORV.

Jake turned to look, weapon ready, but the shooter had ducked behind one of the buildings.

Quickly, Jake jumped out of the vehicle, grabbed two of the plastic gas cans, and rushed them toward Templar.

"Is that the Bell from last night coming back?" Templar asked.

"I don't know. Why wouldn't it land back here on the helipad?" Jake dropped two of the propane lighters on the ground.

"Could be reinforcements. We need to hurry," Templar said. "Did you find the backup generator for the fence?"

"Not yet. We'll look for that next. It's probably nearby," Jake said, as another shot came from the same general direction as the previous one. "Assuming we don't get killed first."

"Can you hold them off while I get a can of gas into the generator's fuel tank? The heat of the engine should be enough to ignite the rest of the diesel once the gas gets things going," Templar said. "Then we'll trail another can of it a fair distance away from the leak in the fuel line and ignite it."

Jake stared at him. "And then what?"

"Then we get the hell out of here," Templar grinned and went to work.

A shooter stepped out from the corner of the building and fired again. Jake spun around and returned fire.

Jake's bullets hit the mark.

The shooter went down.

A second shooter picked up the attack and fired from behind another corner of the building.

Jake crouched low near the driver's side of the ORV, returning fire after every third round to conserve ammo.

Templar hurried toward the ORV, trailing a line of gasoline in the gravel from the second plastic can. When he reached the ORV, he jumped into the passenger seat.

Jake shot toward the second man, who ducked behind the building again.

Jake jumped into the ORV. "Ready?"

Templar pulled the trigger on the lighter and pushed the lever to hold the flame.

He tossed it onto the gasoline trail he'd laid on the gravel.

"Go, Go, Go!" Templar shouted.

Jake floored the pedal. The ORV sped away from the generator as fast as it would travel along the gravel drive between the outbuildings.

Two sets of shooters were firing bullets toward Jake and Templar as the flaming gas rushed toward the generator's fuel leak, and the ORV sped away as fast as it could go.

"How long will it take—" Jake managed to shout before the generator's massive explosion drowned out all other noises, including the approaching helo.

The first explosion was followed by at least three smaller ones.

"Did we cut the power to the fence?" Templar shouted over the din.

Jake shrugged, keeping his eye on the driveway ahead.

Another ORV revved up somewhere out of sight on his right.

The helo should have arrived at the helipad before the explosion, but it must have set down somewhere else instead.

Where was the standby generator for the fence? It should be somewhere close by. He hoped.

Templar dropped his handgun on the floor of the ORV and bent to retrieve it while Jake raced the ORV away from the explosion's heat.

Smaller explosions followed at irregular intervals.

Jake mentally crossed his fingers that one of them was the standby generator for the electrified front gate.

If not, maybe the electrified back gate was now offline.

He'd figure it out.

He had to.

"On my way, Mom," he muttered under his breath, watching all sides of the driveway as he floored the ORV, full speed ahead.

Jake didn't see the man who stepped out from behind one of the buildings until it was too late.

In one well-practiced fluid movement, the man settled into a solid shooter's stance and took aim directly at Jake.

CHAPTER 46

KIM DREW HER WEAPON and ran between the residences close behind Burke and Turner. They'd covered less than a hundred yards when a massive explosion from the back of the property shook the ground and sent hot flames into the air.

The first explosion sent the trio to the ground. They lay flat out, covering their heads to avoid flying debris.

The stench of petroleum assaulted her senses. Kim breathed evenly through her mouth, attempting to keep air moving freely through her body. She counted six smaller explosions following the first. The smoke stung her eyes, causing them to water and making it difficult to see clearly.

Burke hopped up and ran toward the blasts. Turner veered left. Kim followed Burke.

Kim was a trained runner, and Burke wasn't back to full capacity yet. But he had a significant head start. She gained ground as she followed, but he held the lead.

When the roar of the explosions subsided, Kim heard another loud noise. An engine of some kind headed toward them.

She rounded the back corner of the largest residence. Straight ahead was a gravel drive that circled behind the seven residences and led to the outbuildings and the rear exit gate.

Headed along the drive was an off-road vehicle running full out. Occupied by the driver alone, the ORV sped toward the front gate.

Kim blinked to clear her vision. The driver was a hulking big man. Six feet five, and two hundred fifty pounds at least. Fair hair. Hands gripping the steering wheel were as big as catcher's mitts.

Everything about the driver looked like Reacher.

Was that Jake?

Or Jack?

Burke had seen the ORV and the driver, too. He dashed to the edge of the drive and stood in a shooter's stance, waiting until the ORV was within unmistakable range and aiming directly at the driver.

"Burke! Stop!" Kim yelled. "Don't shoot!"

Whether he heard or not, her partner's aim was set and he didn't waver.

Turner must have heard the ORV, too. She came into view on the other side of the drive where she had to see Burke's actions.

"Burke! No!"

Kim sped up, closing the distance between her and her partner. She yelled ahead, ordering him to stand down. Twice.

Burke didn't waver.

He shouted back, making his intentions clear. "It's Reacher!"

Kim looked at the driver again. She couldn't get a positive ID. Burke could be right. The driver could be Reacher.

The gap between Burke and the ORV narrowed.

Turner ran toward Burke from the opposite direction.

Kim's vision seemed to clear and sharpen. She pushed through the smoke and the noise and the fear that roiled her belly and quickened her heartbeat.

Shots rang out from two different directions.

One man seemed to pop into the ORV's passenger seat from somewhere.

He fired back.

More gunfire was exchanged, and the passenger fell back into the ORV, below Kim's sightline.

A big man Kim had not seen before stepped out from the cover of one of the smaller outbuildings.

Her sightline wasn't perfect. Too much interference between her and him. Was her mind playing tricks on her, or was that Reacher?

Now there were three men shooting toward the ORV, two from the cover of nearby outbuildings and Burke from the opposite side of the gravel driveway.

Burke moved slightly, prepared to fire directly at the ORV driver.

He held steady, awaiting the perfect moment.

Breathing hard and fast, Kim ran flat out toward Burke to stop him.

Time seemed to slow, and events merged together like a languid dance.

Burke's lazy pull of the trigger sent four heavy shots in lethargic succession.

The ORV moved sluggishly past Burke's position as if the driver were bulletproof.

The big man near the outbuilding raised his weapon, aimed at Burke, and fired with dead-on accuracy.

The two shooters near the next outbuilding fired off several bullets each, and all pointed toward the ORV and Burke.

Kim tackled her partner to the ground.

Burke had already begun to fall before she reached him.

She was too late.

His lifeless body, eyes open, heart still, landed hard with Kim on top of him.

Her partner was dead.

His killers were still free.

Kim rolled off to one side, raised her gun, and returned fire. She hit both shooters with three bullets, center mass. For Burke.

They were both dead before they hit the ground, just like Burke.

The speed of the world returned to normal.

Kim touched Burke's carotid pulse to confirm. He was gone. Her perfunctory reflex was unnecessary.

Burke's body was riddled with at least six bullet holes.

The kill shot was the first one. Fired by the big man with precision, it had slammed through Burke's chest and his heart. Death was close to instantaneous.

The other bullets fired by less accurate marksmen were wasted, although they had also hit the target.

She could not save her partner.

Kim turned her attention to the big man, but he was no longer there. He had disappeared. For now.

Turner ran up and offered Kim a hand. "Come on!"

She scrambled to her feet and followed Turner to cover behind a huge tree close to the largest residence.

They waited a few moments, breathing hard.

"Why did Burke shoot at Jake?" Turner asked.

Kim shook her head, bewildered.

Burke had tried to kill the ORV driver. Did he know he was aiming at Jake? Or did he think the driver was Jack Reacher?

Either way, Burke's actions were inexcusable. He'd gone rogue again.

And this time, he'd paid for it with his life.

A thousand thoughts ran through Kim's head at lightning speed. But they all boiled down to one illogical thing.

Burke's death was her fault.

He was her number two. Her partner. She was responsible for him. She owed him. Simple as that.

Loss and failure overwhelmed her, even as she knew her guilt was misplaced.

Kim hadn't killed Burke even though she had failed to stop the man who did.

She wasn't the first field agent to lose a partner to enemy combatants, and she wouldn't be the last.

The sound of gunfire near the front of the compound penetrated the thick fog of her thinking and reached Kim's ears.

The gun battle had merely paused. It wasn't over yet.

"Hear that? Jake and Margaret are still in trouble." Turner shook Kim's shoulder. "Come on. Let's go."

Kim nodded, weapon drawn. She crouched low and led Turner along the path of the ORV toward the melee at the front gate.

CHAPTER 47

Thursday, May 26
White Kings Palace

"TEMPLAR! ARE YOU OKAY?" Jake shouted into the wind as he drove the ORV like a madman toward the front gate. Gunfire had erupted there.

Templar was hit. He'd fallen back into his seat. Jake couldn't stop to help him amid the gunfire. They'd made that deal on the front end.

Templar, face ashen, waved Jake's concerns away. Blood bloomed through his shirt on his left shoulder. He slapped a palm over the wound, attempting to stop the blood, but the bouncing ORV made his effort useless.

Jake took the corner at the end of the gravel driveway too fast. He grabbed the steering wheel to stay in his seat. Templar barely remained upright.

As they sped past, he saw the empty helo sitting in the middle of the big green lawn between the front gate and the residences. Too bad he had no idea how to pilot one of those birds.

The scene at the front gate was chaotic.

Margaret and Adams were hunkered down too close to the exit near the right side of the gate behind a large boulder. There was very little available cover to protect them.

A man Jake had never seen before stood with them, armed and firing back.

On the left side of the gate were four White Kings.

Jake recognized Jones and Coda. The other two were unknown faces.

The four huddled together using two more ORVs for cover, shooting toward Margaret and her protector.

Jake drove the ORV between the combatants to offer Margaret and her unit of three some cover. He couldn't see her well because she was face down on the gravel. But she was still alive.

Jake shoved Templar off the passenger seat onto the gravel drive. The man ducked out from behind the boulder and helped Templar down the embankment out of the line of fire.

Then Jake hopped out of the driver's seat and dashed around the back toward his mother. He scrambled down on the gravel into the ditch.

He took a quick moment to hug Margaret before he assessed the situation.

Adams crouched like a schoolboy hiding under his desk. He'd covered his head with both arms as if that might protect him from speeding bullets.

He was simultaneously babbling and crying, while Margaret tried to comfort him and keep him under control.

"I'm Jake Reacher," he said to Margaret's protector.

"Michael Flint," the man replied, handing Jake another pistol. "Bad news is, there's four of them, all shooting this way."

Jake nodded. "There's good news?"

Flint grinned. "They're lousy shots."

"Right. Well, even a blind pig finds a truffle sooner or later. We can't wait for them to run out of ammo," Jake replied.

Templar grimaced with pain. The blood on his shirt had spread during the final, bumpy sprint in the ORV.

"You don't look good, man," Flint said.

"The only easy day was yesterday," Templar replied. "Did we cut the power to the fence?"

Flint said, "Mission accomplished. A squirrel bounced along the bottom unharmed a few minutes ago. The gate is no longer energized."

Templar replied, "So why aren't you out there instead of still in here?"

"We haven't been able to get past the sentinels over there to push the gate open," Flint replied, handing Templar a gun, too, just in case he had the need to use it and the ability to do so.

Jake nodded. "There's four of them. Two I recognize as the bosses around here. One of them is wounded. And the other two I don't know."

Flint said, "Copy that. Can you cover me while I open the gate?"

"Yeah," Jake replied. "Tell me when you're ready."

"No time like the present," Flint said as he crouched low and pulled an M-67 grenade from his pocket. He showed the grenade to Jake. "We need to even the odds here."

"You just happen to carry those around in your pocket?" Jake said with a smile.

"I was a Boy Scout. Be prepared and all that," Flint replied. "I'll toss this into their nest, on the side of the gate. I'll warn them and give them a few seconds' notice before the blast. They'll run the other way. You two can pick them off. Or at least some of them."

"That'll work. But let me take the gate. I've been through the gate before. I know how it moves." Jake turned to the others. "Stay down until Flint gives you the all-clear. Cover your heads. Got it?"

Margaret and Adams nodded.

Templar said, "I know the drill."

"Here we go." Flint looked each one in the eye and waited for a nod of comprehension.

He yanked the pin and tossed the grenade across the driveway into the shooter's nest.

He yelled, "Frag out!"

Everybody hit the deck.

The grenade exploded slightly less than five long seconds later.

The explosion was loud but somewhat muffled. Almost like one of the White Kings had thrown his body over the grenade but didn't quite cover it completely.

Then Jake ran like hell away from the blast and toward the gate.

Jake laid his shoulder along the gate's edge and shoved hard to open it from a squatting position, using his full strength to force the heavy iron along the track.

He kept his focus on the job even as the gunshots resumed.

CHAPTER 48

Thursday, May 26
White Kings Palace

KIM RAN TOWARD THE gunfire. She hurried along the gravel driveway near the residences until she reached the corner of the building closest to the front gate. Turner was right behind her.

She flattened her back against the wall and turtled her head around the corner to see the situation.

Turner ducked out to look, too.

The ORV had arrived and stopped in the middle of the wide gravel drive near the front gate. A second ORV was across from the first.

Men behind each of the vehicles exchanged bullets.

Kim saw an M67 frag grenade lobbed from behind the ORV closest to the gate. and someone yelled "Frag out!" just before it landed behind the opposite ORV.

"That's got to be Flint," Kim said to Turner as she flattened her back against the wall again.

"He's flushing them out," Turner said. "Three one thousand, four one thousand."

Three men dashed from behind the ORV. One was limping. Probably the one Burke shot at the helo in DC.

Flint poked up from behind the ORV and shot him moments before the blast. The grenade fragments did the rest.

Kim jerked her head back behind the wall. The sound of the blast was strangely muffled.

"I've heard that sound before. More than once. In combat," Turner said breathlessly. "Sounds like some idiot threw himself on that grenade. But he did it badly."

"Could he have survived?"

"Not likely," Turner replied.

The remaining two White Kings continued to dash across open ground.

Flint raised up to shoot.

Before he got the chance, shots came from another direction. Two shots. Two men down.

Jake had the gate open wide enough to walk through. He signaled to Margaret and Adams. Margaret grabbed his arm and pulled him along as she ran to the outside.

Jake went back for Templar, who had lost a lot of blood, but he was still vertical and able to walk leaning on Jake.

When all four were beyond the gate, they disappeared into the woods, likely headed toward Jake's Jeep.

The gunshots had stopped.

Kim and Turner were a long, open distance from the residence to the front gate.

Kim scanned the area. Dozens of possible sniper nests overlooked the dead bodies near the two ORVs in the driveway.

The longer the cease-fire continued, the less likely, it seemed, it would resume.

Kim sensed it might be safe enough to cross the open space.

Turner was peering toward the rooftops and the porches and into the gaps between the buildings. Both women kept all five senses alert.

Locating no further threats, Kim was ready to cross. But The Boss's burner phone vibrated in her pocket before she had the chance.

"Otto," she said when she answered.

"We don't know how many White Kings were onsite when you landed. Infrared body heat cameras suggest at least two dozen are still there. All located in the biggest mansion opposite the front gate," Cooper said. "They could have come out to join the fight any time. But they didn't."

"So you're saying we've eliminated the threat here, then?" Kim asked.

"Possibly," Cooper replied. "Reinforcements are on the way from Fort Jackson. They've got DEA onboard. Maybe fifteen minutes out. You and Flint need to be out of there before they arrive."

"How'd you manage that?" Kim asked, making no effort to hide her annoyance. "And why didn't you send help sooner? Burke might still be alive if we'd had a little help down here."

"If you're blaming yourself for Burke, don't. You could not have saved him even with a dozen backup agents," Cooper sighed. "Burke was on the path to self-destruction long before you met him."

"My partner is *dead*. How am I supposed to live with that?" Kim demanded, her anger barely controlled.

"Not everything is about you, Otto. You should have learned that long before now." Cooper paused briefly to respond to a question from someone else in the room with him. "I didn't say I sent reinforcements and DEA. I said they were on the way. And I have no idea why they didn't arrive sooner."

"If you didn't send them, then who did?" Kim demanded, irritated with his refusal to speak plainly.

"My guess? Lieutenant Colonel Susan Turner. Why don't you ask her? And then get the hell out of there. Unless you want to be tied up by the DEA and the DoD for the next five years." Cooper hung up before she had a chance to ask him about Reacher.

Kim heard the distant whap-whap-whap of helicopter rotors approaching.

Turner looked up toward the noise, seeming not the least surprised.

"Turns out there's twenty-four or more live bodies in the big residence building," Kim said as she dropped the phone back into her pocket. "They're probably not on their way out here to kill us. But we'll know for sure in about five minutes when your reinforcements arrive."

Turner nodded. "I should have told you they were on the way. If I'd known Burke was going to get himself killed, I would have."

"Meaning you didn't trust Burke?"

"Not even a little bit." Turner frowned. "Don't tell me you trusted him, either. You're smarter than that."

"So all this was what? Some sort of test for Jake Reacher?" Kim frowned. "Some army bullshit to prove he's career officer material?"

"Not at all. I told you I wanted to save Jake's career. That was all true," Turner replied, shaking her head. "I had no way of knowing he'd get himself into a war with the White Kings before we had a chance to pick him up."

"So you're saying this all had nothing to do with Jack Reacher." Kim cocked her head and looked Turner in the eyes. "He's not here, on this compound. He didn't get on that helo and lead you here with that red beacon in his pocket. You haven't seen him, haven't talked to him, and don't know where he is. That about the size of it?"

Turner raised her right hand, palm out. "I swear, I don't know where Jack Reacher is."

The two big helos from Fort Jackson were hovering overhead. One set down on the helipad in the back of the compound. The other was searching for an open space large enough to land the big bird.

Kim didn't believe Turner for a minute. But Kim figured she wouldn't say more, and the overwhelming noise silenced all further conversation.

She made her way to Flint's helo on the front lawn just as he was spooling up for takeoff. She climbed into the passenger seat and fastened her harness. She settled her headset and flipped it on.

"Any interest in a quick trip to Houston?" Flint asked with a grin.

Kim shook her head. "Not today. Can you drop me back in DC? I have a few loose ends to clear up before I head back to Detroit."

"You bet," Flint replied as they lifted off quickly and headed northeast in the clear morning sky.

Kim glanced at the screen on the instrument panel that had led them here with the stationary blue and the blinking red beacons.

The blue beacon was still there but it was no longer fixed. It moved slowly away from the compound. Jake's Jeep was headed out of the nightmare. Kim felt an overwhelming sense of relief that Jake, Margaret, and the others would be okay.

The red beacon had disappeared from the screen.

CHAPTER 49

Thursday, May 26
Washington, DC

THE OBSERVER STOOD ACROSS the street from the Four Knights Club, hands in his pockets, watching the DEA agents swarming around the interior and exterior of the building.

They were looking for evidence they wouldn't find. He'd already cleaned up.

Their search would be more than satisfied by new evidence they hadn't anticipated instead.

The opium and the paraphernalia associated with it had already been removed and relocated.

All traces of illegal and immoral activity at the Club were gone. CCTV files had been uploaded to secure servers and replaced with chess tournament video. Local law enforcement would spend hours watching nothing but gambits and checkmates.

In the videos he'd planted, the White Kings always won. Altering reality videos was easy to do these days. He grinned.

Dover's body had been retrieved and dismembered in the butcher shop. The various pieces were now resting at the bottom of the Atlantic. That is, whatever was left of them after the predators had their fill.

Zed had proved invaluable in the cleanup, proving he had career advancement aspirations. And he might have been a suitable replacement for Dover.

But a clean sweep was the safer play.

Which was why he'd terminated the NSA insider who compiled the dossier on Burke for Otto. He'd destroyed the dossier and all the backup intel used to create it as well.

All known traitors had been eliminated.

When the cleanup work was completed, Zed and Patton were the only remaining loose ends.

Which were tied up when Zed was killed by a heroin overdose upstairs in the Washington bedroom at the Four Knights Club.

The necessary changes were made in all the databases to transform Zed's digital and physical characteristics into Patton's.

The body's fingerprints were magically Patton's fingerprints.

The body's DNA was now positively identified as Patton's DNA.

Instantly, Zed disappeared as if he had never existed.

The body became Patton.

No questions would be asked.

When identity and cause of death were confirmed by biometrics, and Patton had no living relatives or friends to claim him, the body would be cremated.

Later, when it was safe to do so, all traces of Patton would be erased from all databases, too. Like Zed and the NSA traitor, Patton would never have existed at all.

It was unlikely that a friend or relative of Zed's or the NSA traitor might come looking for them someday. When and if that happened, it would be dealt with.

He waited and watched from his perch across the street until one of the local police officers found the body in the Washington bedroom.

The medical examiner's office arrived on the scene. The body would be pronounced dead and the crime scene sealed for processing.

After the medical examiner's flunky left the scene, the observer smiled, nodded, and walked away.

Senator Templar would be relieved that Patton no longer had his boot on the senator's neck. He wasn't likely to make any waves.

The Patton/Zed chapter was closed.

The Sullivan/Reacher story was just beginning.

CHAPTER 50

Friday, May 27
Washington, DC

KIM SPENT THE ENSUING hours writing her reports and dealing with loose ends. She closed most of the gaps in her intel. But a few were still open.

She planned to deal with the final issues tonight.

Turner had been reassigned to a post in South Korea. Late Thursday afternoon, she'd shipped out. There had been no time for that long debrief Kim had planned.

Before she left, Turner had assumed responsibility for Jake and Margaret.

Turner assured Kim that Margaret would get home to New Hampshire safely, Templar's wounds would be handled by the navy, and he'd be returned to active service.

Turner had also debriefed Jake quickly, satisfying the army that he wasn't involved with the White Kings and was a hero for helping to take them down. She'd reported to her CO that Jake had behaved like a proper army officer candidate.

Which wasn't too far from the truth to be believable.

Turner said the final answer was that Jake would be sent on his way to Fort Benning, as scheduled, with Turner running interference for him, should that be necessary. She didn't expect any problems to arise.

Turner continued to deny all knowledge of Jack Reacher's whereabouts, but Kim didn't believe her. Evidence of Reacher's handiwork was thick on the ground at the White Kings Palace.

Kim believed, but couldn't prove, that Jack Reacher had fired the shot that killed Burke. He'd done it to save Jake. Or at least, that was the best possible spin Kim could put on events of the day, and Turner didn't disagree.

The matter of Petey Burns was still dangling. Gaspar had finally located Burns, still headed toward his mother's home in Marietta, Georgia.

Kim had failed to recapture Burns herself, but she was FBI.

"The FBI always gets our man," she'd said to Gaspar, tongue-in-cheek before she turned the matter over.

Burns had stolen another Mercedes for the final leg of the trip. A bright red sedan. Unmistakable to the agents in the FBI's Atlanta Field Office.

Kim got the call hours ago. Burns was recaptured and would be returned to prison, where he belonged.

She pressed the redial to call Gaspar. He picked up right away, as was his habit.

"What's up, Sunshine?" he said with a smile in his voice. "Got everything settled to your satisfaction?"

"Almost, Chico. Burns is in custody. He gave up without too much resistance," Kim replied.

"You feel better now? You lost him, and you found him. Makes a nice, closed circle, right?"

She smiled. "Well, I couldn't have found him without your help."

"Doubtful, Suzy Wong. But I appreciate the thought," Gaspar replied with his usual Latin grace. "So now what?"

Kim took a deep breath. She'd already downed several gallons of coffee, and she was bone weary. When her eyelids drooped, she forced them open again.

"What about that NSA report on Burke?" she asked.

Gaspar sighed, and she could feel his resistance across the miles.

"I need that report to finalize my paperwork." After a pause, she added, "And I just need to know the weak spots in his background. And who exploited them and assigned him to my team. I'm lucky he didn't manage to get me killed. I can't let something like that happen again."

Gaspar's answer was long in coming. Finally, he said wearily, "I tried. The report was there under a dozen layers of encryption and bureaucracy. It took me too long to dig it out. But before I got there, Burke was already dead, and the report had vanished."

Kim blinked as if doing so might clear her hearing. "Vanished? What do you mean? How could the report be gone?"

"Dunno. The inside man we were using to compile the report has been reassigned. I've looked everywhere, contacted every source we have. He's so deep off the grid that none of my databases can find him at the moment. The report itself and all the underlying intel was deliberately deep-sixed." Gaspar let out a long pent-up breath. "I'll keep looking. But it's not likely anyone will ever find the source or the report, Kim. I'm sorry."

Kim took in the words, soaking them up like a sponge.

Burke was dead.

The NSA source and the report were both eliminated.

But she couldn't let it go. The stakes were too high.

Which left her with only one choice. She made the call and scheduled the meeting.

To handle the final option well, she needed sleep. First things first.

CHAPTER 51

Friday, May 27
Washington, DC

THE DAY AFTER SHE, Burke, and Turner had stepped into Flint's helicopter atop their budget hotel, Kim rode up from a different lobby in a private elevator to a penthouse suite at the Four Seasons in Washington, DC.

When the car slid to a gentle stop, the doors parted, revealing an open foyer with a spectacular view of the city.

"Good evening, Agent Otto," Russell, the Secret Service agent, smiled. "Good to see you again. Dr. Finlay's waiting in the dining room."

"Thank you, Russell. I'm starving," Kim replied with a grin and followed him through. She liked Russell. He always seemed like a man she could count on.

Russell stopped at a pair of double doors and knocked before he opened one and ushered her through. "Enjoy your dinner."

The door was opposite a wall of windows with the same breathtaking view as the foyer.

Lamont Finlay, Ph.D., waited alone at the head of a long mahogany table set for two, as relaxed as if he owned the room and the building and everything in it.

Perhaps he did.

He stood up as she entered.

"Good to see you, Otto," Finlay said, in a deep voice which would make women around the world swoon and men buy anything he was selling. "Thanks for joining me."

Kim walked across the shiny parquet floor to her chair. "How could I refuse? The cuisine here is likely to be much more impressive than the burger I ate the last time I was in DC."

He smiled as they shook hands. His paw was as big as a catcher's mitt. She could have placed both fists inside his big palm.

He waved her to the table and they both sat.

He'd already poured two glasses of Brunello, her favorite red wine. Barolo was said to be the King of Wines, but Kim preferred Brunello, and Finlay knew it.

Gaspar would have been worried that Finlay bothered to cater to her tastes, but Kim's mind was elsewhere tonight.

"How may I be of service to you?" Finlay asked after they'd settled and tried the first sip.

Kim placed the crystal wine glass carefully onto the tablecloth and turned to face him. "You know my partner died."

"Burke. Yes. I'm sorry for your loss," his voice rumbled with mock sincerity.

"Are you?" Kim cocked her head. "Sorry, I mean?"

"A man died. Why wouldn't I be sorry about that?"

"It took me way too long to figure this one out. But you knew Burke had been assigned to kill Reacher," Kim replied, hiding her annoyance as well as she could.

To his credit, he issued no denial or attempt to change the subject. "I didn't know for sure, no."

"You could have told me."

He said nothing.

"Did you give the order to kill Reacher?" she asked.

"Me? Of course not. Why would I want Reacher dead?" He arched both eyebrows at once, which was a significant indication of surprise for him. "I'm the one who suggested you go to Fort Jackson to extricate Jake from the White Kings. You think I did that because I wanted Reacher dead?"

Kim was still annoyed.

But what he said made sense.

If he'd wanted Reacher dead, there were easier ways to make that happen than sneaking a Judas onto her personal team.

She chose to believe him at least until she had contrary proof.

Which, at the moment, she didn't have.

Gaspar was still digging for that NSA report and for the confidential source who compiled it. They'd find both. Eventually.

If the report or the source implicated Finlay, all bets were off.

From the start, Finlay had been helpful in her search for Reacher. In his own way.

Even though Gaspar didn't trust him, she'd be sorry to learn she'd been wrong about Finlay all this time.

If she were wrong.

Big if.

Their conversation was interrupted when the waiter brought salads and placed them on the table.

Finlay said, "Please leave us until the main course. I'll let you know when we're ready."

The waiter nodded and then retreated into the kitchen.

Kim didn't touch her plate. She was focused on finding answers.

"We agree that Burke was assigned to kill Reacher. You didn't give the order. So who did?" Kim pressed, determined to get to the truth.

She didn't know what she'd do once she got there.

One thing at a time.

"I thought it was Cooper initially." Finlay took a deep breath and wagged his head. "I wasted too much time chasing down that blind alley before I concluded that he was not responsible."

"Why did you cross Cooper off your list of possibles?"

"Because of the DEA involvement. Cooper hates the DEA," Finlay said. "He would never have put a DEA informer inside the Four Knights Club. He'd have put one of his own guys in there instead."

"What DEA informer? What are you talking about?"

"Rupert Adams the Fourth," Finlay said. "Turner didn't tell you?"

"Tell me what?"

"Seven years ago, Turner and Reacher worked together to close down an opium den. They thought it was done and dusted. It wasn't," Finlay explained, refilling his wine glass. Kim's was still untouched. "Adams was a member of the club. He got himself in trouble with the DEA. They turned him. He became an informant."

"What does that have to do with Turner and Reacher?"

"Turner found out about it. She was pissed. She'd thought they closed the lid on that particular box of crap. It was personal for her. She told Reacher. He was pissed. Same reasons, I guess." Finlay shrugged and held both palms up. "So they decided to put the Four Knights Club out of business. Again. Forever, this time."

This was a lot of new information to think through. But the intel connected several dots in Kim's head very quickly.

"Cooper got wind of this new Turner/Reacher plan and brought Burke and me to DC because he knew Reacher was already here. The night Turner got called out to the Four Knights Club...." Kim cocked her head and closed her eyes, visualizing the memory. Then she nodded. "She was on her way to meet Reacher."

"I talked directly to DEA's team leader. They were planning to raid the place the next day," Finlay said, nodding. "But that night, Adams heard they were getting a delivery of new product and reported that to Turner. She and Reacher rushed over there. You know the rest."

"Why did Reacher jump on that helo? And who gave him that beacon to guide us toward the White Kings?" Kim asked.

"The beacon was DEA. They didn't know where the White Kings were processing the opium into heroin," Finlay explained. "Reacher's plan was to jump on the helo with the beacon to lead Turner and DEA to the compound."

"Did Reacher know the White Kings had kidnapped Jake?"

"I guess you'll have to ask him." Finlay shrugged. "But my guess is probably not. I don't believe DEA knew the Four Knights and the White Kings were connected until Reacher led them to that compound."

"Chess connections not withstanding?"

Finlay shrugged.

Kim considered the angles and decided Finlay's story made sense. She nodded slowly. "So someone planted Burke on Cooper's team for the purpose of killing Reacher. Cooper didn't make that decision himself."

"That was my conclusion," Finlay said. He paused and sipped the wine, stalling.

"I agree. I've talked to Cooper. The man's a snake. But he doesn't want Reacher dead," Kim replied slowly. "He's got something in mind that he wants Reacher to do. Until that happens, Cooper wants Reacher alive just as much as we do."

Finlay nodded. "That's my take."

Kim asked, "So who has enough juice to do something like that? Who would give an FBI agent an illegal order to kill a civilian who also happens to be a war hero? Even in DC, the list of suspects has to be fairly short."

Finlay shook his head, drained his glass, and refilled.

Kim's glass was still full. She wanted a clear head to process the facts.

The longer he stalled, the more her patience thinned.

She prodded, "You didn't give Burke the order to kill Reacher. Cooper didn't do it. So who did?"

"Honestly, I'm still not sure." Finlay shook his head as if surrendering to one of the great mysteries of the universe. "But the evidence we've been able to uncover suggests a guy named Patton was probably responsible."

"You sound like that's not helpful intel," Kim said.

"It's not. Patton is dead. Whatever answers he might have offered died with him."

"We're sure he's dead?"

"Totally sure. Saw the body. Checked the biometrics myself," Finlay replied. "Checked them several times, in fact. A dead mastermind wasn't the solution I wanted."

"Why did Patton want Reacher dead? And what was his leverage over Burke?" Kim asked.

"Excellent questions. For which I have no answers," Finlay said as he raised a glass to his lips in a way that suggested Kim should do the same.

Maybe he was just hungry. Or he could have more meetings scheduled tonight.

"But you'll keep digging until you find out," Kim said flatly.

"Of course."

Kim nodded, lifted, and sipped the Brunello. The exceptionally bold fruit flavors danced on her tongue. She detected wild berry and tart cherries, along with dusty spices and something else. Just a hint, but it was there.

She sipped again, giving the cool red wine a chance to warm up in her mouth until she identified the taste.

She nodded slowly, appreciating the flavor and the appropriateness of the sentiment.

Blood oranges.

The other big news is Diane Capri—a friend of mine—wrote a book revisiting the events of KILLING FLOOR in Margrave, Georgia. She imagines an FBI team tasked to trace Reacher's current-day whereabouts. They begin by interviewing people who knew him—starting out with Roscoe and Finlay. Check out this review: "Oh heck yes! I am in love with this book. I'm a huge Jack Reacher fan. If you don't know Jack (pun intended!) then get thee to the bookstore/wherever you buy your fix and pick up one of the many Jack Reacher books by Lee Child. Heck, pick up all of them. In particular, read Killing Floor. Then come back and read Don't Know Jack. This story picks up the other from the point of view of Kim and Gaspar, FBI agents assigned to build a file on Jack Reacher. The problem is, as anyone who knows Reacher can attest, he lives completely off the grid. No cell phone, no house, no car…he's not tied down. A pretty daunting task, then, wouldn't you say?

First lines: "Just the facts. And not many of them, either. Jack Reacher's file was too stale and too thin to be credible. No human could be as invisible as Reacher appeared to be, whether he was currently above the ground or under it. Either the file had been sanitized, or Reacher was the most off-the-grid paranoid Kim Otto had ever heard of." Right away, I'm sensing who Kim Otto is and I'm delighted that I know something she doesn't. You see, I DO know Jack. And I know he's not paranoid. Not really. I know why he lives as he does, and I know what kind of man he is. I loved having that over Kim and Gaspar. If you haven't read any Reacher novels, then this will feel like a good, solid story in its own right. If you have…oh if you have, then you, too, will feel like you have a one-up on the FBI. It's a fun feeling!

"Kim and Gaspar are sent to Margrave by a mysterious boss who reminds me of Charlie, in Charlie's Angels. You never see him…you hear him. He never gives them all the facts. So they are left with a big pile of nothing. They end up embroiled in a murder case that seems connected to Reacher somehow, but they can't see how. Suffice to say the efforts to find the murderer and Reacher, and not lose their own heads in the process, makes for an entertaining read.

"I love the way the author handled the entire story. The pacing is dead on (okay another pun intended), the story is full of twists and turns like a Reacher novel would be, but it's another viewpoint of a Reacher story. It's an outside-in approach to Reacher.

"You might be asking, do they find him? Do they finally meet the infamous Jack Reacher?

"Go…read…now…find out!"

Sounds great, right? Check out "Don't Know Jack," and let me know what you think.

So that's it for now…again, thanks for reading THE AFFAIR, and I hope you'll like A WANTED MAN just as much in September.

Lee Child

ABOUT THE AUTHOR

Diane Capri is an award-winning *New York Times*, *USA Today*, and worldwide bestselling author. She's a recovering lawyer and snowbird who divides her time between Florida and Michigan. An active member of Mystery Writers of America, Author's Guild, International Thriller Writers, Alliance of Independent Authors, Novelists, Inc., and Sisters in Crime, she loves to hear from readers. She is hard at work on her next novel.

Please connect with her online:
http://www.DianeCapri.com
Twitter: http://twitter.com/@DianeCapri
Facebook: http://www.facebook.com/Diane.Capri1
http://www.facebook.com/DianeCapriBooks

Made in the USA
Monee, IL
15 June 2023

35756522R00187